Noah Potter has come to Hong Kong to find his missing sister, Lianne, who disappeared after leaving him a voice mail pleading for his help. Unfortunately the Hong Kong police are unwilling to help him, so Noah has to find her himself.

Noah's search for his sister brings him across Wei Tseng, leader of the Dragons, a group of dedicated men and women willing to do whatever it takes to keep their district safe from the violence and triads that plague the rest of the city's underworld. Wei is a man of violence but also one of incredible compassion, and his history is one that resonates with Noah, igniting a passion neither man expects.

Together they search for Lianne, a search that will lead right into a conflict with the Dragons' greatest rivals in the city.

Published by
NineStar Press
PO Box 91792
Albuquerque, New Mexico, 87199
www.ninestarpress.com

Warning: This book contains sexually explicit content and depictions of rape and murder, which is only suitable for mature readers.

Print ISBN #978-1-945952-70-8
Cover by Natasha Snow
Edited by Sam Lamb

A MATTER OF DUTY

Hong Kong Nights

J.C. Long

PROLOGUE

Rain battered the street relentlessly. It was that season in Hong Kong, with summer storms cropping up unexpectedly to drive people off the street, even the ever-present food vendors with their carts promising the best pork buns, the most delicious noodles, and the most delectable fish. The occasional car would streak by, headlights on against the encroaching night and the curtain of water falling from the sky.

Not a single driver noticed the lone woman, ash-blonde hair plastered about her face and clothes clinging to her like a second skin, as she stumbled down the streets of North Bay. Anyone who *did* see her would probably assume she was drunk. They wouldn't notice the blood at the edge of her mouth, the swelling of her lips, or the dark red mark of a hand mostly hidden by the hair plastered against her face. They would not be able to distinguish the tears staining her cheeks from the rain.

The girl stopped her stumbling walk, leaning against the corner of a building, a sob bubbling up in her throat. The strength threatened to leave her legs. She didn't know how long she'd been moving, or how safe she was. Was there such a thing as safe in this fucking city? The surface was beautiful, alluring, and exotic, but it hid a festering darkness, a cancer in the heart of the city itself.

The bitter thought stoked the dampened fire of anger in her belly. She clung to that anger, letting it reinvigorate her. Gritting her teeth against the sudden pain in her side—the ribs were bruised, if not broken, of that much she was certain—she pushed herself away from the wall and continued. Not much farther now.

The pain increased with each unsteady step she took until every single breath was agony. Every stab of pain reminded her of *them*, of their hands, of their angry words. The memories clawed at her, but she fought through it. She would not give in, not now. She just needed to reach her phone.

Finally, she was in sight of her goal. She avoided the restaurant, avoided Pam's knowing gaze, and took the side door into the building. When she came face-to-face with the stairs, she wanted to cry. She wasn't sure she could tackle them, not three flights, but she had no choice.

Halfway up the first flight, the pain doubled her over, and she clung helplessly to the precarious railing. Despite the pleading of her body, urging her to stop and threatening more damage, she made herself move one step at a time, climbing those stairs that might as well have been Everest.

By the seconding landing, she was on her knees, but she could not stop. Tears flooded her vision and cold spasms racked her body, but she continued on, crawling up those stairs. The pain in her chest was so intense she did not even feel it when she tore off a nail on the uneven wood of beneath her.

At one point, she lost consciousness. When she came to, she almost didn't have the strength to go on. Her body was rebelling against her, unable to function past the pain that tugged at her vision, luring her back into that unconsciousness—at least there would be no pain then—but the sight of her apartment door spurred her on.

She reached the door after what felt like hours. The first thing she saw was her bed, and it was almost too inviting to resist—but no, she didn't have much time.

She stumbled to her desk, where she found the cell phone she'd left behind tonight—and thank god she had, or it would have been over—and picked it up. The wind outside blew the rain against the window, the sound making her jump, eyes wide as she glanced at the door. Not yet. She had a little more time.

Though she did her best to fight her fear back into controllable bounds, her body refused the forced calmness. Her hands shook relentlessly before the phone dropped from them. A sob tore through her throat. She bent down to pick it up, trying to steady herself on the desk. A spasm ran through her side from her chest up to her shoulders, and she collapsed forward, slamming to the floor, the phone caught beneath her. She worked herself over onto her side as her ribs cried in protest. She grabbed the phone once more, dialing the number she knew by heart. *Please*, she thought, squeezing her eyes closed lest the tears pour out, and then she wouldn't be able to stop it. *Please.*

Two rings and then voice mail. Goddamn it. *Goddamn it.* She had no choice, though. She had to try. When the beep came, she struggled to speak, finally managing a few words.

1

"I'm just... I really... I'm in trouble, Noah."

Noah sat on the airplane as it taxied to its arrival gate at Hong Kong International Airport, memories of the last voice mail left by his sister and the last moments he'd spent with her darkening his mind despite the bright September sun pouring through the airplane window. He hadn't answered the phone when she'd called that night three weeks ago—not because he was busy and couldn't take it but because he didn't want to. He was still angry with her at the time. Angry that she ran off to Hong Kong with pretty much no warning. She ran away and left him behind. He never did that to her, despite how very much he wanted to sometimes.

So, acting like a petulant child instead of a twenty-six-year-old man, he'd hit reject, ignoring the call and the alert the phone had made almost three minutes later signifying that someone actually left him a voice mail. If he had been in a clear headspace—if not for being a complete asshat—the amount of time that passed between hitting the reject button and the message arriving would have surprised him. No one left voice mails anymore, much less three-minute-long ones.

Acting like an asshat, he'd ignored that voice mail for one week, first out of anger but later because he'd forgotten about it. He didn't listen to it until he'd become annoyed at the stupid notification at the top of his phone.

"I'm just... I really... I'm in trouble, Noah." A disturbing tremor sat in Lianne's voice, underscoring her words.

Pain flared through Noah's hand, and he realized his fists were clenched so tight his neatly manicured nails almost punctured the skin. He took a few calming breaths, pressing his head back against the seat. Even though he flew first class the cabin space suddenly seemed too small. He closed his eyes against the claustrophobia that washed over him.

Keep it together, Noah. You can't help her if you're dead.

Noah forced his eyes open and stared at the slowly approaching airport. It was a beautiful structure, slightly curved protrusions echoing the feel of Australian architecture. All glass and modern lines, as beautiful as any airport he'd ever seen—more beautiful than the droll monstrosities of most American airports. A gateway in so many ways: opening out to the foreign city-state but also the gateway to finding Lianne. She was here, somewhere, and he was going to find her and take her home. He would protect her, like he always had.

"I'm just... I really..." She went silent for a long moment, the only sound her labored breathing. *"I'm in trouble, Noah. I met this guy, and... Jesus. I don't know what I'm going to do. I don't know—you have—you have to help me. Please."* The part that cut straight to Noah's heart was there at the end. *Please.* Lianne Maureen Potter didn't say "please." She didn't ask for help. Of course, she usually didn't need to when it came to Noah; he had a way of knowing what she needed and providing it. The fact that she'd asked...there was no doubt in Noah's mind she'd found trouble.

That in and of itself wasn't unusual. Lianne had a way of drawing trouble to her, a magnetism geared directly to its frequency. Trouble found its way to her eventually. If she didn't find it first, anyway. But this seemed different. She didn't sound like she'd made some dumb mistake, gotten too drunk, or gotten lost. Noah heard fear, real and raw, in her voice. He'd never known his sister to be truly afraid of anything. Whatever had happened, it was bad news.

"Sir? Excuse me, sir?" A pretty and perky cabin crew member—most likely of Chinese descent, though not entirely, he'd guess—leaned slightly forward, brow wrinkled ever so slightly in well-practiced, polite concern. "You may disembark now."

Surprised, Noah looked around and saw that the first-class cabin was now empty. While lost in his thoughts, the plane had come to a stop, the captain had given his final speech, and the other first-class passengers had gathered their bags and departed. He would have to be careful not to let something like that happen again. He was in a new city, an unfamiliar—and dangerous, if the things he'd heard were true—place, and he could not afford to get so distracted. He had a job to do.

Smiling sheepishly in apology, he got up, gathered his carry-on bag from the overhead compartment, and made his way off the plane, joining the trickle of souls making their way toward the queue of immigration.

Above a door just ahead of him marked "International Arrivals" in four different languages was a sign that said "Welcome to Hong Kong— City of Dreams".

"Yeah right," he muttered to himself, shouldering his bag and marching under the lying sign. City of Dreams, *my ass. For Lianne, seems like it was a city of nightmares instead.*

2

Hong Kong International Airport sat on a small island all its own, like most airports in Asia that Noah had visited. To enter the city proper, one needed to take the metro system or hail a bus or a cab. Noah knew all this when he arrived; he'd prepped for this the moment two weeks ago when he'd tried to call his sister back and received no answer any of the one hundred seventy-two times he'd called over the course of two days. That made him realize he needed to come to Hong Kong and find his sister. He needed to bring her home, if he could.

No, no *if*—he would bring her home. He'd just stepped off the plane, there must be no doubt in his mind; if he did not have hope, he might as well give up right now.

The interior of the airport's beauty matched its exterior. Skylights hovering high above his head cast afternoon sunlight down on him, bathing him in its warmth. The architecture was modern, all sleek glass and deceptive perspectives, but even here, surrounded by large numbers of tourists pouring into the city at the end of their summer vacation, hoping to enjoy Hong Kong's best summer month, he could not mistake this for the West. Everything felt different; a foreign flavor filled the air, swirling in Noah's lungs and coating his tongue. Announcements made over the airport's intercoms came in Chinese, Korean, Japanese, and English. The signs read in those languages and more—German and French and Vietnamese as well.

There was a sort of magic to this place, magic he felt being in the airport, not even truly out in Hong Kong yet. The airport dominated a man-made island, and as he took it all in, Noah felt the strangest sense of anticipation. Part of Noah could not wait to see what the rest of Hong Kong felt like once he was out amongst its crowded streets, deep within the pulse of this city with the highest population density on the entire planet. He did his best to repress that part, though; this was no pleasure tour. He was not a tourist like those who passed him, whiling away their Septembers before slipping back to the mundane banality of their lives.

He envied them that, wished he could explore the avenues of a new place before slinking back home, back under the thumb of his cold, uncaring father.

Noah had a task to do, though, so he would have to control the wanderlust that gripped him as tightly as it ever gripped Lianne.

He reached the escalator that would descend deep underground to the metro. As he waited, he dug into his backpack, seeking out the crumpled paper where he'd jotted down instructions on how to get where he needed to go, making sure he did not get lost. It was merely reflex, however; he'd committed that paper to memory a week ago.

Noah hadn't spoken to Lianne right before she left. He'd been angry and made damn sure she knew it. He hadn't known where in Hong Kong she went, what she'd do when she got there, or even how to contact her once she got there, other than the cell phone—and how reliable would a cell phone be? Hong Kong was basically China, right?

Before she left, though, she'd left information about her flight with their father, along with an address for a room she'd found online. It was in the Eastern District, so all he had to do was find it and see what was going on.

People and their luggage crowded the subway. Though the surface hadn't seemed so bad, the subway car was stifling hot with so many bodies crammed close together. Noah felt the earlier claustrophobia's nauseating grips on the corner of his mind and forced himself to focus on the different colorful advertisements all along the upper portion of the subway to distract himself. It was a forty-minute subway ride according to the app he'd downloaded on his phone, and he would have to transfer once he reached a place called Center. He needed to keep it together until he did.

Impulse driving him, he dug his iPhone out of his pocket and stared at it. His background picture was, as usual, a picture of himself and Lianne together. Though she was four years older than him, some people thought they must be fraternal twins since they looked so similar. Both had pale skin that tanned to a beautiful copper in the summer sun, similar brown-blond, almost ash-gray hair, and the same round blue-green eyes they'd inherited from Vivienne Maureen Potter, their beautiful mother.

According to the top of the phone's screen, he had service—he'd made damned sure he'd be able to use the cell phone once he got here in order to contact his sister. Without consciously choosing to, his fingers hit the call button on his sister's name. He watched as it said connecting, hoping she would answer the phone, explain that she'd gone off to visit some other place for a few weeks and was back now, safe, and the voice mail was some angry reaction to a breakup with the fifth boy she'd been dating since her arrival in Hong Kong. He prayed she'd pick up, like every other time he'd tried to call her in the last two weeks.

Hands shaking slightly, he brought the phone to his ear. Straight to voice mail, just like every time since he received her message. It didn't even give him the benefit of hearing her voice, either; it was one of those generic "This number is not available. Please leave a message after the tone" messages. The hope that had been growing in his heart crumbled to dust, just as it had each time before.

It took every ounce of control he possessed not to redial the number immediately, but he managed. A man could only take so much disappointment at a time.

3

The apartment his sister selected turned out to just be a cramped room above a small noodle shop crammed into a back alley street in North Bay. It was a pain in the ass to drag his luggage all the way there, but he didn't want to waste time going back toward Center to put his bags in his hotel room. Noah checked the information on the paper Lianne had given their father twice to make sure he was in the right place.

Looking at his surroundings, he found himself not the least bit surprised his sister had ended up in trouble of some sort; it didn't seem to be a reputable area by any means. Directly across from the noodle shop there sat a parking garage, its walls tagged with spray paint a hundred times over. The different marks overlapped at times, as if someone had attempted to cover the previous tag with their own, claiming the territory in the same way a dog might use urine to cover the scent of another dog and claim an area. Trash littered the alleyway, the air heavy with the mingling scents of piled garbage and the more palatable but still foreign smells coming from the noodle shop.

The building with the noodle shop consisted of four floors, the restaurant itself on the first floor. The three above it were plain-looking brownstone. Grimy windows looked out onto the alleyway, most of them reflecting smudged fingerprints in the sunlight. A few had curtains or blinds up. The sound of a television commercial drifted down to him from an open window on the third floor.

A few people walking by looked at him askance, and he realized he must look like some sort of Peeping Tom, standing there looking up at these windows. Blushing bright red—which probably didn't help the pervert image—Noah made his way up toward the restaurant.

A small bell over the door rang as he walked in. An intense smell rolled over him like waves on a beach, and the temperature ratcheted upward in the close confines, spices and meat and that hard to describe smell that comes from cooking noodles. It wasn't too bad outside, probably close to eighty degrees, but it seemed to reach a hundred in the still air of the noodle shop. There restaurant had seven tables: two big round ones in the center that sat eight people, three four-top, and two two-top tables crammed along the wall. People sat at three of the tables; four older gentlemen at one, steaming bowls of noodles in front of them along with several bottles of Tsingtao beer. At another, an older woman, her daughter, and a girl of about five—three generations seated together. Two men probably a few years younger than Noah took one of the two-seaters. Both were sporting dirty tank tops that showed a variety of tattoos on their arms. They both turned their eyes to Noah standing there, and he quickly looked away. Something about those men screamed *danger*.

A rather plump woman came up to him then and started to ask him a question in Cantonese before realizing from his blank expression he had no idea what she was saying and switching to accented English. "Just one? Come this way. We have a lunch special. Large noodles only fifty-five dollars. Here, we can put your bag here." She took his bags from him and placed them behind the counter.

Noah started to tell her he wasn't there to eat, but his stomach chose that moment to assert itself with a loud rumble. It was just after two o'clock in the afternoon Hong Kong time, and the last meal they'd served on the plane had been a breakfast around six that morning.

Well, I can't find Lianne if I die of hunger first. He would question the waitress about her over the meal, and just maybe Lianne would come in herself while he ate and they would have a cheerful, tear-filled reunion. Stranger things had happened. Probably.

The other two-person table was directly across from the table where the two men sat. As he took the seat facing the door—he hadn't fully suppressed the foolish hope of Lianne's arrival—Noah felt the heavy gazes of the two men. The hair on the back of his neck stood on end. He picked up the menu—a single piece of unornamented paper that listed the names of the dishes in Chinese characters with romanized pinyin below it and no indication of what was in them besides noodles. At least he knew the noodles.

Noah pretended to study the incomprehensible menu, chancing a glance at the men. Both were of average height, one a little taller than Noah, one a little shorter by the looks of it. The one facing the same direction as Noah had short-cropped hair, the other long, stringy locks. Both were dark tones, though the shorter hair was an inky blue-black, the other man's closer to brown. They ate in silence, absorbed in their meals with little time for anything else. Noah was pretty sure their appearance of being unaware was a deception; he'd wager all the money in his bank account that they knew exactly what went on around them. These two men seemed unlikely to be caught unawares.

Short Hair's eyes turned away from his meal at that second and met Noah's for the briefest moment before Noah turned away, heart pounding inexplicably. He was grateful for the waitress's arrival.

"What do you want?"

"Uh..." Noah turned his eyes helplessly back to the menu he could make neither heads nor tails of. Sensing his distress, the waitress reached a pudgy, sausage-like finger to the menu, touching each item that she listed. "Noodles with shrimp, noodles with pork, noodles with beef—that one is spicy—wanton soup."

"I'll have the noodles with beef," he said. He reached into his pocket, pulling out the picture of his sister. "Do you know—" He stopped short as the waitress walked away. Resigned to wait, he placed the picture on the table and poured himself a glass of water, its cool taste welcome in the hot restaurant. He hadn't realized it until that moment but a damp sheen of sweat coated his skin. It wouldn't be long before he became sticky and uncomfortable. *I hope I packed enough deodorant.*

The waitress returned with his order—a large, steaming bowl of what looked like noodles in a dark red broth, whose scent spoke of spice and pleasant burning. He saw various vegetables floating along with the noodles, and the slightest probing with the ladle-shaped soup spoon or chopsticks exposed tender bits of beef—he was instantly salivating.

Noah was so caught up with the arrival of the food he forgot the picture until the waitress moved off to deliver the check to the four-top of old, drunk—by now—men.

"Damn it," he muttered, placing the picture down on the table. At this rate, he had no hope of finding Lianne in a hurry. Foiled again, he picked up the soup spoon in his left hand and chopsticks in his right. He began by first ladling up a bit of the broth and giving it a sip. The waitress hadn't been exaggerating; the heat of it rolled over Noah's tongue in waves, chili and other seasonings he couldn't identify biting his tongue. The unexpected strength of the heat caught Noah off guard and set his throat tingling, but he refused to cough and show sign of weakness. He didn't want to look like the stupid white guy who couldn't handle a little kick in his noodles and covered it up by nonchalantly sipping water. He wasn't careful, and his elbow nudged the picture of his sister to the ground.

Noah put the glass down and started to reach for the photo, but a tattooed arm beat him to it. The short-haired guy, coming from where a sign said the bathrooms were, passed the table and picked the photo up. His eyes studied it for the briefest of moments, unreadable, before he handed it politely back to Noah, muttering, "You dropped this."

"Thanks," Noah stammered, watching as Short Hair rejoined his companion, and the two of them made their way to the front where a small register stood near the door. He didn't know what it was, but something about the entire encounter left him chilled. It was probably an overreaction—the guy had just picked up the picture for him, that was it—but he couldn't shake the strange feeling that gripped him. He watched the two men until they were gone, and even then his eyes lingered on the door as if he expected them to return.

4

He ate his lunch without paying it much attention and, gathering his bags, hurried to the counter, determined to get his questions answered now. The same chubby lady met him at the counter and took the receipt from him.

"Fifty-five dollar," she said. Noah dug the money out of his wallet and handed it to her. As he waited for the change, he turned the picture for her to look at.

"Do you know this girl?"

The waitress's hand froze in the process of handing Noah his change, eyes narrowed at the picture. She took it in her pudgy fingers, studying it closely. "Nice girl. She lived upstairs for a while."

Noah frowned. "Lived? She doesn't live there anymore?"

The waitress shrugged a bit, still looking at the picture. "I haven't seen her for around a month. One day she just didn't come home."

Despite the heat, Noah felt like someone doused him with ice water. "What do you mean 'one day she didn't come home'?"

"One day she went out, and nobody saw her come back. Left all her things there, too. No one knows anything." She looked at Noah and then at the picture. "You look like her."

"She's my sister," Noah explained, surprised he was able to speak. His throat felt tight, as if a hand had gripped him, cutting off the flow of air. He swallowed several times, but that did nothing to help. For a moment, he was afraid he was going to faint.

"You want see her stuff?"

"Her apartment is still empty?"

"She paid for three months up front." The waitress turned, motioning for him to follow her. She led him past the cramped kitchen where he heard the loud clamor of pots and pans and voices calling back and forth in Cantonese. There was a small door right next to the bathroom that she led him through. The small stairwell they entered felt ten degrees cooler than the heat of the noodle shop. Noah was grateful to be out of there. The staircase he went up was dubious-looking, the wooden steps warped and bent in a few places and the banister cracked and covered here and there with what looked like mold.

Noah followed the waitress to the third floor and into a hallway lit by a single light swinging on a chain above them. The walls here might have sported a coat of paint, once, but time had bleached the color from them. Dark brown spots on the walls and ceiling spoke of trapped rain water. There were four doors here, two on either side. They stopped in front of the first, closest to the stairs. It was a green door, wood, reminding Noah of the doors at a cheap motel. The waitress simply pushed the door open and motioned him into the room.

Trembling suddenly, Noah went inside. The room was what he expected: small, sparse. There was a single full-sized bed, a shaky wooden desk, a small bookshelf, a single dresser for clothes, a dusty mirror, and a small television set that looked like it came from the nineties. Despite the cheapness of the surroundings, Noah could see signs of his sister everywhere: a thick and obviously expensive comforter covered the bed, the desk bore the sorts of knickknacks his sister had a habit of purchasing when she traveled. The window had been meticulously cleaned—Lianne loved to just sit and stare out windows; she could do it for hours. Beneath the window sat both of Lianne's expensive Louis Vuitton luggage pieces. He had no doubt that if he opened the dresser he would find some of her clothes.

Noah was on the floor, uncertain how he'd gotten there. The cool wood soaked into his jeans but he paid it no heed; it was nothing compared to the chill that had settled into his bones.

He felt a heavy hand on his shoulder and looked up into the waitress's face. He'd thought her plain before, but he could see in those almond eyes a spark of *something*. Perhaps she wasn't so plain, after all. Genuine concern lined her round face. "You okay?"

"Can—can I stay here?" He hadn't known he was going to ask that until he did; he already had a hotel booked, but now he found himself wanting nothing more than to be in this space, surrounded by his sister's belongings. Maybe that would help him feel some sort of connection to her, however tenuous.

The waitress thought for a moment and then nodded. "She paid up until next Friday."

Noah took her offered hand and pushed up from the floor. "If I'm still here then I'll pay whatever the rent is." As the waitress turned to go, Noah called out. "Wait, what's your name?"

"My name Pam," she answered without looking back. She closed the door behind her as she left, and Noah was left alone in the room. The room where his sister had lived for nearly three months.

Noah slowly sat on the bed, struggling for control of his emotions. He lay back, staring up at the spotted ceiling and the slowly rotating blades of the ceiling fan that stirred the air. For a moment, he thought he could smell his sister's usual perfume, and the dam broke, tears flowing freely down his face. He had no doubts now, not that there had ever really been.

Lianne was in trouble.

5

"You sure?" Short Hair leaned back in the passenger seat of the beat-up car as it drove through North Bay's busy streets. They had the car windows rolled down to let out the smoke from their cigarettes and provide a relief from the heat—the shitty car's shitty air conditioner didn't work. He took a deep drag of his cigarette before he answered his long-haired companion's question, the words coming out in a plume of smoke as he exhaled.

"I'm fuckin' sure, man. I told you when he came in, the *gweilo* looked familiar. That hair, them eyes, hard to miss, ya know?"

Short-Hair hocked a wad of spit and tossed the butt of his cigarette out the window as they came to a red light. "What, you gay for him, Ming?"

"*D'iu lay, puk gai.*" *Fuck you, asshole.* Ming punched his companion in the arm hard. "You saw it, too. Don't lie, shithead."

"Yeah, I saw it. Still, you sure? There's gotta be at least a million *gweilo* with that hair and those eyes. That ain't enough, especially if you wanna tell Leo 'bout it."

Ming frowned at the thought. But no, he was sure. There was no chance he was wrong. That was good, because Leo Tong was not kind to people who gave him wrong information. "Dude, listen. He had a fuckin' picture on the table. It was a picture of *her*, man."

Short-Hair's head jerked around sharply, his hard eyes drilling into Ming's, asking some question. He found the answer he sought there and nodded. A car behind them honked, the light having changed to green during that silent exchange. Ming threw his middle finger up out the window as Long-Hair took his foot off the break and jerked the car into a U-turn, nearly clipping another car but paying no attention. Both of them remained silent the remainder of the ride, thinking about what lay ahead for them in the Wai Chen district.

6

"See, Wei, I told you," Conroy Wong said in a low voice, eyes focused on the basketball court across the street and the three men standing there. "These *sei bat po* are dealin' in *our* territory."

Wei Tseng nodded, side of his fist against his mouth as he watched the three men from the corner of his eye, much more discreetly than his companion did. A tall fucker at six foot three, and quite handsome at that, so *blending in* had never been one of Conroy's skill sets. His brown eyes, a color that could look so ordinary on others, looked like liquid sex according to one person—and Wei knew Conroy had attracted his fair share of company with just a smoldering look and a quirk of his full lips. More than once someone had taken a look at Conroy and immediately assumed him to be some celebrity they hadn't seen before. Wei knew Conroy loved the attention, and he set out to get it—despite his fighting abilities, he kept his hair always styled just so, his clothing meant to draw attention to his height and muscular frame. Today he'd chosen to wear nothing more than a white tank top as a shirt, clearly exposing the colorful dragon tattoo that climbed up his back and revealed its head on his shoulder. A mark of the Dragons.

No, Conroy wasn't famous for his discretion, but Wei didn't need him for that. He'd have brought along someone else—someone like Tony or Chris—if discretion was his aim today. Conroy was strong as an ox, as the expression went, and damn good with his hands. He was exactly the kind of guy Wei wanted at his side if it came to a fight.

Funny thing was it seemed to come to a fight much more frequently with Conroy present than when he wasn't there. Take it for what it was.

Wei was shorter than his friend, just under six foot even, but he was no less dangerous. Growing up in the New Territories across Victoria Harbor, in the slums of a city riddled with triad members, he'd been fighting for as long as he could remember. He wasn't a gym buff like Conroy was, didn't spend all of his free time working out, but years of fighting had honed his body all the same. While he lacked Conroy's bulk, every inch of him was hard muscle, and if anyone doubted him because it wasn't immediately obvious, they realized their mistake soon after.

Some guys would feel inadequate sitting next to Conroy, but not him. Wei didn't get called handsome much, but he got called sexy on occasion, a more subtle attraction than what drew people to Conroy. One partner told him he exuded an aura of magnetic power that was impossible to resist. He didn't know about all that. He let his hair be messy atop his head, controlling its length so it did not go to wild. While most of the Dragons had inky-blue hair, Wei's was jet black, hair that absorbed light and refused to lighten. His eyes were dark black as well, the smallest of scars splitting the growth of his left eyebrow near where it ended at the center of his face, a memento of one of his many fights. Small black studs sat in either ear, occasionally catching the light. Unlike the other Dragons, Wei also seemed to have a perpetual case of five-o'clock shadow—something for which many of the guys, especially the younger ones like Jesse and Winston, envied him.

The three men across the street were definitely going out of their way to stand out. They huddled together behind the basketball hoop at the end of the court closest to the small café where Conroy and Wei were watching them. Every now and then they would look around suspiciously before ducking their heads back to what they were doing. Keeping an eye out for the cops, no doubt. They were all three young, no older than nineteen, and they had the looks of people who wanted to *look* like they were part of a triad but really weren't. They wore baggy jeans, baseball caps, but no shirts in order to show off their ink. The tattoos they had were designed to enhance their tough persona, a mix of imagery they thought would be intimidating. There was no passion, no *meaning* behind the ink.

They definitely weren't triad. That was good.

"Time to go over there and knock some heads?" asked Conroy hopefully, glancing at his leader. It was a position Wei had earned more than once, one conferred on him not just by age—at twenty-nine he was the oldest member, aside from Raphael, who was more a member by proxy, having married in—but by the absolute loyalty of his men.

Wei shook his head. "Right now we got nothing on them other than they're standing around acting suspicious. They might just be dumbass kids. We haven't been able to catch a single sign of whoever is dealing in our turf. We've got to be sure." These three were definitely not professionals, if they *were* dealers; they were meeting in broad daylight in a very heavily trafficked area, in territory known to be claimed by another group. That was stupid. Their very body language screamed *Look at me, I'm up to no good!*

Conroy looked as if he wanted to argue the wisdom of *being sure* but decided against it. Instead he said, "That tall *ga tsan* in the middle, he's the leader."

Wei didn't bother asking him how he knew. He trusted Conroy to know these things. If Conroy said that fucker was the leader of the three, then he was. That's the one they would hit the hardest. They couldn't have these young wannabe triad members bringing drugs into their territory. There was already enough going on as it was.

After about ten minutes, they were rewarded. A figure dressed in dark jeans and a black hoodie, despite the late summer warmth, came walking toward the basketball court. He had his hood pulled up and dark black sunglasses on his face that made his features indistinguishable. Wei didn't care; he wasn't interested in the buyer—if someone wanted to fuck up their own life that way, so be it. It was the seller he wanted. They were just wolves, preying on the weak and downtrodden. They caused nothing but pain and misery. He thought about the three women found dead over the past few months, official cause of death drug overdose, even with their families insisting the girls would never do that. He remembered the agonized sobs coming from the families, the mothers in particular, remembered the looks of desperation on their faces as they demanded to know how Wei could let that happen.

Wei clenched his teeth so hard he expected them to crack. He never wanted to have to face that again, never wanted to see someone else suffer that loss. He couldn't bring those girls back, couldn't magically find whoever did what they'd done, so he was going to bust some punks spreading their poison in *his* territory.

"It's goin' down, boss," Conroy said in a low voice, drawing Wei back to reality. He saw the quick movements of hands, money traded for a small baggy.

"You know I hate when you call me that," Wei grumbled as he rose to his feet, slipping his cell phone back into his pocket and settling his own shades on his face. A look and a nod from Conroy and they were making their way across the street.

The trio's "customer" was already retreating quickly, cutting across the basketball court and behind a low brick wall to disappear out of sight. Wei didn't pay any attention to his departure.

Once the trio realized Wei and Conroy were coming their way, they squared their bodies, looking them up and down, testing to see what was coming. They certainly didn't *look* like customers, but they didn't look like cops, either.

Wei quickly sized the three up to get an idea of what he was dealing with. The one that Conroy had pegged as the leader was somewhere between Wei's height and Conroy's with a lot of muscle mass that quite likely came from steroid use. His face was narrow and haggard despite his body size. To his left was a scrawny rat of a guy. He was much shorter and skinnier than either of his companions, the kind of person whose feelings of inferiority of his size would drive him to lash out in violence to prove he was just as tough as people around him. The third guy was on the chubby side, his hands crisscrossed with tiny scars that looked like they had come from knife fights or something similar. All three were wearing pants that were three sizes too big for them, held up tenuously somewhere around their lower thighs by inefficient belts.

As Wei expected, it was Skinny who stepped forward to challenge them. "What you *sei gei lou* want? Get the fuck out of—" Conroy's fist slamming into his jaw silenced him, sending him sprawling to the ground, blood spurting from a busted lip. Wei was fairly sure he'd have a few loose teeth after that blow.

Wei wasted no time, going right for the leader. Thinking he had the height advantage, Tall Guy swung a left hook, but Wei knocked it away with very little problem and drove his fist into the guy's gut, hard, once and then again. As he doubled over, Wei grabbed the side of his head and shoved him to the ground hard.

"What the fuck you *puk gai* think you're doin', huh?" Wei shouted. He started to bend down but Skinny barreled into him from his left side, slipping by Conroy while he was busy smashing Chubby's face a bit. Wei hit the ground hard and instantly brought his legs in, arms tight to shield his head from the rain of erratic blows Skinny was pelting down on him. The kid didn't even know how to fucking fight.

Wei waited for his opening and then raised up, intentionally taking a weak, glancing left hook to the mouth—weak but enough to bust his lip—and retaliated by slamming the heel of his right hand into Skinny's solar plexus, knocking the wind out of him.

The small fries dealt with, Wei rose and walked back over to where Tall Guy was still on the ground, clutching his stomach. He looked down at the man with disdain, brushing dirt from his shirt and jeans.

"Shit, I liked these jeans," he muttered darkly.

"Yea that's right, you better fuckin' run!" Conroy shouted. Wei looked over and saw Chubby sprinting across the court, his face already swollen and bruising. He had to hold his baggy pants up in order to run. Conroy laughed at the sight. Wei didn't share his amusement, though.

"You dumbasses know where you're at, right?" Wei crouched down near Tall Guy's head, taking his hat and tossing it aside so he could pull his head up by his hair to look at him. "Didn't anybody fuckin' tell you that you should stay out of the Eastern District, huh?"

Tall Guy moaned. "Shit, man, nobody told us nothin'. We thought this place was up for grabs, man."

Conroy spat derisively. "Up for grabs? You think the Eastern District is up for grabs?" He came up behind Tall Guy, violently kicking him in the kidney. "This is fuckin' Dragons territory, you hear me? The goddamn *Dragons* own this place!"

"Conroy." Wei's tone cut through Conroy's anger. For a moment, Wei thought it wouldn't be enough to cool him down—he'd gotten a small taste of violence in that excuse for a fight, and he'd be raring to play out some more—but his phone rang, saving Wei the trouble of having to deal with him.

Conroy suitably distracted, Wei turned his attention back to Tall Guy. He bent down and reached into his pockets, searching. When Tall Guy tried to squirm free, Wei grabbed his balls through his jeans and twisted sharply. After that, he meekly let Wei empty his pockets. Three more little baggies filled with powder, identical to the one that they'd just sold, along with about seven hundred dollars. Pretty lucrative for such obvious novices.

Wei held the baggies, his disgust plain. "Who supplies you with this shit? Who fuckin' supplies you?"

"I don't know," Tall Guy moaned, repeating it again and again, his voice escalating as Wei drew back his fist. "I don't know. I don't know. I don't fucking know!"

"Hey, Wei," Conroy called.

"I'm a little busy here, Conroy."

"That can wait, boss."

"Conroy, you know I hate when..." Wei trailed off as he turned to see Conroy, and his face told him everything he needed to know. "There's been another."

7

"Want to run that by me again?" Noah demanded, nearly spilling the glass of wine he'd been drinking from as he gaped at his sister. Lianne merely smiled at her brother. She'd expected this reaction; she knew him far too well to be unable to predict his moods and how he'd take news, especially news of this caliber. How could she not? She'd helped the housekeeper, Mrs. Faye, raise him.

Patiently she repeated, "I'm going to Hong Kong for a while. I don't know how long I'll be there—definitely for the ninety days the visa gives me, and I'll probably grease some official's palms and stay longer."

Noah blinked at her rapidly, no doubt trying to process what he heard. This was the first time she'd mentioned anything about traveling again—she'd only been back from Argentina for a few months—and she, unlike her brother, had never shown any interest in the Asian countries. Finally mustering his thoughts together, he managed to dumbly repeat her. "Hong Kong."

She nodded.

"But...but *why*?"

"Do I ever have a reason, Noah?" Lianne lifted her own glass of wine to her lips and sipped, the strong flavors spilling over her taste buds, activating them in the most delicious way. She watched her brother sitting across the dinner table from her with some amusement. It was rare to see such confusion on his handsome face.

"You should stay longer," her brother insisted, gulping deeply from his own glass, a small red flush creeping into his face, though she knew he was by no means drunk. Noah liked wine, though, and she'd supplied a very good vintage in hopes of easing her brother through the news. "You've only been home a few months. You need time to plan, anyway— we both know you'd never like Hong Kong—"

"It's already planned," Lianne interrupted, catching her brother's eyes and holding them with her own. "The ticket's booked."

Noah leaned back slowly, understanding blossoming behind his eyes. Understanding and hurt. "When did you decide?" His voice was terse, now, the build up to the storm of anger that was sure to come. Lianne had learned to read those tells as surely as a fisherman learned to read the sky and winds before a storm. It was always better to be aware of the oncoming storm.

"Not long after I got back from Argentina." There was a flicker of guilt in her voice, guilt that her brother latched on to like a pit bull.

"You decided that long ago? Without even telling me? What the hell?" Noah's voice grew louder with each word. "I didn't even know you were *considering* another trip! You haven't said anything at all, not even hints that you'd just be leaving." The end of that sentence hung heavy in the air between them, the crux of her brother's growing anger. Leaving *me*.

Lianne felt terrible for hurting Noah's feelings like this, she really did. Even though she'd known this would happen, known he'd be hurt, seeing it made it worse. She ran a hand through her hair, praying to whatever god might listen that she could head this off before it grew into a full-fledged battle. That was like taking a bite of a salad and hoping for steak instead.

"I need to get away, Noah. This place, this house can be so...toxic, you know?"

Noah laughed mirthlessly. "Of course I do! You think I can blame you for wanting to escape as much as you can? You think I don't know how poisonous it is to be in the same *room* as Father? I don't know anyone who's ever met the man who doesn't feel the same damn way—if they don't, they're probably just as bad as he is, or worse." Noah was standing now, pacing back and forth with empty wine glass in hand. Good thing it was empty, too; he was waving it around to emphasize his words.

"What makes me mad," he said at last, turning to face her, eyes blazing brightly. Noah's eyes always amazed her; they were capable of so much expression while hers were just...colorful. They might have had the same color eyes, but no one would ever mistake the two. A million words could be said and understood just through Noah's eyes. Lianne's eyes were pretty; Noah's were magical. "What makes me mad is that you didn't say a word to me. Of all people. I helped you plan Argentina—shit, I helped you plan Brussels and Spain and France. Why this time? Why did you shut me out this time?"

"I'm not shutting you out," Lianne insisted, crossing the distance between herself and her brother. He was taller, but only just, so it was easy for her to lean her head against his like she used to do when they were young, and she comforted him. "I felt that it was time for me to be an adult and do my own planning, being thirty years old and all."

She felt the tension begin to leave her brother's body and thought maybe the worst of it was over.

"Does Father know yet?"

Lianne nodded, still leaning her forehead against Noah's. "Of course he does. You know the way he watches our accounts. He knew the moment I booked the plane ticket." As soon as the words left her mouth, she wished she could take them back. Just when she'd been about to sidestep the landmine, she'd stepped right on it, and it exploded. Noah jerked away from her, eyes blazing up once more.

"He knew before me? *Father* knew before I did?"

Lianne wanted to melt through the floor, anything to escape the look of hurt on her brother's soft features. She started to reach for him, but he jerked out of reach and instead turned to the dinner table and quickly filled his glass nearly to the brim with wine and emptying it once more.

"When?" Noah demanded, voice jagged from the wine he'd just slung back like water.

"Last Wednesday," Lianne said meekly.

"No, when do you leave?"

Lianne took a ragged breath. "The day after tomorrow." She expected another explosion of rage, more vehemence, more declarations of her betrayal, but what happened instead was so much worse. Noah calmly sat the wine glass down on the table and turned on his heel, barely glancing in her direction as he stalked out of her apartment as she called after him.

"Noah! Noah, come back, please! Noah, please!"

8

"Noah, please!" Lianne's voice had shifted, suddenly weak and dripping a palpable pain that spoke of torture and unknown horrors—

Noah jerked awake, fighting away the mix of memory and dream. He tossed the comforter off and sat up, disoriented and expecting it to be night outside. Bright sunlight poured through the window instead, dust motes dancing in its rays as it illuminated long patches of the wooden floor. He checked the time on his phone as he stumbled toward the small door he'd noticed the day before near the dresser and into the utilitarian bathroom. It was eleven in the morning. Jet lag and emotions must have caught up with him, and he'd slept clear through the night.

His sister's voice still clung to his mind, a darkness that even the too-warm light of the sun couldn't banish. The intensity of the dream, the way his heart still hammered in his chest after waking, combined with his conscious fears continued to plague him even now. He'd failed in his duty as a brother, failed to protect his sister.

If I'd answered the phone the first time she called... Guilt, hot and burning, tore at his stomach, bringing tears to his eyes and threatening to overwhelm him. He didn't think he would ever be able to forgive himself.

He deserved the pain of that guilt, so he simply sat there on the bed, shoulders hunched, looking blindly at his hands resting palms-up on the comforter in his lap. That guilt was selfish, he knew, more about him than about her, so he only allowed himself a few minutes to indulge it. He didn't have time for much more, not if he wanted to help Lianne.

He refused to believe her beyond help.

While the bathroom lacked an actual bathtub it had a small shower stall, so Noah took a hurried shower, keeping the water cold to combat the heavy air in the apartment. It didn't have an air conditioner and the ceiling fan could only do so much. He didn't know how anyone had survived summer before the invention of the air conditioner. Probably wasn't as bad as it is now, though; global warming had taken an obvious toll on the planet. That had to be it, nothing else made sense.

Noah usually liked to luxuriate in his showers, but he kept this one utilitarian—washed his hair, soaped up, rinsed, done. As he dried off, he booted up his laptop, thankful that Hong Kong's access to the Internet wasn't as restricted as in China, like he'd expected it to be. Once dressed, he opened Google and began to search.

It took little work to find instructions to the nearest police station, once he'd figured out what jurisdiction his sister's disappearance would fall under. His first instinct was to go to the American embassy or to the federal forces, but he imagined that would create some hostilities, step on someone else's toes. He didn't want to do that, so he'd start local.

His sister's residence was in the Eastern District, not far from the district called Wai Chen to the west. If he could trust what he read, the Eastern District precinct of the Hong Kong Police Department was about a thirty-minute bus ride from where he was. That was where he'd start.

Making sure he had his wallet, the picture of his sister, and his passport for identification purposes, Noah headed out the door.

9

It didn't take long for him to find the Eastern District police station. The building, a colonial-era structure, had tall, imposing columns. It looked utterly out of place surrounded by the other buildings. To one side of it was a coin laundry and a bookstore, to the other several restaurants. Across the street from it, several food peddlers had set up stalls and called out loudly, competing with each other to attract buyers for their goods.

Noah, who hadn't had breakfast, forked over the twenty-five dollars for one of the steaming pork buns and was immediately glad he did. The bun itself was hot and chewy, the stuffing succulent pork, dripping tasty juices. He gobbled it down, humming appreciatively as he did. He finished in three bites. For a moment, he debated buying another but decided there would be time for that later. Right now he needed to focus on his reason for being in front of the police station—and for being in Hong Kong.

Touching the edge of the picture in his pocket for comfort, he went inside.

Surprisingly, the interior of the station looked like it might have been a set for any old nineties police drama in the States. Other than the décor, though, everything was modern. The computers looked to be state-of-the-art. Everything had an intense efficiency to it, a sense of controlled chaos. Everything had a purpose, and everything was operating like a machine.

The officer behind the counter was average in just about every way, nothing that would make him stand out in memory. He seemed surprised to see a foreigner walk through the door.

"Can I help you?"

"I would like to talk to someone about a potential missing person."

The officer looked him over critically, as if gauging how serious he was. "Just a moment, please." The officer disappeared for a moment and returned, followed by a nonuniformed officer. The inspector, probably in his very early thirties if not late twenties, was dressed in a pair of dark-wash jeans and a plaid button-down, its sleeves rolled up past his elbows. Not the image of a higher-ranking officer Noah had in mind.

"I'm Inspector Hong. Officer Tsai said you wanted to discuss a missing person?"

"Yes. My sister."

Inspector Hong nodded and motioned for Noah to follow him. He led Noah through the bullpen. Phones were ringing nonstop; a few officers took statements from witnesses while another had a man handcuffed to the chair across from him, clearly processing him for some crime—a petty one, Noah hoped, eying the flimsy-looking chair with some trepidation.

Inspector Hong's desk sat a mere three desks away from the chained man, the last on his row. About ten feet away was a closed office, the door marked HENRY DANG, SUPERINTENDENT.

While the inspector dug around on his desk to find paper and a pen, Noah took the opportunity to study him: his hair was almost long enough to be considered unprofessional, but not quite. His eyes were a pale brown mixed with hazel beneath strong eyebrows. His cheekbones were high—the man had bone structure that a model would kill for. Aside from his good looks, he radiated this sense of trustworthiness that made it difficult *not* to warm up to him.

Paper and pen retrieved, Inspector Hong directed his gaze at Noah. "All right, tell me why you think you're sister has gone missing." The tone of voice he used communicated a distant but somehow sincere interest in Noah's situation; Noah suspected it was a technique meant to set the listener at ease, to make them feel safe and respected, so they could open up easier.

Instead of speaking right away, Noah pulled his cell phone out of his pocket and quickly geared up the message, putting it on speaker phone so the inspector could hear it, too.

The message was just over one full minute of silence, the sound of breathing, heavy, someone trying to speak a few times before manage it at last. "Noah. It's me. I'm just... I really... I've gotten in some kind of trouble, I don't know. I met this guy, and... Jesus, Noah. I don't know what I'm going to do. I don't know—you have—you have to help me. Please."

"When did you receive this message?"

Noah explained everything, then, about his sister's departure, the silence between the two of them, and the sudden phone call. He also added what he'd learned from Pam at the noodle shop.

"Do you have a picture?"

Noah nodded, digging into his pocket and handing the picture to Inspector Hong. He studied it closely for a moment before setting it down on the desk between the two of them. "Other than what you've told me, you don't have any idea where she might have gone or done? Any friends in Hong Kong who might know where she is?"

Noah shook his head. "I don't know. She didn't tell me anything about her time here, so I have absolutely no idea what she was up to. If I know Lianne, she was at a lot of night clubs. She enjoyed going out, seeing the nightlife in a new place."

Inspector Hong pursed his lips. "That's not much to go on, but it's a—" He stopped talking, eyes moving over Noah's shoulder as a sudden ruckus rose behind him. Noah turned to see what was going on as he heard the officer at the front desk say, "You can't go back there!" to a man who clearly had no intention of listening to him.

The man was one of the most striking people Noah had ever laid eyes on. He would not be surprised if his mouth hung open as he looked. Not much taller than Noah, the guy had something about him, this raw, masculine power that drew Noah in quickly. He could almost smell the testosterone and sensuality that radiated from him. His face was a bit too hard to be called handsome—but he was all the more sexy for it. The tight gray material of his shirt displayed his body nicely, the right arm giving the barest flashes of a tattoo beneath the sleeve as it moved with him.

Noah had never gotten so instantly erect just from *seeing* a guy before. The guy that caused that boner moved right toward him, too. A sudden surge of fear replaced the arousal; he wouldn't call the look on this guy's face a happy one. Noah didn't think he'd like to make enemies with this guy.

"Another one, Hong," the guy spat, storming up to Inspector Hong's desk. Hong rose, meeting the challenge with an almost bemused expression. He didn't seem intimidated by this newcomer, though Noah sure was. Noah was very glad to be ignored right then. "You don't look surprised, so I guess you already fucking knew. Already ruled a goddamn overdose? Are you fucking kidding me?"

"They *were* overdoses, Wei," Hong said patiently, crossing his arms across his chest.

"Don't call me that, like you know me, like we're friends," the other guy—Wei—hissed. Noah guessed there was some history there. "The newest girl—she was fucking eighteen, by the way, Allen, *eighteen*—barely just turned up and you fuckin' bastards have already 'closed the case'? What is this bullshit? What's it gonna take, huh?"

"You want to talk about this rationally, fine, but as you can see—" Inspector Hong gestured at Noah with his right hand, and Noah wished he hadn't, because those blazing, furious eyes were on Noah, and he felt himself shudder—from what, exactly, he couldn't say. "—I'm with someone."

"Oh, I get it," Wei said bitterly, looking at the picture of Lianne on the desk. "Looks like the fucking Hong Kong Police Force can't be relied on to investigate the shit happening to their own people, but let a foreigner go missing and it gets top-fucking-priority." Wei stepped in close to the inspector, and Noah's breath caught in his throat. For a moment, he thought the men would come to blows, but they didn't. "What if these girls' skin had been white, huh?"

"That's enough! This is a police station, not the sort of alleys and playgrounds you thugs are used to!" The superintendent's office door was now open, the man inside drawn out by the noise in the bullpen. The superintendent didn't look like much to Noah; he was a man probably in his sixties, bald except for a few tufts of gray hair over his ears on either side of his head, with thick, unkempt eyebrows that gave his face a comical cast. He was skin and bones; the suit he wore might have looked good on someone who could actually fill it out, but it simply hung loosely from Henry Dang.

"Superintendent Dang. Always a pleasure." The words and eyes said it was anything but.

"My officers have better things to do than listen to your brutish yelling, Tseng. Why don't you run along? I'm sure you can find *something* to occupy you." The amount of sheer venom that could be imbedded in such few words shocked Noah, but there was no mistaking it; just a look at the superintendent's eyes at that moment would let anyone around know he loathed the man in front of him.

"You're right, I *do* have things to occupy myself, like protecting the people of this district—something you *claim* to be doing."

Dang laughed, an unpleasant sound that set the hair on the back of Noah's neck on end. "Is that really what you think? You and those thugs who follow you might think of yourselves as some modern heroes, fighting the good fight, but that's bullshit. You and the rest of the Dragons are just thugs, no better than any other gang out there."

Noah caught Inspector Hong's eyes for a moment and saw what must have been in his own eyes: the look of someone caught in the middle, hoping to avoid the conflict.

"Is that what you think, you pompous ass? No better than any other gang out there? When the Nine Stars ran this territory, how many people died every day? How many cops were gunned down in the line of duty? How much drugs flowed on these streets? Since the Dragons took over, you guys have become glorified meter maids!" Wei slammed his hand down on Hong's desk, the motion bringing him forward and into Noah's personal space. The scent of him suddenly flared in Noah's nostrils, a fresh smell of cedar soap with the slightest hints of sweat and a massive amount of something he could only identify as *male*. The man's pheromones made Noah feel almost light-headed, and his cock throbbed painfully, uncomfortably trapped within the confines of his jeans. His pulse quickened; he could feel the flush of red as it creeped up his neck and into his cheeks. "We keep our territory safe—we keep the other triads at bay. *We* do, not you."

Superintendent Dang just shook his head. "You're a delusional prick, Wei Tseng. You think this is 'your' territory, and that's the problem. Instead of relying on the police, you act like you're above the law, just like every other piece-of-shit triad out there."

Wei threw something on Inspector Hong's desk. "Maybe that's because you *can't* be relied on. I'll leave you to investigate your precious missing *gwei mui*." He pushed away from the desk, his angry eyes catching Noah's for a moment and holding, and inside them was the flicker of something Noah couldn't name. As suddenly as he entered, he left, though his scent lingered, as did the effects seeing him had on Noah.

"I'm really sorry for that, sir," Superintendent Dang said in a simpering voice, giving Noah an apologetic bow that did not seem the least bit sincere. "Now, am I right in understanding you're here looking for someone?"

"I was just about to take a report, sir," Inspector Hong started to explain, but the superintendent held up a calloused hand, silencing him.

"Yes, but I'd like to hear it again. It's the least I can do considering the trouble that miscreant you used to run around with caused with this fuss." Noah didn't miss the look on Inspector Hong's face at the superintendent's words; they were like a physical slap to the face, and he paled a bit. Noah was pretty sure the superintendent noticed it, too.

He didn't have much choice, so he explained everything to the superintendent, who took a seat at Inspector Hong's desk across from him. He started to play the voice message again, but Dang stopped him. "That won't be necessary, Mr. Potter. I understand your concern for your sister's safety, but I have to say that what you've given us is...very little to go on. I'm not even certain we can say she's gone missing at this point."

Noah felt like he'd been punched in the gut, the wind knocked out of him for a moment. *Not sure she'd gone missing?* How could that be? "The voice mail," he said at last, reaching numbly to start the message. "You have to hear the message."

Dang nodded his head in polite acquiescence, though the look on his face said he was sure this would be a waste of time. Noah played it again, watching the superintendent's face as he did, but it was a mask, giving away nothing of what he was thinking. Inspector Hong, on the other hand, just looked uncomfortable.

When it finished, he placed the phone down on the desk with a clatter. "You see?" There was no way the superintendent couldn't see now, no way he couldn't understand after listening to Lianne's voice on that message.

"While I do agree that she sounds to be in a state of emotional distress, Mr. Potter, it doesn't sound like she's fearing for her life. If that were the case, why was there such a long pause at the beginning?"

The blood drained from Noah's face, and he felt dizzy. They didn't believe him. The police, the people who were responsible for the safety of the district, didn't believe him.

"I think it much more likely," the superintendent went on, oblivious to the effect his words had had, the numbness that was seeping into Noah, "that this trouble with a boy has led to some...er, consequences...and she is dealing with those."

"Her things are still at her place." Noah's voice sounded flat, foreign to his own ears.

"She may be on a fling with the boy she mentioned," Dang said patiently. "Or else decided to take a short trip—from what you've told us that is not unlikely, given her nature."

"A trip? No, her luggage is still in her room."

Dang sighed, losing patience with a matter he deemed closed. "She may have bought new luggage, Mr. Potter." He rose, and Noah knew it for the dismissal it was. "Please, continue to keep us informed, and if any new evidence comes to light, share it with us. If proof is found that, like you say, your sister is in danger, we will of course exhaust all of our resources to find her. However, until then, we need to focus our manpower on real cases."

Noah mumbled his thanks, reaching down to pick up the photo of Lianne. He paused for a moment when he saw what Wei had thrown onto the desk. It was a photo, much like the one he had of Lianne. It was of a beautiful young girl with happy eyes, a heart-shaped face, and a big, toothy smile despite the braces she wore still.

Noah didn't pay any attention to what Inspector Hong was saying as he escorted him to the door, didn't really notice the business card being shoved into his hand before the inspector walked helplessly back to his desk. Didn't notice the superintendent standing at his open door, watching him.

The police didn't believe him. He could not fathom it. He'd been taught he could always reach out to them when he needed help. Maybe in Hong Kong it was different. There was no one, then. No one who could help him and Lianne. He was on his own.

10

Outside the precinct, Wei smoked a cigarette and paced the sidewalk angrily. That smug bastard Dang's words still echoed in his mind. So, no better than any other gang out there, huh? He called them thugs, miscreants, compared them to the triads. He didn't care that since the Dragons had come to power, defeating the Nine Stars in what was a necessary but undeniably bloody street war, crime rate in the Eastern District had become almost minimal. Theft still happened, as did the occasional drunken brawl in the street or crimes of passion, sure, but triad crime—drugs, prostitution, murder—had all but disappeared, because Wei wouldn't tolerate it. He would keep these streets safe for the people who lived in them.

And yet he hadn't been able to do that like he wanted. Young women were turning up dead, victims of supposed overdoses.

This was happening in his territory while the cops who claimed to have the same agenda as Wei simply dismissed them, shutting the cases as nothing more than drug addicts who happened to let their habit get the better of them before the cases even opened. One less drug addict wasn't a bad thing, according to those fuckers.

It didn't matter that the families swore up and down that they didn't have a drug problem, didn't matter that they were *people*, even if they happened to be drug addicts, which Wei didn't think they were. Didn't matter that families had lost something irreplaceable in their girls.

But fine. Wei expected the police to just sit on their asses and do nothing while something like this happened. Wei and the Dragons would take care of it themselves, and to hell with the police and anyone else who got in their way.

The station door behind him opened, and Wei glanced over his shoulder as the white guy who'd been at Hong's desk came out. Wei had noticed him the moment he'd set eyes on Hong's desk—hard not to, really; the other man had these hypnotic blue-green eyes that reminded him of the ocean. They were more than just a pretty color, though; in the brief instances he'd made eye contact, Wei could see that they were vibrant, alive. Eyes like that could tell a hundred stories without the mouth ever needing to speak.

What he'd seen in those eyes had been pain, pain and a hope born of desperation. Wei remembered the picture of the pretty white lady on the desk. Her eyes had been the same as this man's.

Those eyes right now showed dejection. *So, turns out not even being white can get a proper investigation going.* He immediately felt guilty for the thought. It wasn't this guy's fault that Dang and Hong—his jaw tightened when he thought about that bastard—wouldn't lift a finger to help his people. This guy was just like the families he'd visited, dealing with his loss and searching for answers, searching for help that seemed unlikely to come.

Fucking cop bastards.

Wei watched the man descend the precinct steps and stand there on the sidewalk, looking back and forth on the road, hunting a taxi most likely. If Wei had been younger, he might have catcalled. The guy was slender, which always appealed to him. His face was attractive—sensual, pouty lips that looked utterly kissable and would probably look amazing engaged in other activities. He had broad shoulders despite his slender frame, and his legs looked well-toned in the tight-fit jeans he wore. Wei's gaze traveled up those legs and came to rest with a quiet, appreciative grunt on the other man's ass. Nice and round and would fit perfectly in his hands, no doubt. Wei had to quickly tug at the growing bulge in the front of his jeans, angling his cock toward his navel and giving it more room to grow. What about this guy spurred this kind of reaction in him simply from *looking*?

Wei took one last drag of his cigarette, flicked the butt away, and walked down to stand next to the other guy. He was definitely aware of Wei's presence; Wei saw the way his muscles tensed, heard the slight intake of breath. From reading his body language, Wei guessed he'd had some martial arts training.

"When did your sister disappear?"

The question seemed to catch the other man off guard, his head jerking to the side to look up—though only slightly; there was barely any difference in their heights—those expressive eyes showing his shock and a bit of suspicion. "How did you know she's my sister?"

"The eyes," Wei replied. The other guy nodded as if he'd been expecting that answer.

"Everyone always says we have the same eyes."

"They're similar," Wei conceded. *Similar, yes, but not the same. I don't think there's a set of eyes out there than can match the fire in yours.* "So, when did she?"

The other man looked down at the sidewalk for a moment. "I'm not entirely sure," he confessed. He explained his story, the lack of communication with his travel-loving sister, the phone call and voice mail, the disappearance. Though he clearly struggled to keep his voice emotionless, Wei sensed the pain underneath the words and found himself fighting the urge to reach out and comfort him.

Instead, he simply said, "I'm Wei."

The other man looked at him, an eyebrow, slightly darker than the rest of his hair, cocked. "I'm Noah." Noah turned his attention back to the road, craning his neck to see the vehicles coming and going.

"You're going to have a hell of a time getting a taxi to pick you up here," Wei commented. "If you want, I can give you a ride wherever it is you're going."

He didn't mistake the suspicion in those eyes as they looked him over—but there might have been something more, as well. Wei wanted to say he saw a flare of interest, but decided he was attributing that to his own burgeoning arousal—he was still hard as a rock in this guy's presence.

"Why would you do that?"

"To make up for the way I acted in there," Wei replied, pointing at the station behind them with his thumb over his shoulder. "Not saying those cop bastards didn't deserve it," he added quickly, "but you didn't have anything to do with it, and I shouldn't have put you in the middle." He couldn't help teasing the other man a bit. "Plenty of people would kill to get this offer, you know."

Noah snorted. "I'm sure." He shook his head. "It was nice of you to make the offer, but I'll catch a taxi. Never take a ride from strangers and all that good stuff."

Wei smiled, his lips widening into a grin when he saw the slight hint of a blush on the other man's cheeks. So that flare of interest wasn't his imagination, after all. He wouldn't push, though, and he had things to do. He'd need to meet up with the boys and let them know what had gone down at the police station—not that they wouldn't have already guessed, since it was the fucking Hong Kong Police Force they were dealing with.

"You can at least let me wait with you until a taxi comes."

Noah pointed behind Wei at an approaching vehicle. "Looks like you're in luck. Here comes one now." He flagged it down. "Thanks for keeping me company."

Wei couldn't help himself, and he winked. The flush returned stronger than ever to Noah's cheeks. *Definitely not imagined.* "No problem. Maybe I'll see you around."

Noah muttered out something Wei didn't catch and pulled the door closed. Wei stood there, watching until the taxi turned out of sight.

Noah was certainly an intriguing prospect, but he mustn't lose focus at this point. He had things to look after. A leader's work, it seemed, was never done.

11

Wei collected his motorcycle parked nearby, donned his helmet, and rode off to meet his fellow Dragons at their usual place. The ride gave him a chance to sort through some of his thoughts. His rage after his confrontation with Hong and that piece of shit Dang hadn't abated. Dang he understood, but Hong? He sped up without really thinking about it, his anger fueling his speed. He couldn't think about Allen without getting pissed off even after so much time had passed.

Wei didn't need to ride angry, not if he wanted to arrive in one piece, so he turned his thoughts away from assholes he wanted to beat the shit out of to the interesting man he'd met today. Just thinking about those damn eyes had his cock stirring to life once more—Jesus Christ, he couldn't think of the last time someone had that effect on him. Well, he could, but it was a place in his mind he absolutely refused to go. He kept it sealed off, tighter and more secure than any high-security vault in any bank in the world. Besides, it was much more pleasurable to think about the here and now.

The more he thought about Noah's story, the more wary Wei became. The story sounded remarkably similar to the kind of disappearances that happened in other parts of the city. Those most often came down to human trafficking, connected to the triads. Wei didn't hold with that, and anyone attempting that sort of action in his territory would be swiftly punished. The fact that she disappeared on his turf did not sit well with him. Combine it with the overdosing women turning up on his streets and it screamed of a rival gang moving in on the Eastern District.

Nothing good could come of that.

The implications of such an event still weighed heavily on his mind as he brought his motorcycle to a stop outside the coffee shop owned by Constance Chang. It was a nice-looking coffee shop, not quite upscale but not a cheap hole-in-the-wall, either. Located near the heart of the Eastern District, the coffee shop was the seat of power for the Dragons. It had a simple and refined exterior, no complicated decoration or flourishing ornamentation, just a few tables under green patio umbrellas and a simple sign that said "Coffee by Constance."

Two young women sat at one of the outside tables, probably in the first year of university, identical pairs of large sunglasses on their faces and backpacks slung over their chairs as they shared iced coffee. They both looked Wei over appreciatively, obvious even behind their sunglasses. He flashed them a little smile, though they weren't his type. Without the sunglasses, their eyes wouldn't be...alive.

Not like a certain pair of ocean eyes. He killed the thought before it rekindled the desire he'd only just managed to push down. No way would he go into a meeting with his boys with a fucking hard-on.

Coffee by Constance boasted an interior as simple as the exterior, to wonderful effect. The walls were all beautiful dark-stained wood, as were the counters. The tables were similar, though a shade lighter to stand out against the room itself. Constance had placed live potted plants strategically throughout the shop. Classical jazz music wafted gently from the speakers, turned down low enough to be a pleasant background drone, never loud enough to stifle conversation. People sat at three of the café's nine interior tables, enjoying their coffee or one of Constance's desserts, which had become more famous than her coffee. Her strawberry-cream-stuffed buns were a staple of the community around the shop. Few people came in that didn't order one.

Constance's daughter stood behind the counter. Shelby was seventeen, a pretty girl with a mass of curly hair that she had dyed the color of dripping honey, which annoyed her mother to no end. Shelby waved at Wei as he came in.

"How's it going, Shelby?"

"I'm stuck behind the counter in this place, how do *you* think?" Despite the petulant tone of her words she smiled. Wei knew she loved the coffee shop and enjoyed working there with her mother.

"I tried to put you in the back, but you let everything burn." Constance Chang emerged from the kitchen, hands on her hips as she scowled at her daughter. Constance, a strong woman, in her early forties—though no one would remind her of it lest they enjoyed physical pain—was not much taller than her daughter, around five foot five, though her presence rivaled Wei's. Straight black hair reached just below her shoulders, though at the shop she usually kept it pulled back into a tight ponytail. She had eyes as sharp as a hawk's; she missed very little, did Constance. Her size made her seem fragile, but Wei knew better. Constance had been instrumental in the Dragons taking control of the Eastern District. She was not a woman to be fucked with.

Constance turned those sharp eyes on Wei and tilted her head toward the back. "Everyone else is up there," she said. Wei nodded and started into the small kitchen. "Oh, and Wei," Constance called behind him, "send Winston back down when you get up there." Her tone brooked no argument, and Wei grinned. Winston was going to hate that.

He made his way through the narrow kitchen—its surfaces gleaming on either side of him; Constance kept her kitchen immaculate—and out into the small fenced-in back alley behind the coffee shop. To the left of the door was a rusty metal staircase that ascended to the second floor and a red door. Constance owned the second floor, as well, and Wei and the Dragons used it as their primary meeting place.

He entered the upstairs room and found the other Dragons there already, chatting and messing around. They all fell silent when Wei walked in, eyes turned to him. He noted each of them. Steel and Chris, Conroy and Jesse, Kevin and Walker, Smile and Tony, and Winston. This was his family; these were the people who cared for him, who were there when shit hit the fan. These were the people he'd fought side by side with—and would do so again without a second's hesitation.

"Yo, Wei, how'd it go with the cops?" Conroy asked by way of greeting.

Chris snorted, not giving Wei a chance to respond. "How the fuck do you think it went, man? Fuckin' Hong Kong police can't do shit."

Expectant eyes turned from Chris back to Wei, each of them, waiting for an answer. Before he would give it to them, Wei's sought out Winston—there he was, leaning against the wall at the back of the room between Kevin and Walker. Twenty years old, soon to be twenty-one—that meant he was a man. He still resembled a child, but he would grow out of it. He was a bit on the scrawny side, but he'd been hitting the gym pretty religiously with some of the other Dragons closer to his age, like Jesse and Steel, and the effects were starting to show. As he slowly bulked up, his body grew from that of a teenager to that of a man. He kept his hair shaggy, always falling into his face, though it wasn't unkempt—Constance would never allow that. His eyes matched his sister's, the same slightly oval face, the same surprising expression of innocence.

Wei caught his eyes and something in them flickered, the look on his face becoming pleading. *Please,* it said. *Please don't shut me out.* Winston wanted so desperately to be a Dragon, to belong in their world, be part of the family. He didn't realize that lacking the tattoo didn't make him any less of their family. That alone told Wei Winston wasn't ready, not yet.

"Winston," he said, his voice even, carefully communicating this was nothing personal. "Go on downstairs and see if your mom needs any help."

"She's got Shelby," Winston said quickly, not succeeding in hiding the whine from his voice. "She's fine."

Wei barely restrained a sigh. He definitely wasn't ready. "This is a Dragons meeting." He didn't say it, but he knew Winston would pick up on the subtle *and you're not a Dragon* attached to those words.

Face growing stony, Winston kicked off the wall, crossing the crowded room and skirting the big poker table in the middle of it. "My mom told you to send me down, didn't she? You don't have to say anything. I already know. For fuck's sake, I'm twenty years old. I wish she'd just get out of my life!"

A muscle in Wei's jaw twitched at that. He waited until Winston was out the door and stepped out behind him, closing the door firmly—he didn't want to humiliate the younger man in front of the entire family. He grabbed Winston's shoulder, turning him to face him and keeping his own face inscrutable as he met the furious gaze from the younger man.

"You're the boss of the Dragons. You could tell her no." It was an accusation—the accusation of a bratty child, and Wei saw that even Winston realized that, but was too far in his feelings of hurt to really care.

"Yeah, but I won't."

"Why not?" Winston exploded, jerking his shoulder out of Wei's grasp. "I'm a grown man now. She can't just treat me like some little kid forever!"

"If you don't want to be treated like a little kid, then stop acting like one," Wei said bluntly. Winston opened his mouth to argue, but something he saw in the Dragons' leader's eyes seemed to make him think twice about it; his mouth closed with an audible snap. "You're ready to join the Dragons, huh? You can't even take fuckin' orders. The men in that room have earned the right to question what I say—but they still *follow orders*. If you join the Dragons right now, you'd be a grunt, the low man on the totem pole. You wouldn't have a voice—you haven't earned it yet. If some new Dragon responded like that to me, you know what would happen?" Winston's eyes glanced away from Wei's, his jaw set, but Wei wasn't going to allow it. The message needed to get across. *"Do you know what would happen?"*

At last Winston met his eyes again. "You'd lay him out."

Wei nodded, glad Winston understood. "You're damn right I would. No way can I have that kind of challenge to my authority. You said I could tell your mom no—"

"But you won't. I get it," Winston said bitterly.

"Do you know *why* though?" Winston shook his head. "I didn't think so. Your mother has done more for the Dragons than just about anyone else—including the people in that room up there. She's earned my respect a thousand times over—and she damn well deserves yours. Don't you ever let me hear you disrespect her in any way again, you understand?"

Winston nodded wordlessly and turned to go, but Wei grabbed him, softer this time. "Listen to me. You'll get your chance, Winston. You're too good a soldier for me to want to keep you out forever." Wei was pleased to see that his words bolstered Winston somewhat.

He stood there at the top of the stairs, watching until Winston disappeared into Coffee by Constance's kitchen, and then turned back. There was a lot he needed to discuss with the Dragons.

12

Noah couldn't get Wei out of his head. The weight of Wei's gaze on him or the smell of him when he'd leaned over Inspector Hong's desk, the powerful muscles of his arms straining...it all played on repeat in his mind, driving him to a point of arousal he hadn't felt in a long time. Hell, he wasn't certain *anyone* had ever had this sort of effect on him; the memory of something as mundane as a silly wink made his cock throb, demanding attention.

He'd picked a hell of a day to wear slim-fitting jeans.

He rode in the taxi back to Lianne's place, trying not to fidget uncomfortably and give away his condition. Hopefully the taxi driver would think the flush in his cheeks was from the heat and not because he was so turned on even the friction of his underwear was driving him wild.

This didn't make any sense; why should a perfect stranger affect him this way? He'd only laid eyes on the guy twice, and he couldn't say his first meeting inside the police station had left him with a great impression. Yet the man outside the police station had seemed entirely different, like there were two distinct individuals within the same shell of a man. How did they mesh as one person?

It's not like I'll ever see him again, he reminded himself, settling back against the hot leather of the seat and forcing his eyes to concentrate on the scenery as it passed, though seconds later, he had no memory of any of it. He thought back to the confrontation between Wei and the police. *If what they said is to be believed, he's just a gangster.* If so, Noah was better off never seeing him again.

Even if he is sexy as hell...

Noah cleared his throat and shifted, tugging discreetly at the fabric of his jeans, hoping to conceal the bulge of his erection. He didn't want to have a boner when he paid the cab fare.

Noah thought about where he'd come from, where he'd met Wei, and a wash of guilt surged through him, immediately killing any remnants of arousal. He was a terrible brother, getting so distracted by his penis that he momentarily forgot Lianne was in danger somewhere. How could he be so dismissive of his own sister?

To fight the guilt, he forced his mind to focus on the situation at hand—not that there was much to focus on, really. He knew next to nothing, other than the fact that Lianne hadn't returned to the room she was renting after leaving him a distressed message. He'd been there less than twenty-four hours, and he'd already exhausted his leads.

Well, he decided, *I'll just have to open up some new leads.* Noah wasn't about to let a little setback or a man like Superintendent Dang— he wouldn't say it, but he was pretty confident Wei's opinion of the man, that he's a pompous ass, was accurate—hold him back, not with Lianne at stake. He'd hoped to get a little more support from the police, but that wasn't an option.

He might go to the US embassy, see if they would apply pressure to the local government, but he didn't see how that would help; it would probably make the police resentful and lead to shoddy work to get the case closed, and America had to tread carefully along jurisdictional lines where China was concerned. The Mainland probably wouldn't look too happily on the interference of a government they viewed as hostile in their territory.

Going above the superintendent in the Hong Kong police structure would probably be just as ineffective; Dang had jurisdiction, and that was that. He didn't have anyone to rely on; he would have to do this himself.

That thought didn't intimidate him as much as it might have other people; he was used to being alone, used to relying on no one—no one, that is, except Lianne. They only had each other after their mother died—they never counted the nanny, being that their father paid her, making her the extension of his will; neither child fully trusted her for that. They always turned first to each other, no matter their problems.

When Lianne's first major boyfriend cheated on her, she turned to Noah. When Noah realized he was different, that he liked boys and not girls, he turned to Lianne. So went their history, a repetition of the same pattern. It continued even now.

If Lianne was in trouble—and Noah had zero doubt she was—she didn't turn to the police, which might have been the more logical choice. No, those patterns established in childhood were too hard to break. Lianne once more turned to her brother. He would make damn sure she didn't regret it.

13

He'd formulated a plan by the time the taxi reached the noodle shop. He paid the fare and quickly made his way into the restaurant. He waved Pam away politely when she approached him with the intention of getting him lunch, and instead made his way into the stairwell leading to the apartment.

He didn't know anything about his sister's life in Hong Kong, what she did there, what her routine was. He could guess a few things easily enough, knowing his sister as well as he did, but he would need more specifics if he had any hope of tracking her down and helping her. He was an idiot for not thinking about it before; Pam seemed to know something about his sister from working in the noodle shop below the apartment—imagine what her neighbors might know. They were the only chance he had of figuring out if there were any clues in Lianne's life that might help him.

He started with the people on the same floor his sister lived, the most likely to know anything about her. Her direct neighbor did not answer the door or else wasn't home.

The room across the hallway was occupied by a tired-looking woman who greeted him with a squalling baby slung on her hip. Her sleep-deprived gaze took him in without showing any sign of emotion. Noah showed her the picture, explaining the situation and hoping she could speak English, knowing the chance of that was high. Luckily for him she could. Unluckily, she was not able to tell him anything; she'd seen Lianne from time to time but had never spoken to her and didn't really know what Lianne did when she came and went.

Noah thanked her and moved on.

The final room on the floor was occupied by at least two people— Noah could see male and female shoes in the small area where shoes were meant to be removed. It was a man, mid-forties, who opened the door. The first thing Noah noticed about him was that his clothes were food-stained and filthy. The second thing Noah noticed was that he was piss-drunk this early in the day. He even had a bottle of some sort of Chinese alcohol in his hand when he opened the door.

Noah started to show the picture and explain, but the guy just shook his head, wagging his hand for emphasis, muttering something to him in Chinese. Noah assumed it was something along the lines of "I don't speak English" or "Go the fuck away"; it was really hard to tell with the man so inebriated. Either way, he wasn't going to get much out of him, so he made his way to the second floor.

"She's so loud," complained the heavyset woman of indeterminate age who lived just below Lianne's apartment.

"Loud in what ways?" Noah inquired, breath catching ever so slightly in his chest. Maybe she would have something for him, something that could help.

"She always play music, no matter what time it is. Sometimes I have to bang on ceiling with my broom, but she just keeps the music on. Sometimes," her voice now dropped to a conspiratorial tone, and she leaned toward Noah, taking him into her confidence as she shared a juicy tidbit of gossip she just couldn't hold back, "she would bring over men. Could hear their heavy footsteps. Could hear them...having sex, too, sometimes."

Noah wasn't surprised by that information. His sister had had an active sex life since she'd first begun having sex senior year of high school. Being in a foreign country wouldn't curb her sexual appetites— might have the opposite effect, in fact.

He thought for a moment about the wild flaring of sexual desire he'd felt for Wei just seeing and smelling him, and his face flushed red with shame. He needed to get this lady onto more fruitful topics.

"Can you tell me anything about her habits? Any places she was likely to go? Any routine she may have had?"

The woman shook her head. "I really only notice her if she being loud, so I don't know what she do when she not stomping and screwing up there."

Noah tried to hide his disappointment, but he must have failed because the woman added, "I'm sorry."

Noah thanked her for her time and moved on. The occupants of the other three rooms on that floor were just as unhelpful; two of them weren't home and the one that was, a mousy thing of a man with thick Coke-bottle glasses and a head shaped like an egg with a thinning frazzle of hair resting atop it, didn't even realize a foreign girl lived in the building.

He could do nothing but return to Lianne's room, dejected. He'd been so certain he would get something useful out of these people, but he'd only hit a roadblock. He was having bad luck every step of the way.

Once he returned to Lianne's room once more, he crossed to the window, feeling the heat of the sun across his face as he stared out at the city. Large portions of the view were obscured by taller buildings, but it still was lovely. He hadn't seen it last night, having passed out, but he imagined that at night it was even more beautiful.

How many times had Lianne been at this window, staring out at this place that was so familiar and yet so different?

For a moment he could almost sense his sister right there with him. Traces of her lingered all around this place, the paths she traveled from the bed to the window, the window to the bathroom, the bathroom to the desk, the desk to the door. It was difficult for him to imagine the vibrancy that was his sister contained in such a small space. It was somewhat like putting a polar bear in a small tank. It would survive, but it wouldn't thrive.

He turned away from the sun and walked listlessly through the room. He stopped in front of the desk, examining the smattering of papers upon it. Many were receipts for purchases Noah didn't understand— they would be useless to him; he had no way of knowing where they were from.

He opened one of the drawers. It was empty. The second drawer contained more papers, things that looked like ticket stubs and several of those paper wristbands given at some clubs to mark people who were old enough to drink once inside. They were each torn neatly; Lianne was one of the people who liked to keep mementos of her nights out to look back on later.

Most of them were from the same place, he realized, a nightclub called simply "K." Noah held the thin slips of paper in his hand, staring down at them. There were seven from K; she went there a lot. A clue, right underneath his nose, if he'd bothered to look earlier.

Maybe his luck was turning after all.

14

Noah'd departed America on Wednesday, and he'd arrived on Thursday Hong Kong time. After his long nap, it was now Friday, a perfect night to go check out a club. The plan didn't have his full confidence; he didn't know what he could learn from a night club that would be helpful, but he had to start somewhere.

He hadn't really packed any clothes that would be appropriate to go to the club in; the night life had been the last thing on his mind. He would have to make do with some of the clothes he'd brought; some must work in conjunction together, he figured.

In the end, Noah settled on a pair of dark gray jeans that hung low on his hips and a navy-blue V-neck long-sleeved shirt, something he'd packed in consideration of his return flight; he always froze on airplanes. He checked himself out in the mirror beneath the harsh, unflattering light of the bathroom. It would do. He'd brought some of the basics he'd need for hair and skin care, and the pack included some gel, so he made his hair presentable at least. The interior of a night club would be too dark for anyone to really see him anyway.

Everything in order in regards to his appearance, he turned his thoughts to the next small hurdle: finding the place.

That turned out to be very little problem. He took one of the bands from Lianne's drawer with him to the taxi and showed the driver, who recognized it immediately. K was quite the hot spot of the moment in the Eastern District, attracting large crowds of people. Its popularity made it a well-known spot for the taxi drivers.

Noah found it difficult to pay attention to the twists and turns of the streets of Hong Kong and stopped bothering trying to keep track of the path. He trusted the taxi driver to get him where he needed to be.

Outwardly he remained calm, just another tourist on his way for a night out, but inside his mind swirled, a growing hope that something would come of this journey meshed with the very real—and quickly growing—fear that this too would be another setback. He fought against the anxiety, reminding himself he'd only just begun his search. If he gave in to despair now, he might as well have failed.

The farther into the heart of the Eastern District the taxi drove, the brighter the night became; neon signs of various sizes and colors blazed on all sides, bathing Noah in showers of multicolored light. The streets were full of people going to and fro, young and old alike. He saw groups of friends standing around the sidewalk, couples in each other's arms.

This was the entertainment district of the area; bars lined the streets, stacked on top of each other, each offering a different experience. The small bars soon gave way to bigger clubs, the music reaching him even inside the taxi. Despite it being only nine o'clock, people already formed lines outside some of the clubs.

The taxi finally came to a stop behind two others in front of a big building. It was fairly nondescript, a large awning extending from the body of the building, marked with the old-fashioned marquee-style lights. A single stylized "K" glowed bright pink on the wall. Like many of the other places he'd seen, a bouncer stood guard at the door, and a queue formed, awaiting admittance.

Noah paid the cabbie, checked to make sure he had Lianne's picture and his passport for ID, and climbed out of the taxi.

The night air was actually not stifling, the first hint Noah had seen here that summer was at its end and soon would be making way for the fall. A light breeze teased his face as he joined the line. It relieved him to see most people dressed similarly casual—the guys, at least. The girls all dressed to play, tight dresses or pants, low-cut tops exposing ample cleavage, short skirts designed to tease.

The line moved quickly, and soon Noah was showing his passport at the door, paying the thirty dollar cover charge, receiving his own thin paper bracelet marking him as legal to drink—his green whereas the one in his pocket from Lianne's drawer was red; maybe they had different colors for different days?—and walking inside.

The moment he moved through the door, the sound of electronic dance music assaulted him, the bass rumbling in his bones, the rhythm taking up residence in his skull, throbbing behind his eyes after mere moments. The entryway was a short, dark hallway. At the halfway point was a coat check to the left, the bathrooms to the right, the far end lit by a pale glow. As soon as he stepped into the light, he found himself in an elaborately designed interior: a swooping staircase to the far end led up to a second level, strategically placed tall, mirrored columns walled off a few areas. A round depression in the center of the room acted as the dance floor, inset with flashing lights beneath glass tiles. Just beyond the dance floor was the area where the DJ played his tunes. Directly to Noah's right, three bartenders worked hard to provide drinks to the crowd of people.

The inside was already full—milling, sweating bodies on the dance floor, lounging at nice tables around the perimeter, crowding around the bar for their drinks. As he stood there in the opening into this teeming world of noise and movement, Noah felt momentarily overwhelmed.

How am I ever going to find someone that can help me in all this?

15

Wei hated places like K, where the environment overloaded the senses. It dulled reactions, being unable to adequately hear or see what might be going on around you. He didn't like being put at a disadvantage; in his position it might be fatal.

He ignored the noise as he made his way through the back corridor to where the offices were. He and Chris, who he'd brought along for extra muscle, passed several workers, but they all knew him and knew that his expression meant they should stay the fuck out of his way.

He found the main office where the club's owner, a little shit of a man named Jean-Paul Georges, handled business. A muscle-bound white guy stood next to the closed door. He spotted Chris and Wei and moved to intercept them. Wei didn't blame him; he'd cultivated a reputation and image of toughness, and Chris, though he had what they all teased him as "anime hair"—it was currently copper-red and long enough to need to be tied back in a small man bun at the back, two long bangs pushed behind his ears—could pull a knife faster than anyone Wei had ever met. Wei shoved the guard away, throwing open the door and storming into the office.

It was utilitarian and out of fashion, the furniture within it all bought secondhand. The chairs boasted an ugly tan color that would have been at home in an elderly woman's living room. There were no decorations to speak of, Georges being too cheap to splurge on something that wouldn't bring money back to him. The interior of the club in view of customers, sure. His office, not a chance.

Jean-Paul Georges was the definition of sleazy. He was a portly French expat in a green tweed suit he thought looked sophisticated but gave him the appearance of a swollen balloon instead, the jacket unable to button because of his extended gut. His face had developed jowls and was constantly red, even more so in the summer. He sat behind the desk, on the phone with someone and speaking French, but he fell silence when Wei entered, the guard at the door coming behind them.

"Hang up the phone," Wei demanded.

"I'm really sorry, sir," the guard apologized. He grabbed Chris by the arm. "You two should leave."

Georges simply continued to stare at them.

"Are you fucking deaf?" Wei demanded. Chris shook the guard's hands off of his arm, glowering at him. "Hang up the goddamn phone, Georges."

As if his name were some sort of trigger word after being hypnotized, Georges shook himself from his stupor, muttered something into the phone, and hung up. "It's all right, Bruno," he said, his French accent heavy on certain words. The guard stopped his efforts to remove the intruders.

"Bruno?" Chris snickered. "Did your mother hate you?" The guard just stared impassively at him.

"Chris," Wei chastised gently; the last thing they needed to do at the moment was to patronize Georges's guards.

"What? It's a weird name—Bruno. Sounds like the villain in a bad spy flick." Chris caught Wei's glance and nodded, still smiling slightly. "All right, sorry."

"You may go, Bruno," Georges said, leaning back in his chair, the leather creaking beneath his weight. "And do try to keep anyone else out." A subtle reprimand, but Wei was familiar with that tone. It meant he'd get it worse later, after Wei departed. Bruno knew it too, judging by his face as he met Wei's eyes before closing the door.

"You've hired some new blood since I visited last," Wei commented. He took a seat without waiting for Georges to invite him to do so. Chris remained standing behind his chair.

"Faces come and go in zis line of work." Georges dug in his desk and removed a cigar, extending it to Wei. "Cigar?" Wei shook his head, so Georges set about preparing it, biting off the butt and spitting it back into his palm before placing the cigar in his mouth and lighting it. When he seemed to be satisfied with it, he took a deep puff and exhaled the rich-smelling smoke. "I didn't expect a visit so soon; you didn't call ahead."

"I don't have to call ahead," Wei said, crossing his legs and resting his elbows on the arm of the chair. "This is my territory, Georges. Never forget that. You might pay most of the rent, but it's on my turf."

Georges nodded so quickly his jowls quivered. "Of course, of course." Wei had no idea how much of that compliance was for show and how much was legitimate; Jean-Paul Georges was a spineless man in the end, but he was a master of self-preservation; he'd been doing business with the triads in Hong Kong and China long enough that he'd learned quickly what was necessary to keep his neck off the line.

"What can I do for ze Dragons, Monsieur Tseng?"

Wei pulled out the photos of the four women who'd gone missing and turned up dead and placed the pictures down on the desk for Georges to look at. "These four women, do you recognize any of them?"

Jean-Paul Georges took his time examining each one—overacting, probably, wanting to show Wei just how seriously he considered matters the Dragons brought before him. After looking at the last one he shook his head quizzically. "Not that I can recall, no. What's zis about?"

"Each of these women visited K in the last several months, some of them quite frequently, based on what the families have told us." Comprehension sparked in Georges's eyes. Spineless and unscrupulous, yes; an idiot, no. "They each disappeared for a few days before turning up dead of a drug overdose, each with no prior history of drug addiction."

"And ze only connection you can see is K," Georges finished, stroking his ample chin. "*Oui*, that is troubling, indeed."

Wei smirked. "I'm glad to see you understand the situation, Georges. Since the connection exists, I decided to drop by and see if you know what exactly is going on in your club."

The Frenchman's eyes bulged and he reminded Wei of a bullfrog. "I 'ope you are not implying that myself or my employees are somehow involved in these deaths, Monsieur Tseng. I assure you that is not the case! That would be quite bad for business."

"I suppose it would," Wei conceded, hiding his grimace of distaste at just what part of the disappearances had been objectionable. He'd zeroed in on how it would not benefit him financially, not the fact that four women had lost their lives. Wei couldn't fathom seeing the world in that sort of light, but that worldview helped Jean-Paul Georges thrive in the underworld of the triads. It took a special kind of person.

"Would it be possible that something is taking place here without you knowing?" Wei inquired politely, keeping his face tranquil. Wei might find Georges to be a disgusting excuse for a human being, but that did not mean he was unnecessary. Georges currently led the Eastern District's illicit markets, controlling everything else that went on beneath him to some degree. Wei needed someone easily controlled pulling those strings, and that description fit Georges perfectly.

Needing him didn't make Wei want to punch the fat Frenchman's face any less, though. He just had to control the urges, one of the necessary evils of maintaining control over the district. And he *had* to maintain control.

"It is theoretically possible, *oui*," Georges conceded, the admission sounding particularly painful for him. "I am always up here in my office. But ze staff would never let something like that happen. Whatever their morals might be, they all are fearful of the wrath of the Dragons."

"Instruct your staff to keep an eye out. Increase safety precautions— have someone check the bathrooms every ten minutes. If something *is* going down here without anyone's notice, the bathroom would be a place for it."

Georges nodded his understanding, and Wei stood, the fat Frenchman following suit. "While ze circumstances are regrettable, it is always a pleasure to zee you, Monsieur Tseng."

They walked to the door, Chris a few steps behind them. "Make sure to have your people on the lookout, and let me know if you hear anything new."

There was that too-eager head-bobbing again. Wei wondered if Georges could feel the skin of his jowls moving independently to the rest of his face. "*Mais oui*, Monsieur."

Wei and Chris excused themselves, Chris giving Bruno a mocking salute as they disappeared down the hallway. Once out of earshot of the bodyguard, Chris leaned in to Wei. "Do you believe him?"

Wei sighed. "I'm not sure. Probably. Even if I do, though, I'm pretty sure K is involved somehow, I'm just not sure how."

Chris nodded, crossing his arms over his chest. "So what do we do now?"

Wei took the four photos he had, handing two to Chris and keeping two for himself. "Now we go around and talk to the staff, see if any of them recognize these girls. If they came here frequently, a worker is bound to have seen them and might have information for us. This is the best lead we've got, and since the cops won't do their fucking jobs, we'll have to do it for them."

16

Wei and Chris showed their pictures to everyone they could think of, all the employees, customers who might be regulars, even the DJ, but none of them had anything useful to say. Most of them couldn't recall one way or another if they'd seen any of the girls, the others gave a definite no.

Wei had a slight headache growing behind his eyes from the noise in the club, a steady buildup of pressure that right now was just uncomfortable but had the potential to become a real annoyance.

God, he was ready to be out of this noise, but he had a job to do, and he was damn well going to do it. He owed it to the families and to the girls themselves. Someone had to put in the effort. Someone had to care.

At a lull between songs voices drifted down to Wei from above, and he glanced up toward the slightly curtained off VIP area.

That was somewhere he hadn't checked yet. He found the stairs leading up to it being overseen by a second bouncer who immediately stepped into his way, a challenging look on his face. "You going somewhere?"

Wei narrowed his eyes. "Yeah. Up."

The bouncer scoffed. "I don't think so. This area is VIP only."

Wei stepped up until he was almost nose to nose with the bouncer. "Do you have any idea who the fuck I am?"

"No, and that's why you're staying right down here."

Wei gritted his teeth, but before he could say anything, Chris came up behind him, grabbing his shoulder. He had to tug several times before Wei turned away from the bouncer, who had a smirk on his face. Wei wanted nothing more than to wipe that smirk away, with his fist, preferably.

"What?" Wei snapped, irate. He saw the hurt reflected in Chris's eyes and sighed. "What is it? Did you find something?"

Chris looked over Wei's shoulder at the bouncer before leading him away. "I was talking to the bartenders, and they told me I was the second person to come around with pictures asking questions tonight."

Wei's eyebrows shot up. Had there been a death he was unaware of? Had someone taken it upon themselves to investigate, not trusting the Dragons to be able to do it? That would be a disaster. Wei and the Dragons controlled this territory by proving they could protect the people and the turf so they didn't need to rely on fear to keep order. If people began to doubt their ability to protect them, it would make the way for other gangs to try to pull through and take the turf for themselves. It would lead to more violence and bloodshed. He had to avoid that at all costs.

"Did you find out who it was?" Wei started toward the bar, Chris falling in behind him.

Chris shook his head. "The bartenders couldn't say anything other than that it was a foreigner. With pictures of a white girl."

Wei came to a sudden halt, turning to look at Chris. There was no way... It couldn't be him, could it? What the hell were the odds? But then, how many white people had gone missing in the Eastern District?

Heat suddenly rushed through his body at the thought he might get to see Noah again; he was grateful it was dark in the club, and Chris would easily mistake the redness in his face as a trick of the light.

When he spoke, he sounded far calmer than he felt, with his heart racing in his chest. "We need to find this foreigner."

17

"Does this girl look familiar to you at all?" Noah asked of one of the three bartenders, holding Lianne's picture in the light for the guy to see. The bartender, one of the tallest guys Noah had ever seen, seemed taller with his hair shaved into a long Mohawk, spiked straight up, the tips of it dyed a light blonde. He had several piercings in his ears and nose.

The bartender shrugged, noncommittal. "We get a lot of people in here," he explained. "It's hard to remember one face."

Noah glanced around; he didn't see many—or any—other foreigners in the crowd. *How hard could it be to remember the beautiful white girl?* As it passed through his mind, he flushed with shame. He was ashamed of the mindset behind it that implied that white people were special enough to stand out, even if that wasn't the sense he'd meant it in.

Instead he said, "She's been here a lot—at least seven times." The bartender indulged him, taking the photo once more, squinting at it carefully as if willing himself to recognize it, but shook his head as he handed it back.

The other two bartenders were really busy, so Noah decided to wait at the bar until they had a down moment to ask them. He rested his elbows on the bar surface, glancing around at the clubbers. Bodies jam-packed the dance floor, partners pressed right against each other, their bodies moving as one. More than a few people on the floor were kissing. At a row of tables near the bar, there were a few elegantly dressed girls with men much too unattractive for them; the way a special waitstaff kept bringing them bottles, though, and the way money flowed so openly, Noah had no problem guessing why they were there.

"Can I get you anything, sir?" A voice came from over his shoulder, and he turned around rapidly. As he did so, he knocked over a man's beer, spilling it down his shirt and pants. The man, already drunk, sprang unsteadily off his stool, cursing in Chinese and glaring daggers at Noah.

"I'm so sorry," Noah apologized, cursing himself for being so careless. "Let me get him another beer," he said, turning to the bartender, a petite, heart-faced girl with a nose ring, bright blue lips, and blue color contacts. He turned to apologize again, but the man and the guy who'd been there with him were making their way through the crowd toward the bathroom, glaring back at him over their shoulders.

"I'm really sorry," he repeated to the bartender who just waved it off. "I know you're busy, but I was wondering, have you seen this girl?" He held the picture out to her, holding out very little hope that she had. It would be similar to her coworker, he was sure: too busy, too many faces, too hard to remember.

He almost fainted when she said, "Yeah, I've seen her here a few times."

"You have? Is there anything you can tell me?" Noah inquired eagerly, heart beating a mile a minute in his chest. *Someone had seen Lianne!*

"Not much, really. I don't leave the bar when I'm here." She saw the crestfallen look on Noah's face and must have felt sympathy for him. "If you want to ask someone else, go ask Vaughn. He's the bouncer for the VIP section. Whenever that girl was here, she always ended up there."

"Thank you so much," Noah said, slipping her a tip for her help.

It wasn't hard to find the VIP section; there was a small staircase leading up to another balcony area, separate from the one he'd noticed when he first came in. A cloth curtain obscured anyone's view of what was going on up there, offering some semblance of privacy in this very public place.

There was a bodybuilder of a man standing in front of the stairs, his features handsomely illuminated by the lights of the club. He sported a super-short haircut, akin to five-o'clock shadow on his head. His eyes narrowed on Noah when he walked up.

"VIP section only," he said politely but firmly.

Noah nodded his understanding and held up one hand as an offer of patience while he handed the other picture to the man—Vaughn, he guessed. "I know I'm not on the list, and that's fine. I just wanted to ask you a quick question. Do you recognize this girl?"

Vaughn frowned as he studied the picture. Something flickered behind his gaze, and for a moment, Noah was hopeful, and then he shook his head, handing the picture back to him. "I'm sorry. I don't think I've ever seen her."

"Are you sure?" Noah hated the pleading tone to his voice, but he didn't care. This was his last chance to find out something.

"I'm sure," Vaughn said shortly. "Sorry, but I've got work to do. If Mr. Georges sees me talking to you when I should be on duty, I'll be in deep shit."

Recognizing it for the dismissal that it was, Noah turned away, defeated. He'd talked to everyone in the building, then. *Well*, he thought, *almost everyone.* He still had one shot. He made his way to the main hallway. Anyone entering or leaving the club had to go through there, so the person working the coat check might have seen *something.*

"Yeah, I recognize her," the coat check girl said almost as soon as she set eyes on the picture. Noah's heart leapt into his throat, but he tried not to show his relief. "She was a regular here for a while, always coming on Friday and Saturday nights—sometimes Sundays, too. Usually left with the same guy."

"Do you know who the guy is?" Noah asked. *A guy, huh? That could be nothing—Lianne has a healthy sexual appetite—but it could be something. At any rate it's one more person out there who might know something.*

The girl shook her head and handed the picture back to Noah. "He's a regular, but I don't know his name. Don't think I could tell you much about him; average height, average face, nothing unique. Well, I guess that's not true," she amended, thinking. "He had a small scar across his cheek—pretty faint, not too noticeable. Especially in a dark club."

"When was the last time you remember seeing her?"

The coat girl shrugged elegantly. "I don't know. I went on vacation about three weeks ago. When I got back, I didn't see her around."

Noah nodded his thanks and started to turn when another question came to him. "Sorry, just one more thing. What about the guy you usually saw her with? Did he stop coming, too?"

"No, he still comes around pretty frequently."

Noah thanked the girl and turned away. So, there was some guy involved. He was the logical next step in his search—he still came to the club, too; he hadn't disappeared like Noah's sister. Now he just needed to figure out how to find him.

He stepped into the bathroom, fighting an inner despair that reared its ugly head suddenly, striking as swiftly as a cobra. How could he find one average-looking guy in a club this full? There must have been upward of a thousand people passing through on any given weekend night. It might be easier to find a needle in a haystack.

Noah ran cold water in the sink, splashing his face before looking up into the mirror. *I found this out,* he reminded himself as he watched droplets of water fall from the end of his nose. *I know she came here a lot, and I know she was always with the same guy. The guy is a regular, though, so he comes here a lot.* If it were necessary, Noah would brave the chaos of this place every night until he finally caught sight of the guy matching the coat check girl's description. He had the financial means to do it, and he had the time—*he* did, but did Lianne?

Thoughts of his sister spurred him in to action. He wiped his face with a paper towel and stepped out of the bathroom. He nearly ran into someone on his way out and mumbled an apology. As he started to step by, though, the guy stepped into his way. Not wanting to meet this guy's gaze, he glanced down—and saw a stain on his shirt and pants. A sinking feeling in his gut, Noah looked up.

Sure enough, it was the guy whose beer he'd spilled earlier. Behind him was his buddy. Both of them leered unpleasantly at him. Noah tried to step to the other side, but the man's buddy stepped into his way.

Noah tensed, knowing confrontation was coming and there was nothing he could do to avoid it. He could only do his best to make sure it was short and no one got hurt too badly—the last thing he wanted to was to end up back at the police precinct; he couldn't find Lianne from behind the bars of a jail cell.

"Is there a problem?" Noah asked politely, casually widening his stance into a more defensible one.

"Yea there's a problem, fuckin' *gweilo*," hissed Stained Shirt. "You British *puk gai* think you can come everywhere and you own it, yea? This isn't your fuckin' city anymore!"

"I'm not British. I'm American," Noah explained. He slowly took out his wallet, removing a few bills from it. "I'm really sorry I spilled your beer on you; it was an accident. I hope this will make us even." He held out the money, praying the drunk idiots would take it and go.

"You think you can buy us, rich man?" Stained Shirt's buddy laughed loudly. He jerked the money out of Noah's hand. "Money solves all problems? Makes us even?" Before Noah could stop him, he snatched the wallet from Noah's other hand. "Maybe this makes us even."

Noah took a step forward to grab the wallet, but Stained Shirt shoved him back hard. He nearly fell through the swinging door into the bathroom but kept his feet.

"Fuckin' *gweilo*!"

Noah didn't know what a *gweilo* was, but he figured it wasn't a nice term. He'd had just about enough when a muscular arm grabbed Stained Shirt's friend from behind, twisting his arm until the wallet fell to the ground, a second hand coming up to hold his head down, bending his body at a ninety-degree angle. Stained Shirt's friend howled in Cantonese.

Noah's eyes widened when he saw Wei's familiar face. A tingle of desire started just below his navel, spreading outward from there despite the circumstances.

Stained Shirt turned to confront the new arrival, but a second guy stepped out from behind Wei, intelligent eyes full of potential violence. Stained Shirt hissed something at the new arrival in Chinese only to stiffen at the response he received.

"You two are gonna apologize to this nice foreigner here," Wei said, voice oozing danger. Wei spoke in a low voice, but no one in the vicinity had any problem hearing him even over the thrum of the club's music. "Then you're gonna go back inside and enjoy your fuckin' night and we're not gonna make anything of this, right?" When he didn't immediately receive a response, he bent Stained Shirt's buddy's arm back even farther, eliciting a cry of pain. "You don't want me to make an issue of this. *Right*?"

Stained Shirt's buddy said something in Chinese several times before finally switching to English. "Right! Right! Jesus fuckin' Christ!" Wei released him, and he staggered forward, falling to his knees. He scrambled up quickly, glaring murderously at Wei. Stained Shirt tugged on his arm, muttering something. Finally, the two disappeared back inside.

That dealt with, Wei scooped up Noah's wallet and handed it back to him. Their hands very nearly touched in the process, and Noah almost felt tiny sparks leap the inch between their skin, an electric sensation he'd never known before. He had the wild urge to slide his finger up *just so* and make that contact, but before he could decide whether or not to act on it, Wei withdrew his hand.

"You sure know how to make friends," Wei commented dryly. Despite the buildup of tension from the near violent situation—or perhaps because of it—Noah laughed.

"I've always been mister popular," he managed.

Wei turned back to his companion, handing him two photographs. "Go back inside, keep asking questions. Report back to me later." A question hung unanswered between the two, but finally his companion turned, going back inside.

His friend gone, Wei turned back to Noah. "Must be fate, us running into each other twice in one day."

Noah arched an eyebrow. "Fate, or you're a stalker."

Wei snorted. "Okay, let me get you home."

"I'm not done here," Noah protested.

"Those guys are going to go back in there, drink more, get even more stupid drunk, and eventually the alcohol will override their fear of me and they'll try something again."

Noah looked at the slightly taller man icily. It sounded like Wei thought he couldn't look out for himself. "I'll handle it if they do."

Wei rolled his eyes. "They're bound to have friends in there, and there will be people who don't even know them who'd love the chance to beat up on a foreigner. It would be better for you if you extracted yourself."

Noah wanted to argue more but realized Wei was right. "Fine. I'll go catch a taxi."

"At this hour? Not a chance. I'll give you a lift."

Noah's heart fluttered at the thought of being in a confined space alone with this sexy but clearly dangerous man. "That's a lot of trouble to go to."

"It's no trouble." Wei made for the door, the matter seemingly already settled in his mind. Well, Noah guessed it had.

They emerged into the slightly cooler night and the neon brightness that seemed like day to Noah for a moment in comparison to the darkness of K.

As soon as they emerged, Wei lit a cigarette and then offered one to Noah.

"No thanks, I don't smoke," Noah said politely. In the better light outside, he could really see Wei for the first time that night, and he let out a small grunt of approval. Wei was wearing a pair of dark corduroy pants and a white T-shirt beneath a black short-sleeved button-down, unbuttoned. The material of the T-shirt clung to the muscle beneath, outlining nice pecs and a hard stomach. It was a body that was without a doubt forged by violence. Noah watched those muscles move beneath the fabric as Wei raised the cigarette back to his lips and inhaled.

This guy is unbelievably sexy, Noah marveled. *Does he have any idea how hot he is?* Noah shook his head, feeling completely stupid to be standing there ogling this Asian Adonis in front of a nightclub.

"Let's go," Wei said, tossing his cigarette butt to the ground and stomping on it to put it out. "So, where am I taking you?" When Noah explained, he nodded. "I'm pretty sure I know where that is."

"Where's your car?" Noah asked as Wei led him around the corner.

"You'll see," Wei replied with a grin Noah could only describe as mischievous.

He led Noah into a dark alleyway. Noah hesitated at the mouth of the alley, uncertain. This wasn't the sort of place one usually parked a car. What did Wei intend, exactly? "You leading me into a dark alley to have your way with me?" Noah joked, certain that his anxiety was clear in his words.

"When I have my way with you, it won't be in a dark alley," Wei called back. A sudden single bright light illuminated Noah as a vehicle roared to life in the alley. Noah covered his eyes against the brightness as Wei drew up beside him atop a sleek, jet-black motorcycle. "Hop on."

"I've never ridden a motorcycle before," Noah said nervously.

"There's a first time for everything," Wei replied with a wink. It had the exact same effect as the first—Noah's cock stiffened without warning, suddenly struggling against the confines of his pants.

Noah climbed on behind Wei, trembling slightly from nervousness. "What about a helmet?"

"I'll be careful," Wei promised, and his voice was so absolutely sincere that some of Noah's nervousness eased. "Just hold on tight—that's right," he said as Noah wrapped his arms around Wei's middle. His hands came together at Wei's abdomen—the heat of his flesh through the white T-shirt was intense, and Noah's arousal grew.

God I hope he can't feel that.

Noah let out a very unmanly squeal as Wei urged the motorcycle into motion without warning. He tightened his hold on Wei, pressing his face into his back to shield it from the wind.

They emerged from the alley completely and merged with traffic.

Noah's eyes widened suddenly as Wei's words dawned on him.

When, he thought. *He said* when *I have my way with you, not* if.

18

Wei's nearness offset Noah's fear of the motorcycle, somewhat—it was hard to maintain that fear when he was in a state of severely heightened arousal. Whatever bits of anxiety that might have remained vanished at the realization that Wei was a superb driver; he handled the motorcycle as if it were something he'd been doing all his life. The slightest movements of his body brought responses from the powerful machine beneath him.

Pressed up against Wei as he was, Noah felt the muscles moving beneath warm flesh, hard steel beneath soft velvet. His face was warm with Wei's body heat, his nostrils filled with the smell of him—that same cedar smell he'd gotten earlier, mixed with sweat and a hint of cologne—his ears filled with the sound of his heart beating in his chest. He didn't know if he was fooling himself, but it seemed to be beating a little fast.

The motorcycle ride was exhilarating—and not simply because he was able to cling to the body of this sexy man—and Noah found himself regretting never having the experience before. The flow of Hong Kong traffic kept their speed in check. *It must be amazing to get out of the city and on the road where you can just...go,* Noah thought wistfully. He would love to tell Wei to just keep going, find somewhere to go as fast as he could. But that would feel like running away, and Noah Potter did not run. This was his fight.

At a red light, Wei leaned forward, looking over his shoulder at Noah. "Tell me why you were looking for your sister at K." Something in his eyes told Noah he had an idea of the answer already and was just seeking confirmation.

"My sister used to go there a lot—I found a bunch of these bracelets—" Noah held up his wrist to indicate what he meant. "—in a drawer in her room. I thought maybe I could find some answers there."

A horn honked as the light turned green, bringing their conversation to a close. Noah found himself wondering as to the importance of K, and what circumstances brought Wei and his friend—was that the right word? It was probably one of the members of his gang, if what Dang said had any truth to it—there. He remembered Wei handing two photos to the other guy. Was it possible they were also looking for information about their missing-turned-overdosed girls there? That would be one really big coincidence.

"So what did you find?" Wei asked at the next red light, picking up the threads of conversation like there hadn't been a pause.

Noah debated how much to tell the other man. Could he trust him? He didn't even know him, not really. What he did know of him wasn't the most comforting information; Dang had called him a thug, a gangster. He'd helped Noah out of a tight spot, true—but even in doing so he'd exhibited that he was definitely a creature capable of violence. And yet when he spoke to Noah, his manner was so different from when he'd spoken to the police or to those guys inside the club. It was civil, gentle. How did he reconcile the dichotomous nature of this man?

It didn't help that Noah found himself wildly attracted to him—it might have made things worse. He couldn't tell how much of his desire to trust Wei was his instincts talking to him and how much was his erection. It definitely complicated matters.

However, Wei *did* save his ass at K, and he'd earned the right to know, so Noah explained everything—how his sister was a regular there for a while before disappearing, how she'd been spotted leaving with the same man, as well as the description of that man.

The light turned green once more and they drove on, Noah hoping he hadn't made some mistake confiding in the other man. He was curious about Wei's interest. It wasn't mere polite conversation-making, of that much he was certain. Did the other man think Lianne's disappearance was in any way related to the girls he talked about at the precinct? It seemed oddly coincidental that they were both at the same place at the same time showing pictures, out of all the clubs in Hong Kong.

A connection seemed likely. Noah was not a man who believed in coincidences. What that meant exactly he wasn't sure.

Wei brought the motorcycle to a stop in front of the noodle shop. It was nearly eleven, and the shop was closed. The nearby streetlights were the only source of illumination, painting the hard angles of Wei's face in a strange orange glow.

"What are you going to do now?" asked Wei as Noah climbed off the motorcycle.

"Take a shower and go to sleep," Noah answered.

Wei's face was serious as he regarded the other man, and Noah felt his cock throb again. There was something intense in that gaze, something stirring just behind those vivid eyes that Noah could not name, something primal. "You know what I meant."

Noah sighed, deflating a bit. "I can't really tell you that," he said, searching for the words to explain himself. "Not because I don't want to—because I don't know. I've spent every phase of this thing so far just focusing on the step right in front of me; I've never had some big picture in mind."

Wei looked at him skeptically, kicking the bike stand down and slinging his leg over the motorcycle so he was leaning slightly against it, easily balancing its weight. "You came across the world with no plan?"

Noah laughed. "It sounds ridiculous when you say it."

"That's because it is ridiculous." Wei chuckled. The deep, throaty bass of it seemed to reverberate across the small distance between them, and Noah found himself wishing he were still on the motorcycle, arms around him, chest pressed against his broad back when he let that chuckle out. He would have loved to feel it vibrate through him. "I'm not sure this is something you can manage without a plan."

Noah knew he was right. He'd gotten lucky with the break at K, but he couldn't—he *wouldn't*—rely on luck to save Lianne's life. It was time he got serious.

"I guess my next step is finding out who this guy is that Lianne was seen at the club with. If I can figure out who he is, I'm one step closer to finding her."

Wei frowned. "You don't know what you might be getting into. This could be dangerous."

Noah met his gaze unflinching. He was not going to back down, no matter what. This was Lianne; this was his sister. "It might be, but that's not going to stop me."

There was something akin to respect in Wei's eyes. "No, I didn't think you would. Do you have a phone with a Hong Kong number?"

Noah shook his head.

"Well, you need to get one. It's dangerous for you to be running around without a phone, especially since you want to investigate your sister's disappearance."

"You were doing the same thing tonight, weren't you?" Noah asked. He saw Wei stiffen and hoped he hadn't crossed any lines. "I saw the pictures you gave to your friend." After a moment, Wei nodded slowly. "Tell me about these girls. Maybe they're connected," he added hurriedly, seeing the way that Wei was about to shut him out. It worked.

"I've been thinking maybe they are," Wei admitted at last, "but the girls I'm looking into, it's different."

"How?"

Wei shook his head firmly. "I'm not going to talk about it out here on the street. It's a sensitive matter." Wei straightened and walked past Noah toward the building.

"Where are you going?" Noah called after him.

Wei turned so he was walking backward, an eyebrow quirked. "Isn't it obvious? Your room." The surprise on Noah's face was enough to make Wei laugh, and he turned back around.

Noah stood there, dazed for a moment. Wei was going up to his room. It was in response to the question Noah had asked, but it didn't matter. This sexy, dangerous man was on his way up to the room Noah was staying in. Noah flushed. He didn't understand why this guy's simple gestures and words cut through him so easily; he'd never reacted so wildly and immediately to another man before. It was like every experience he'd ever had suddenly multiplied a hundredfold. The smallest of quirks were igniting the sexual fires within him, and he didn't know how to handle it.

Lianne's room. The thought killed a bit of the fire, but it didn't still his heartbeat or make him feel any less like an ungainly teenager who lacked experience and was about to be alone with his crush.

A rebellious voice in the back of his mind squeaked, *He's not my crush*, but the rest of Noah's consciousness completely ignored it and walked on suddenly unsteady legs after Wei, who disappeared around the side of the building. When Noah joined him, it was at a side door that led into the stairwell to the rooms without needing to cut through the noodle shop. Noah hadn't even realized it was there.

He didn't say that to Wei, though.

"It's up here," he said, mentally kicking himself for such a flimsy, obvious statement. He led Wei up the stairs, trying to step quietly on them given the hour, but having very little luck. The stairwell was badly illuminated at night; each flight had only a single bulb above it, casting a weak yellow glow that barely pierced the gloom of the place. The sounds of the lives of the other tenants came drifting out as they reached the second landing and then again as they started for the third.

Right before he crested the stairs, Noah stopped dead, so suddenly that Wei bumped into him. "What's wrong?" Wei asked, but Noah couldn't speak. He could only stare at the door to Lianne's apartment, a door he'd shut tight when he left that night.

A door that stood wide open.

19

Noah seemed to be in some sort of state of shock, sitting on his sister's trashed bed, wrapped in a blanket, shaking. As soon as Wei saw the door open, he'd stepped around Noah and entered the room to find the place totally wrecked. Someone had gone in and destroyed pretty much everything. Clothes littered the floor along with broken furniture. The large window that looked out over the back of the building was shattered—outward, not inward; Wei found almost no glass in the apartment.

On the floor in the center of the room was a piece of paper with the words GO HOME *GWEILO* written on it in thick red paint. It seemed like an afterthought to Wei—a way of adding insult to injury. Racism wasn't the primary focus of the vandalism.

Someone doesn't want Noah here, he thought, which only cemented Wei's certainty that there was something going on, something big, involving Noah's sister. And more than likely the missing girls, as well.

Wei pulled his phone out of his pocket, dialing Conroy's number. "Are you calling the cops?" Noah asked in a monotone voice from the bed, startling Wei. He hadn't spoken a word since seeing the place in this condition.

Wei looked back at him, concerned. The light in those blue eyes now looked dim, and Wei hated it. Nothing should ever dim that beautiful, vibrant glow. *It's not the time to think poetic shit like that*, he reminded himself.

"That won't do any good."

"Ah."

"Yo, boss," Conroy greeted in Wei's ear suddenly as he answered the phone. "You still at the club? Those honeys hot tonight?"

"I'm about to send you an address. Get Smile and Tony and meet me here."

The joking vanished from Conroy's tone instantly. "You got it, boss. What's goin' on?"

"Get here," Wei said. "Fast, Conroy."

"What does that mean?" Noah asked in the same deadpan voice. He pointed limply toward the piece of paper Wei had found. He hadn't realized he was still holding it.

"*Gweilo* is a Cantonese word. It's not really polite."

"I gathered that much. But what does it mean? Something to do with foreigners, right?"

Wei nodded. "Really it means *ghost*, but the way it's usually used now refers to foreigners, specifically white people."

Noah nodded, a jerky motion that seemed more appropriate from a ventriloquist doll, not a normally energetic human being. "I get it; white, like ghosts. It's appropriate."

"No," Wei said fiercely, "it's not." He crumpled the paper up, squatting down to be level with Noah's eyes, and catching and holding them with his own. When he was certain Noah was paying attention, he held the paper ball up. "This is bullshit, pure and simple, you hear me? There's nothing appropriate about it. Don't let this shit in your head."

Wei rose, tossing the paper aside. "Come on. Help me find some of your things. We need to pack your shit and get you somewhere safer."

Noah stared at him, confused. "What?"

"Whoever did this isn't going to just stop," Wei explained, shifting through the belongings strewn across the floor for any hint of what might be Noah's. "If they went this far it wouldn't be too hard for them to go further."

"This is my sister's room!" Noah said, heat slowly returning to his voice. "I'm not just going to run away from the one place in this whole godforsaken country where I have a connection to her."

Wei rounded on Noah. "Is that connection worth getting yourself killed? Do you think anyone is going to run to her rescue if something happens to you?" He hated that his voice had to be so sharp, but there wasn't enough time to gently get through to the other man. "No. You're the only chance she's got, Noah. If she's really in as much trouble as you think she is—as *I* think she is, too—do you think the people responsible are just going to leave you to run around and find her?"

"You don't know they're connected," Noah argued, but even Wei could tell he did not believe that when he said it; he'd suggested the exact opposite ten minutes ago outside. "And if they are, all the more reason to call the cops!"

"You saw how helpful the cops were," Wei reminded him. "They'll just use this as a reason to write off what you've said—this note will have them immediately saying it's unrelated even when it should be clear that it isn't.

"Even worse, Dang might decide to 'assign protection' to you, which will make it where you can't do a thing to find your sister. Is that what you want?"

Noah turned his face away from Wei, biting his lower lip. "I don't want to lose this connection to her." The words were barely a whisper, but they struck Wei like the sharpest arrow, making his heart ache.

He understood that deeply personal pain; he'd felt it countless times himself. He wanted to go to the other man and pull him into his arms, soothe away the pain, but he knew he would never be successful. This pain went too deep for physical comfort to salve. It would be easier for him to track down the bastards who'd caused him this pain and make them hurt, but that would have to come later. Right now he needed to get Noah somewhere he could be protected.

That urge was so powerful it overwhelmed everything else. He needed—not wanted, *needed*—to protect Noah, and he didn't have a good reason why. He just knew he would protect him, no matter what.

Finally seeing the wisdom of Wei's words, Noah rose, searching the room until he found the smaller of his two suitcases. The larger one was trashed, its sides collapsed and broken as if someone stomped on it repeatedly.

"Someone who stays in this building is going to notice this eventually," Noah remarked, gesturing with his arm widely to indicate the room. "Especially with that window broken."

"I'll get it taken care of," Wei assured. "I'll have my guys move your sister's stuff to storage and clean this place up. At least make it look like you left. That should buy us some time."

Wei started gathering as much of the clothing strewn around the floor together as he could, feeling Noah's eyes on him the entire time.

"Why are you helping me?"

The question caught Wei off guard, and he didn't have a readily available answer for him. "This is my turf," he said gruffly, hoping that was enough for Noah for the moment. "I can't let shit like this happen in my own territory. It makes me look weak."

"So I'm a way to show strength." The words didn't have any emotion in them—no resentment or bitterness, just an observation of a fact. That didn't make Wei feel less guilty for saying it.

"That's part of it," Wei admitted, reluctant to have Noah believe it was strictly that. The truth was he was beginning to see trouble in his own territory with the girls disappearing and the drug dealers moving into his turf. He needed to take every opportunity he could get to show his strength. "There's more to it, though."

"Like how you think Lianne's disappearance is connected to those other girls."

Wei nodded but didn't say anything more on the topic. This wasn't the place to do so. He hadn't seen any obvious evidence the apartment was now bugged, but that didn't mean it wasn't. There were people out there who would be too skilled for Wei to catch sight of their handiwork. That's why he'd called Tony along.

Wei was clearing through some of the things by the door and stopped when he saw a small rectangular piece of paper facedown on the floor beneath the window. He almost didn't notice it because of the color of the baseboard. Wei picked it up and turned it over. It looked like the kind of pictures that could be taken in those Japanese photo booths with the background and special effects. It was a series of pictures of Lianne and Noah, their blood relation painfully obvious. They could have been twins for all Wei could tell in the picture. Each picture was them in a ridiculous or flirty pose, and they were both plainly barely containing their laughter in each one.

"We took those three years ago on a week-long trip to Tokyo," Noah said softly right behind Wei. It was only Wei's experience grooming the tough persona of the leader of the Dragons that kept him from jumping or showing any outward signs of surprise. Noah took the picture from him, looking down at it. The memories were happy ones, Wei surmised, judging by the smile that widened Noah's lips. "I didn't know she'd kept hers."

"I know what you're going through is hard right now," Wei said, voice breaking a bit before he could regain control of it. "You don't need this place to have that connection—this place, it can only remind you why you're here, you know? But *this*,"—he touched the photo strip gently— "this will help you think of your sister at a happy time and remember her the way she *should* be remembered. Let *this* be your connection to her, not this place."

Those impossibly colored eyes caught Wei's, a question hidden deep within them—a question neither man knew, much less could answer, but it was magnetic, drawing Wei in. Before either knew it, they were standing nearly pressed against each other, the entire world currently narrowed down to just the other's eyes.

Desire coursed through Wei's veins like fire. He wanted nothing more right then than to take Noah in his arms, feel his body pressed against his own, taste those lips, drive the other man to a passion that would make him forget his worries, forget the pain he felt, at least for a little while.

Wei actually leaned in to make some part of that happen, their lips drawing closer and closer together, but a knock at the door jarred the two of them back to the reality of their surroundings, and Noah, flushed scarlet, widened the distance between them, looking toward the door.

"That's my guys," Wei said, voice husky with unspoken and unacted desire.

"They're fast," Noah commented, not meeting Wei's gaze. The flush was slowly fading from his skin, but his voice still held a slight tremor of lust. Wei nodded, not trusting himself to speak at the moment.

Noah turned back to the clothing sprawled out, gathering what he wanted to take. Wei made his way to the door and opened it, letting Tony, Conroy, and Smile—so named because of the fact that he actually never did—into the apartment.

"What the hell happened here?" Conroy asked, letting out a low whistle as he looked around at the chaos.

"Some unruly house guests," Wei said. "No time to explain. I need you three to clean this place up, make it look ready for someone new to move in. Be careful with the things—everything that's left behind once we leave goes to storage. First thing tomorrow, we get a guy in here to replace the window. This all needs to be done as quietly as possible."

Wei turned back to Noah, who was standing beside the black luggage bag and staring at the ground, a dazed look on his face. "Do you have everything you need?"

Noah shrugged. "Maybe. I don't know."

He was going into emotional shock, Wei realized. He needed to get Noah out of there as soon as possible. He took the bag and zipped it up. "This will do for now." He handed the bag to Conroy. "Bring this to the Constance's when you're done."

"Wei, what's going on?" Tony asked, glancing in Noah's direction meaningfully.

"I'll explain everything to everyone, but not now. We need to get this done."

"We're on it." If the three Dragons resented being called in for cleanup detail, they didn't show it; they got to work without complaint.

Noah still stared at that same spot on the ground, seemingly withdrawing into his mind. Wei understood the appeal, but he couldn't let him do that, not yet. He closed the space between them and put his hands on Noah's shoulders gently. When he spoke, he kept his voice soft and soothing. "Let's go."

Noah stiffened beneath his hands and then relaxed immediately, tension draining from his body. The contact—even through the fabric of his shirt—brought a different form of tension to Wei's body, but he paid it no heed. It definitely wasn't the time.

"Where are we going?"

"Somewhere safe, until we figure out what's going on."

Somewhere I can protect you.

20

It was after two in the morning when Wei drove his motorcycle into a parking garage outside a fairly nice-looking building. There were several cars in the parking garage, most of them high-end. Wei brought the motorcycle to a stop in parking space 20-A.

Noah climbed off, his mind in such a fog he had barely noticed the sensation of being pressed against Wei. *Everything keeps falling apart.* He'd been in the country for just a few days and already he'd lost pretty much every vestige of a connection to his sister. On top of that, he was now involved in something that went God only knew how deep and turning to a group of people he didn't even know.

Had he made a mistake in coming to Hong Kong? *What was I thinking, trying to help Lianne in a foreign country when I don't even know how to help myself?* The doubt and fear almost crushed the heart in his chest.

"Over here," Wei said, brushing past him and leading him toward an elevator not too far away. Noah followed behind, barely noticing the tingle that rushed through him when Wei's shoulder brushed against his own.

In the elevator, Wei pressed floor twenty. When the doors opened again, they were in a hallway that went in two directions, ending in a door on either side. A thick beige carpet, so plush that for a moment Noah expected to sink into it, lined the floor. They went to the left and came to a door marked with 20-A. Wei pressed in a series of buttons, and the door let out three short beeps.

Noah stepped into the room first, uncertain in the darkness. A moment later the door shut and the only light was coming through a partially curtained window that looked to be pretty far away.

Noah could not help but become *very* aware of Wei, standing close behind him, their bodies almost touching in the narrow space. That closeness, along with the scent of the other man, came quite close to piercing the shell of despair rapidly closing around him. It spiked when

Wei's hands came onto his upper arms on either side, gently maneuvering him out of the way so he could step past him. A faint click sounded, and light filled the room.

Noah found himself in a narrow entryway lined on either side with a series of cabinets. Noah saw that Wei had shucked his shoes there before continuing into the apartment, so he followed suit.

The small entryway opened up into a large single space. To Noah's immediate left was what he assumed to be the bathroom. A little farther beyond that was a kitchen area. To the right was an expansive living room and beyond that, obscured behind a panel of fogged glass that extended half the length of the room, was what he assumed to be the bedroom. The place was not lavishly furnished but everything in it was of nice quality. A comfortable red-wine-colored couch faced the wall where a large television was mounted. A few chairs of the same color faced inward on either side of the couch, and directly in the center of the three pieces of furniture was a handsome wooden coffee table. Directly to the left of the television on the wall was a six-shelf bookcase of dark wood, filled with books.

The wall behind the couch was mostly window, white semi-transparent curtains drawn to dim the light, heavier curtains of the same red-wine color waiting to be drawn. A few pieces of art dotted the walls, small and unobtrusive. They weren't throwaway choices, not something picked up from bargain sale bins in a home décor store, Noah could tell. Each piece had been chosen for a reason. Wei clearly put some effort into the design and layout of his home.

"This is where you live?" Noah looked around, clearly impressed.

Wei raised an eyebrow. "What, surprised that a gangster lives so well?"

Noah blushed furiously. "What? No, that isn't—I just meant that—I mean—" Wei's laughter silenced his jarred sputtering. "That's mean."

Wei laughed harder, his eyes twinkling wickedly. "I couldn't resist."

Noah couldn't help but smile a little in return. There was something infectious about Wei's laughter, something that took root in his chest and said *Hey, laughing, it's good. We should try, too.* It was yet another facet of the complex man standing before him that he could appreciate. Nothing was ever only what it looked like; there was always another layer, something deeper, something more complex. It only added to the alluring charm of the man, made Noah want to probe further, find out what else was waiting to be uncovered.

"Do you want anything to drink?" asked Wei. Noah was startled to see he was already on his way to the kitchen, his feet soundless on the hardwood floor. He moved with a surprising amount of grace for someone Dang called nothing more than a thug.

The man was complex, multifaceted, like a good wine.

"What do you have?" Noah asked when Wei repeated his question.

"Water, wine, beer," Wei listed, head in the refrigerator. "After tonight I'm pretty sure you could use a beer." Without waiting for Noah's agreement, he emerged from the fridge with two bottles of Tsingtao beer.

"Can't argue with your logic," Noah said, joining him at the countertop island of the kitchen and taking the beer offered him. Wei popped the tops with a bottle opener and held his beer out to Noah for a cheers. "I don't know what there is to drink to," Noah said darkly.

"To first steps," Wei replied. "To finding your sister—which I am going to help you do. You're going to have the Dragons at your disposal for this."

Noah clinked his beer bottle against Wei's and followed him to the couch, taking a seat on opposite ends, neither quite ready to sit so close together, both their bodies still feeling the echoes of their earlier closeness. Noah took a drink of the beer, gathering his thoughts. There was a lot he wanted to ask the other man, and now it seemed he would have the chance.

"The Dragons," he started after a moment. "They're your gang, right?"

Wei rolled his eyes a bit. "In the most basic sense of the word, I guess—but no, they're way more than that. Each and every one of them is family. We've been through a lot together. I know what Dang says, but he's wrong. These people are dedicated to this district, dedicated to the people who live here, ensuring their protection and safety. We've each lived through violence, and know what that can do to people."

"But you're the gang that runs this area." Noah made sure there was no judgment in his voice, just stating a simple fact.

Wei nodded. "There was a gang in power before the Dragons—the Nine Stars. They were monsters. People they didn't like were just gunned down in the middle of the street. Drugs flowed freely in this territory. The Nine Stars demanded crazy amounts of protection money and weren't afraid to make examples of people who wouldn't or couldn't pay. The police and the Nine Stars were engaged in what was basically a war. Cops died almost daily."

Wei fell silent, his eyes lost somewhere in the past. Noah did not speak, merely watched him, wondering what painful memory he was examining. After what seemed like an eternity but was merely seconds, he continued.

"Five years ago, my sister...she was only fourteen, the last true family I had." A shadow passed over Wei's face, fraught with pain. "My parents both died before—my mom during my sister's birth and my dad from heart problems when she was ten. Mei was all I had in this world."

"What happened?" Noah asked, not sure he wanted to know.

"She was caught in a territorial dispute between the Nine Stars and the cops—part of an initiative meant to take the district back. She was shot. Neither group even noticed it had happened. By the time someone was able to get her to the hospital, it was too late."

Wei stared down at the floor, jaw set, fists clenched so tightly the veins in his arm bulged out. Noah couldn't say later why he did it, where the urge came from, but he hated to see the other guy in such pain. He reached out, putting his hand over Wei's. He felt the muscles tighten even more before they began to relax. Wei slowly looked up, meeting Noah's eyes. The pain in them was palpable, so real Noah thought he could reach out and touch it. Noah didn't remove his hand.

Noah knew what the loss of a parent was like, knew the emptiness it caused, and he felt it at that moment, seeing someone else go through it. Noah had only lost his mother, but he never really felt like he had a father. Emotionally, anyway, so he knew what it was to only have one person you could depend on.

When Wei spoke again, despite the pain, his voice seemed stronger. "That was when I—we—decided enough was enough. Most of the Dragons were people I grew up with, people who hated seeing this place like that. We were able to find other people who were willing to join us pretty easily. We formed the Dragons, and we fought the Nine Stars for this territory. It was brutal—I won't lie about that. We did some pretty awful things to get control of the Eastern District. But it was necessary. Once we wiped out the Nine Stars, the other gangs feared us, seeing what we did, and we've kept control since then.

"We made a promise, though. We'd never lead the way the other gangs did. We don't profit from prostitution and drugs. We don't tolerate that in our territory. Anyone selling drugs here is going to face the Dragons. We have a few illegal gambling dens set up, but we keep a tight hold on them. We don't rule through fear—no one will ever be afraid of us if they see us. We lead by helping. We've proven to the people that we can keep the violence away, keep them safe, so they trust us.

"I'm not saying we're good guys," he added, something in his face saying he desperately needed Noah to see them for all that they were. "If someone crosses the line, challenges my authority, I deal with it. But—"

"But you're the lesser of two evils," Noah finished. Wei leaned back, body relaxed once more. Was that relief on his face, or was Noah trying to read too much into it? There didn't seem to be need for it any more so Noah reluctantly removed his hand from Wei's.

"I guess you can say that. I don't have any illusions about what I am. I'm not a good person—"

"I disagree." Noah was surprised by just how intensely he objected to that statement. "You're a good person who has had to do some hard things for the greater good. Nothing is black and white—nothing says that gangsters can't be good people, or that cops can't be bad people."

Wei leaned forward suddenly until he was nearly nose to nose with Noah. Noah all but gasped. It took all of his willpower not to pull back at the suddenness of it. He could feel Wei's breath on his face, feel the warmth radiating from his body—*Damn, this guy must be a heat rock*, he thought. Unbidden, he glanced down toward Wei's lips, so close to his own, so inviting. The arousal coursing once more through his veins was more potent than any beer, and once more Noah found himself throbbing just at the nearness of the other man.

"Do you really believe that?" Wei's voice was husky, his eyes demanding Noah's attention, intense and unblinking.

Noah, sensing this was a serious matter for the other man, did his best to show his certainty on his face. "I do."

Wei's head cocked to the side, a gesture that reminded Noah of Ringo, the boxer his family had when he was young. That image in his head brought a barely suppressed giggle from him. Wei, surprised by that reaction, sat back. "What? What's so funny?"

Noah doubted he would like the comparison to a dog and just shook his head. "Sorry. I think I'm just tired."

Wei looked at the clock on his phone and raised his eyebrows. "I guess so. It's almost three." He stood, finishing off the remaining half of his beer in three deep gulps. Noah watched his Adam's apple bob as he drank, so turned up he was surprised the heat of his body wasn't burning through his skin. If spontaneous combustion were a real thing, he decided, this was probably where it came from.

"Just let me get changed, and you can have the bed."

"What? No, I couldn't take your bed," Noah protested, setting his own beer, still about half-full, on a coaster on the coffee table. "I'll sleep on the couch. You sleep in your bed."

"I'm pretty sure you need it more than I do tonight," Wei said firmly. "We can argue about other arrangements tomorrow after you've had a good night's sleep."

Before Noah could argue further Wei disappeared into the space behind the fogged glass. A light clicked on—a lamp near the bed, he guessed. He could see Wei's shadow moving over the glass as he heard the sound of a closet sliding open. He felt like a Peeping Tom but couldn't help himself; he watched Wei's shadow as he shucked his pants, stepping out of them before pulling on others. The shirt came off next. The whole thing was somehow erotic, a strip tease even though Noah could not see him.

A moment later, Wei reappeared around the glass divide. He was wearing nothing but a pair of dark gray sweatpants low on his hips. Noah's gaze went to the other man's body. His waist was narrow, his shoulders broad. He had well-defined pecs and a flat stomach, the low sweatpants revealing the barest traces of a trail of hair going down to disappear into the fabric. There were a few scars along his stomach, and his right shoulder had what looked like a puckered gunshot scar. What drew his attention most, though, was the dragon tattoo on his chest, a red serpentine beast that seemed to spiral around, its clawed foot directly over his heart. His right shoulder bore a tattoo, two sets of dates in a fifteen year span. Noah had no doubt as to its meaning.

Noah could not help but gape at the body before him. It was perfect, utterly masculine and realistic. It wasn't a cookie-cutter body magazines and porn and literature said was sexy, it was the body of a real man, honed, as he'd thought, by violence. When he realized he was staring, Noah blushed and turned away, looking pointedly at the television. He could feel Wei's stare drilling into his back.

"Your bag will be here when you wake up. Tomorrow I'll take you to meet the other Dragons, and we will get to the bottom of this. For now, you should get some rest."

Noah rose, forcing himself not to look at Wei directly. "Where is the bathroom?"

"Oh, it's right over here." Wei showed him to the bathroom. He nodded his thanks and went inside. The bathroom was nice, the tiles a pale blue that evoked thoughts of springtime. The back of the room was dominated by a large shower. There was no bathtub in sight, unfortunately.

Noah splashed his face with cold water in the sink. The reality of his situation was sinking in, and the numbness was giving way to pain—and fear. He was afraid he would never see Lianne again. He was afraid he was in over his head and was going to get himself killed.

He was afraid of the passion that was growing between himself and Wei. He didn't know how it had happened, but this stranger had wormed his way into Noah's psyche in mere hours. It was foolish—the man was dangerous, and beyond that, he was from another country, a place very different from Noah's own. Their cultures, their lives, their upbringings—they had absolutely nothing in common. Wei had to fight for everything he had—a literal war for survival—and Noah was given everything he could ever want thanks to his father's money.

He gathered his composure and stepped out of the bathroom to find the lights dimmed, only the glow from the bathroom illuminating the apartment. Wei was sitting on the couch, a pillow and thin sheet already spread out.

Wei walked past Noah, into the bathroom. "Try to get some sleep."

Wei waited until Noah was on the other side of the partition before he closed the bathroom door, throwing the room in darkness. Noah sighed, a sense of strangeness tingling through his core as he felt for the bed before climbing into it. It was soft, comfortable, much better than the bed at the apartment over the noodle shop. He collapsed onto the bed as he heard the water start in the bathroom.

Because of the events of the night, exhaustion sunk its claws into him. He wrapped the sheet around himself and nestled into the pillow. His cock stiffened instantly as he was surrounded by Wei's scent, drowning in it. Underneath the wave of arousal was something else, a feeling Noah hadn't felt since he'd stepped onto the plane in America: safety.

It was bizarre to equate a gangster's scent with being safe, but Noah felt protected and quickly drifted off to sleep.

21

Though he'd fallen asleep on that couch many times while watching TV, Wei found that tonight he simply couldn't. Perhaps it had something to do with the fact that a guy he found to be incredibly sexy was at that moment curled up in *his* bed with him relegated to the couch like a husband who'd pissed off his wife. It was maddening, really, for the primal part of him.

He clenched his right hand, remembering how it had felt when Noah placed his own hand over it, the way the other man's heat seemed to flow into him, draining the tension, easing his muscles, relaxing him. No one had ever had that effect on him—many of the Dragons made comments that he would still be tightly wound after getting laid, and they weren't entirely wrong. He bore a tension born of responsibility and a life of violence. During the war with the Nine Stars, he had never known when he would be attacked, if he was getting ready to breathe his last breath. Now, in power, he had to wonder when their rivals would make a move, when the other shoe would drop.

But something was different about Noah.

At the same time, guilt rode close behind those feelings. In a few short days, Noah's life had changed forever, and here Wei was, wanting nothing more than to strip naked, crawl into bed with him, and slide deeper inside him than anyone had ever been, claim him so thoroughly everyone else would know just by looking that he belonged to Wei.

Talk about selfish.

Wei couldn't help the way his body reacted, though, and right then, he ached for some kind of release. He would never take advantage of someone in a vulnerable position, which ruled Noah out. He would have to take care of things manually—not an uncommon occurrence for him.

Not having much choice if he wanted to get to sleep any time soon, Wei threw the sheet off his body. He ran the palm of his hand down the tent in his gray sweatpants, even that tiny sensation threatening to tear a moan from his lips; he'd never been so highly aroused just from being in close vicinity with someone else before.

Face flushed, he pushed the waistband of his sweatpants and his boxer briefs down, hooking them behind his heavy, full balls, his cock springing free to slap against his hard stomach. Wei glanced over his shoulder toward the bedroom area to make sure Noah was still fast asleep before he wrapped his right hand loosely around his erection. He sighed at the sensation, knowing it would be much better if it were someone else's hand but not caring, only needing to work to that release that had been building for so long inside him.

He began to stroke in quick, powerful motions, not trying to savor it but to just get it over with. As he stroked, though, he began to imagine it was Noah's softer hands on his cock, cradling the length, thumb exploring the veiny underside, brushing against the soft, fleshy head. Without intending to, he slowed his pace, allowing his fantasy Noah to explore his length. His left hand came down to tug on his balls, but it was Noah's hand making contact there in his mind, weighing them, feeling the come churning inside them, just waiting to be released.

His pace quickened.

The fantasy evolved; his hand moved from his balls and up his body, caressing the skin as it reached his right nipple, forefinger and thumb tweaking it. In his mind, it was Noah's fingers. He imagined Noah's lips ghosting along his neck—he could almost feel his warm breath. He brought the fingers of his left hand to his mouth, wetting them before returning to his nipple. His mind transformed the wet fingers to those luscious lips of Noah's, imagined his wet tongue teasing him.

Wei's breath came ragged now, the pleasure building in his abdomen, rising steadily toward release. He allowed himself to take the fantasy further. Suddenly it was not Noah's hand on his cock but Noah's warm, wet mouth. The image was too much, and he came hard, hips jerking as he released six shots of hot come onto his abdomen.

He lay there for a moment, limp, still unsatisfied even though he'd alleviated the sexual pressure. That was strange, not to mention troubling. It told him he didn't want to just satisfy his lust with Noah, but that he was wanting something deeper.

Nothing good would come of that.

22

Sleep did not come easily to Wei that night, nor did it stay long when it did finally come. He was awake before Noah and had already showered—where he repeated the events of the previous night, the fantasies of Noah intensifying, though again he came just after imagining Noah sucking his cock—and prepared a pot of coffee by the time Noah came padding around the glass partition into the living room, clothes rumpled, hair sticking up on all ends, and looking a bit confused.

Wei tried to hold in the laughter but failed. Noah just looked too damn adorable. The laughter made Noah scowl, which just made Wei laugh more.

"What time is it?" Noah asked, padding over to the kitchen area where Wei was seated at the small four-person table, a cup of coffee in hand, the newspaper laid out on the table before him.

"Just after nine," Wei answered. "We're going to go and meet the other Dragons around eleven, so they isn't any rush."

Noah ran a hand through his unruly hair. "So I have time to take a shower; that's good."

Wei pointed to where Noah's black suitcase stood beside the couch. "The boys brought your bag this morning, so you can change clothes and everything."

"That's a relief. Do you mind if I take a shower?"

"Of course not; go ahead."

Noah thanked him and entered the bathroom. As the shower came on, Wei made his way to the refrigerator to see what he could offer Noah for breakfast. He didn't have much in there; a few more bottles of Tsingtao beer, some containers of takeout that probably needed to be thrown out, a pitcher of water, and that was it. The freezer was no better, empty except for an ice tray.

I'll just have Constance make something, he decided, closing the fridge. He could stock up the apartment after the meeting. He'd ask Noah what he preferred, do his best to make him comfortable there. It was the least he could do to provide some manner of stability in the other man's suddenly chaotic life.

He heard the shower shut off, and a moment later, the door opened a crack. "Uh, Wei? This is embarrassing, but there's no towel in here," said Noah sheepishly, poking his head through the small opening.

"Shit. I forgot to get you one. I'm sorry. Hold on." Wei went to the ceiling-to-wall cabinet in the entryway closest to the bathroom and opened it. He removed a towel and handed it to Noah. As the other man moved to take it, he caught a glimpse of bare flesh—his chest and stomach with a smattering of hair, closely shaved pubic hair, the flesh at the base of his... Wei looked away quickly, struggling to keep the flush from creeping up his neck and into his face.

That brief look, not even seeing anything truly spicy, was coursing through him, filling his lower region with blood. *Goddamn it, I'm thirty fucking years old. I should be able to control my own body.* His body had other ideas, though; it was much more interested in acting like a seventeen-year-old boy, stiffening at the slightest breeze. He needed to get under control before he met with the other Dragons; they would heckle him mercilessly if they caught on to his situation.

Noah emerged from the bathroom, towel wrapped around his waist, holding it closed at his right hip. "I'm going to change," he said, damp body gleaming slightly. He grabbed his bag and pulled it back behind the divider.

It took every ounce of Wei's self-control not to watch the fogged glass wall in hopes of catching a glimpse of Noah's naked form. He would not resort to peeping; besides, the first time he saw Noah naked, he wanted the other man to be very aware of it.

He was not surprised to find he very much did want to see Noah naked. See and more. The fantasy the night before, as well as the one in the shower, were enough to tell him that. He had never been one to lie to himself. The sooner he accepted the truth of a situation, the easier it was for him. Know thyself and all that.

"Did you enjoy your shower?" Wei asked as Noah rejoined him, pulling a short-sleeved blue button-down over a plain white T-shirt. A pair of simple thin jeans and socked-feet completed the look.

"It was really nice," Noah replied, running a hand through his damp hair in what seemed to be an effort to tame it. "I would have loved a bath, though."

"Maybe we can make that happen later," Wei commented, a plan already forming in his mind.

Noah cocked his head curiously but didn't press, instead patting his stomach and turning the subject to food. "What's for breakfast, then?"

"Kitchen's not stocked," said Wei apologetically. "I don't usually eat here. But where we're going for the meeting will have food, don't worry." As if voicing protest, Noah's stomach gurgled loudly. "Hopefully you don't starve before then."

"I think I'll manage."

Noah turned to the large window that dominated the back wall. Upon waking, Wei had pushed the curtains open to greet the sun. He'd chosen the apartment building because of its beautiful view. It looked out over most of Eastern, and on a smogless day—rare as they were—the coast could even be seen.

"This view is amazing," Noah murmured.

"That's why I got it." Wei walked to stand next to Noah, shoulders almost touching. "The view helps calm me. It's high up enough that the noise of the street isn't too bad, more just a hum, and it helps me think of the city as a peaceful place."

"My sister would have liked it," Noah said, pain flickering across his face. Wei wanted to reach out and comfort him, but he would not make the first move and did not want to scare him off. "She would spend hours picking hotels before we traveled to make sure she could get a room with a perfect view."

They stood there in awkward silence for a moment, Noah lost with the ghost of his sister and Wei uncertain how to help him. Finally, Wei cleared his throat. "We should probably get going if we want to get some food before the meeting starts."

With one last glance out the window, Noah followed Wei to the door.

23

Nervousness and fear replaced Noah's hunger as Wei brought the motorcycle to a stop outside a cute coffee shop called Coffee by Constance. He really had no idea what he was about to step into. The bit of time he'd spent with Wei made him pretty confident he was in no danger—not that Wei wasn't dangerous, just that Wei wouldn't hurt him. The other Dragons, though, he couldn't say the same about them. If they were anything like Wei, Noah had nothing to worry about, but trust wasn't something that came easy to him.

The coffee shop looked nice, the sort of nonchain place Noah loved to frequent in the States. A cute teenage girl stood behind the counter when they came in. She instantly smiled at Wei, a small red glow entering her cheeks that Noah noticed immediately. It was unsurprising that a teenage girl would find the man so attractive. The jealousy, though, surprised him. Jealous of a teenager looking at a guy he had zero claim on. What was up with that?

"Morning, Shelby." Wei approached the counter and leaned against it, smiling at the girl.

"Hey, Wei," the girl replied, blinking her eyes prettily at him. After a moment, she turned those chocolate brown eyes on Noah. "Who is your friend?"

"This is Noah. Is your mom around?"

Shelby nodded, pointing toward a door. "She's in the kitchen."

"Thanks. Come on, Noah." Noah followed Wei behind the counter, feeling awkward about entering an area with a sign that read "Employees Only." The kitchen was nice and neat, precisely what Noah expected based on the outside. A middle-aged Asian woman wiped down a cook surface.

"Morning, Constance," Wei greeted politely, waving Noah in behind him. "This is Noah."

Constance's sharp eyes took Noah in carefully as she finished wiping the surface and deposited the cloth in the sink. "Chris told me you found a foreigner at K," she said. "This have anything to do with those girls?"

Wei nodded. "This does. Any chance of breakfast before the meeting?"

Constance smiled. The change that such a simple gesture brought over the woman surprised Noah. An inner light seemed to blaze behind her skin, her eyes becoming luminous and her face youthful and serene. She was almost a different person, and in that Noah saw where the girl out front, Shelby, got her looks. Constance looked very much like her daughter when she smiled.

"You're going to need to cook at home with a guest," Constance chided Wei as she set about preparing something. "You're a great cook. I don't know why you don't have a stocked kitchen."

Noah turned to Wei, eyebrow raised, and mouthed, *You can cook?* The other man simply shrugged as if to say, *If you're lucky you'll find out.*

Constance pulled a carton of eggs from the industrial refrigerator and set Wei to work making toast. Soon a nice simple breakfast of scrambled eggs, toast, and orange juice was ready. Noah devoured it appreciatively while Constance looked on approvingly.

"The others should be here in the next fifteen minutes," Constance told Wei, who nodded his understanding around a mouthful of toast.

The door opened, and a young man came in, face and hands coated with grease. He held his hands far away from any surface before Constance said anything, as if anticipating her, and made a beeline for the sink. Like with her daughter, the family resemblance was immediate.

"Hey, Wei," the young man said. His eyes fell on Noah, and they widened. "Woah, who's the *gweilo?*" The word wasn't said with malevolence, simply a casual use that implied a familiarity with the word. Despite the clearly casual meaning, the word hit Noah hard in the wake of the previous night.

"Winston," Constance scolded, but before she said more, Wei crossed the space of the kitchen in two long steps, holding the back of Winston's neck to make sure he was paying attention to him.

"Don't let me ever hear you say that word again." His voice was calm, but there was a deadly seriousness that even Noah recognized.

"Sure, of course, Wei," Winston stammered, bewildered. Wei touched their foreheads together and released him. He looked to Noah. "I'm sorry, man."

"It's…it's nothing." Noah finished drinking his orange juice, inwardly cringing at the awkwardness of this moment.

"Are you ready to head up to the meeting?" Wei asked Noah, gathering his plate and cup and taking them to the sink. Noah followed his example, his nervousness growing.

"I guess so. I'm not really sure how much help I'll be."

"There's a meeting?" Winston asked. He was soaping up his hands and couldn't really look back at them at the same time. "Why is there a meeting? And wait, *he's* going to it?"

"He's got something the others need to hear," Wei said patiently. "Let's go, Noah."

"Thank you for the breakfast," Noah said politely.

Constance smiled warmly, the same transformation overtaking her face once more. "You're welcome, Noah." She turned on Winston. "You can just wash those dishes when you get done with your filthy hands."

Noah left the kitchen with Wei, the sounds of Winston's protests following him out.

Wei led him up to a comfortably furnished room above the coffee shop. There were two long couches, several chairs, and even a big poker table in the middle. In the back he saw an open door that led to a bathroom. A refrigerator stood in the corner. A window overlooked the alley at the side of the building. From the window Noah could see a beat-up old car of some model or other, its hood popped open between the coffee shop and its neighboring building.

"That car is Winston's pet project," Wei said, following Noah's gaze. "He's got a real talent for fixing things. There's no place near his apartment he can keep the car, so he keeps it here."

Noah thought about how young Winston seemed. A thought dawned on him. "Is he a Dragon?"

"No, but he really wants to be. And one day he will be. Probably not soon enough for his tastes, though. Come on, the others should be here soon."

Fifteen minutes later, eleven other people came into the room. Most of them were guys of varying age, from around Noah's to a few years older than Wei. He recognized some of the guys—there was the guy from the club the previous night, and the three guys who had come to Lianne's apartment, as well. The others gave him a curious look, but none said anything, probably assuming that Wei would fill them in.

Once everyone was there, they gathered around. Noah, feeling self-conscious and unsure exactly what to do, just stood off to the side, doing his best not to fidget.

"Before we start, Wei, I got some information after you left." The guy from the club stepped forward.

"What is it, Chris?"

"I managed to track down someone who recognized two of the girls, said they were both regulars, went there all the time for a bit, always with the same guy, and then they just stopped going."

"Like Lianne," Noah blurted before he thought better of it. Every eye in the room turned to him. Heat rose in his face, so hot he was sure he'd suffer from third-degree burns. "Sorry."

One of the men said something to Wei in Cantonese. Noah had no idea what, or even the tone it was said in; it was really hard for him to read the mood of Chinese, as it was a tonal language.

"Walker, speak in English," Wei said firmly. "Noah can't speak Chinese." He paused for a moment, seemingly thinking, and turned to Noah. "Can you?"

"I can't."

"I said what is this guy talking about?"

Wei explained his run-in with Noah and then had Noah take over when he finished. After a few nervous false starts, Noah filled them in on the rough details of his sister's traveling to Hong Kong and the call he missed, though not why. He took out his phone and played them the message too.

"I still don't see what this has to do with anything," Walker insisted.

"You might if you'd shut up and listen, Walker," quipped a young man.

"His sister's circumstances are similar to our missing girls," Wei said impatiently. "His sister disappeared after being a regular at K, too. And last night, while searching the club, someone trashed the place his sister stayed at, with a 'go home, *gweilo*' message left behind."

"You think they're connected," said the guy Wei had called Conroy the previous night.

"I'm one hundred percent positive they're connected."

"So what's our next move?" The question came from a dour-looking young man standing in the corner as far from the others as he could be. Noah wondered why he kept himself separate from the others when everyone else seemed so into their bond. Wei hadn't been wrong; they definitely resembled a family.

"I think K has something to do with whatever's going on. If it does, then Georges doesn't seem to know about it."

"Or he's turned on us for the money," Chris offered.

"It would have to be a hell of a lot of money for Georges to cross me," said Wei, unconvinced. "It's more likely that whatever is going on is something he doesn't know about. We should focus on the employees instead."

"Like that VIP section douchebag bouncer?" Chris suggested.

Noah agreed with that sentiment, remembering Vaughn from the previous night.

"Something like that. So we'll start by—"

"Are you really going to lay out our plans right in front of this foreigner?" Walker demanded in disbelief. "You don't even talk about them in front of Winston, and he's more Dragon than this guy."

Noah saw Wei's jawline tighten at Walker's tone. Before he could speak, though, Conroy did. "Maybe he's right, Wei. Bitchily said," he added with a dirty look at Walker, "but right."

Wei nodded jerkily, turning to Noah. "Sorry, but could you wait downstairs? I'm sure Constance, Shelby, and Winston will keep you company."

Noah nodded, grateful for the opportunity to get out of the room. He was uncomfortable around all those people, the animosity from Walker not helping. As he passed Wei on the way to the door, the other man put a hand on his shoulder, his expression saying, *You did well*. The touch sent heat cascading through his body, and he nearly gasped.

How did one man have such an effect on another person? It didn't seem possible. Cheeks aflame for an entirely different reason, Noah stepped outside.

24

Despite the relative heat of the day the air was cool on his warm face. He sighed, leaning back against the door. He heard voices on the other side, but could not make out what they said. Fine by him; he didn't want in on Dragons' secrets.

"They kick you out, too?" Winston sat halfway down the steps, his expression one of dejection.

"Yeah, something about me not being a Dragon." He walked down the steps to where Winston sat. "I don't mind so much, really."

"They're all great people," Winston said. "A little rough around the edges, but great people."

Noah remembered what Wei said about them, the way he spoke of them as family, the vision they shared for their community. Yes, he did not doubt Winston when he said that. Didn't make them less intimidating, though.

"About earlier," he started, rubbing the back of his head like a child apologizing for a misdeed. "I really didn't mean anything by it. I'm sorry if it offended you."

"It's all right. Really. It's just not something I'm used to encountering. I guess I should expect it in a fairly homogenous country, but still it's kind of a culture shock."

Winston stood up and stretched. "There's no telling how long they are going to take. We might as well go into the coffee shop and get a snack. My mom makes great desserts."

Noah followed Winston inside. He liked this guy, he decided. Winston seemed to have a good heart. He was a lot like Wei in that regard.

He had only met Wei yesterday and yet he kept popping into his head at the oddest moments. The attraction that flared between them was surprising in its suddenness and intensity. Noah was not a guy who bought into love at first sight or anything like that. Lust, maybe, but not love.

It didn't strike him as normal lust, though. Lust was cheap, passing, here today gone tomorrow. He'd known lust before, and it hadn't been this...intense. Then again, what was it they said about the brightest flames?

Noah was letting himself get far too caught up in their attraction. He didn't even know if Wei felt the same way in return. Noah guessed he might; he'd caught the occasional glance—like at the bathroom door this morning—and the way he got angry with Winston for using the word *gweilo*—but that could be his own natural hatred for the word and not a need to defend Noah.

"Uh, Noah, was it? Are you coming?"

Noah realized he'd been standing there. God, he must look like an idiot. He ducked his head so Winston couldn't see his cheeks redden and followed him inside.

Shelby and Constance were both behind the counter while a few people sat inside, drinking coffee and chatting. "Mom, two of the strawberry buns," Winston said, leaning against the counter. "You're going to love this, I promise," Winston told Noah. "Mom is famous for these."

Constance placed a stuffed pastry on a plate in front of him, slightly coated in powdered sugar and looking delicious. Noah hadn't had anything sweet to eat since arriving in Hong Kong, so a dessert would be nice. He took a big bite out of it, moaning slightly as the light flaky pastry gave way to a delicious strawberry cream, the richness of the flavor dancing on his taste buds.

"This is amazing," he managed through the mouthful, left hand rising to shield his mouth as he finished it.

"Thank you," Constance smiled. "That one's on the house."

As Noah finished the wonderful dessert his phone rang. It had been so long since he'd heard it that it caught him off guard and he jumped a bit.

Great, now I've looked like an idiot twice in five minutes.

He managed to fish the phone out of his pocket after cleaning his fingers of the remnants of powdered sugar. The number on the ID wasn't one he recognized. Based on the strangeness of it, he guessed it was a Hong Kong number. He answered it, unable to suppress a frown.

"Hello?"

"Ah, Mr. Potter. I am happy you answered." The simpering voice was unmistakable: Superintendent Dang. "You've caused quite a bit of worry, you know."

That was news to him; how had he managed to worry the superintendent? "I have?"

"We received a phone call this morning from a distressed employee at a noodle shop. She claimed a foreign male staying there had disappeared, the room he'd been staying in completely cleaned out. After a few more details were given, we realized it was you. We feared for your safety."

"Why, exactly?"

"Pardon?"

"Why did you fear for my safety, Superintendent?" He regretted saying the man's title as soon as it came out of his mouth. Winston stiffened, Shelby's eyes narrowed, and Constance's face became expressionless. Noah stepped away from the counter a bit.

"Someone spotted men leaving the building, men that matched the description of known associates of the Dragons, a local gang."

"I'm fine, Mr. Dang. How did you get my number, if I may ask? I never gave it to you."

"Your flight records, of course. The card you filled out had it listed. Getting the information from immigration was a simple thing. Now, then, Mr. Potter." Dang's voice changed, becoming heavier, just the right amount of authority entering into it. "My assumption is that you have somehow fallen into the company of the Dragons. While this is inadvisable, it might be beneficial for both of us."

Noah had a sinking feeling in his stomach. "What do you mean by that, exactly?"

"I've been thinking, and perhaps we are in a position to help one another. I might have dismissed your concerns about your sister rashly, hoping for the best-case scenario. I am willing to further investigate this matter, using every resource at my disposal."

"And?"

"And you use your unique position to get me insight on the Dragons. They are far too tight-knit to infiltrate traditionally, but if their leader has taken an interest in you—"

"Oh, please, don't trouble yourself, Superintendent. I would hate for you to waste manpower on something you were so certain was a no-case to begin with." Noah did not bother hiding the anger in his voice. "I'm certain I can make do."

He hung up the phone then, body shaking. Dang only wanted to help him because he thought he could provide valuable information about the Dragons. But was the motivation important? The police must have far more resources than Wei's Dragons—more manpower, more money, more avenues available to search for Lianne. Had he just turned down the best shot at finding his sister? And if so, *why*?

His shaking was mostly anger, anger that Dang would think he would just climb into bed with him so easily, so to speak. The asshole was waving his sister's safety beneath his nose like bait. What kind of person would do that? But whatever the motives, the end result would be the best for his sister if he went with Dang.

The thought hadn't even crossed his mind, though. He hadn't been the slightest bit tempted. The idea of betraying the Dragons—no, the idea of betraying Wei—was so utterly distasteful he'd turned it down without even *considering* what it might mean. He knew Wei to be worthy of his trust, and his instincts told him Dang was not.

He only hoped he hadn't doomed Lianne with that rejection.

25

It was simple enough to outline his plan for everyone. They would take turns staking out K each night and begin a subtle investigation of the employees to figure out what was going on. It was diverting a lot of their attention, but this matter needed to be dealt with as soon as possible. It had the potential to destroy everything they'd worked so hard to build here.

As soon as Wei announced the meeting to be formally over, Walker stalked over to him, as he expected he would. As always, he pulled no punches when she spoke to him. "Do you think it's a good idea to get involved in the *gwai*—in the foreigner's situation at a time like this?"

Wei was patient when he spoke to him, as always. "Noah's situation is connected to what's going on in the Eastern District, Walker."

"That's just what you think. There's no way to know that."

Wei rolled his eyes. "What, so it's just coincidence that his sister went missing in a similar way after also spending a lot of time at K?"

"For all we know, yes!"

"There's no such thing as a coincidence."

Walker scoffed. "You sound ridiculous, Wei. The district can't handle any more girls going missing. This entire place is a powder keg waiting to explode. We won't be able to keep control anymore once it does."

"You're telling me things I already know."

"So act like it!" Walker snapped, louder than he wanted to. He stopped and looked around, seeing that the others were now looking at them. "Stop wasting time with the foreigner and focus on our girls."

"I can accomplish both of those goals at the same time."

"What makes you so sure you can trust him?"

"How often have my instincts been wrong?"

Wei could see that Walker realized he was fighting a losing battle. "Well, I hope it is actually your instincts and not your dick, or we're all in trouble." With that last remark, he pivoted on his heel and stalked to the refrigerator.

Wei's first instinct was to go after him—he'd just accused him of putting the Dragons at risk because he wanted to fuck someone—but a confrontation here wouldn't benefit anyone. Normally he valued Walker for exactly what he'd just done: he was unafraid to speak his mind, and it was invaluable at times. He couldn't be mad at him just because that tendency got turned on him.

"Yo, Wei," Conroy called now that he was no longer engaged in conversation with Walker. "Why don't we introduce our foreigner to some *real* Hong Kong dim sum?"

"Any excuse to eat dim sum, right?" Wei grinned as Conroy flipped him off. "That's actually a good idea. Same place as always?"

Conroy looked at him like he'd grown horns. "Do you even gotta ask? You think we're gonna get dim sum somewhere other than Mama Fo's?"

"You're right. Stupid question. Let's go, bros." Wei led the Dragons down the stairs, a feeling of contentment glowing in his chest. These were his brothers, his people, and when he was with them, he was content. They were a family, and the time they spent together *not* dealing with Dragons business is what solidified that, not their commonly shared cause.

Constance met them in the kitchen. She motioned discreetly for Wei to join her near the refrigerator. The other Dragons went out into the café. Once they were all gone, Constance spoke. "I'm not so sure it's a good idea to say this in front of the other Dragons, but while you we in the meeting, Noah received a phone call."

The look on Constance's face told him that whatever he was about to hear he wasn't going to like, but he couldn't fathom what it might be— unless his sister...

"From the sound of his side of the conversation, it was Superintendent Dang."

"What the fuck did he want?"

"No idea. I'm sure whatever it was it wasn't a social call. You know Dang is a slippery *ga tsan.*"

"And Noah?" Wei's heart tightened for a reason he didn't fully understand.

"He didn't seem too happy at the end of the call, but I don't know him, so it's hard to tell. I figured you should know, in case..." Constance trailed off.

Wei didn't want to ask it even as the words came out, because he knew already. "In case...?"

"In case he's a spy for Dang."

26

Noah sat at a table near the door, a coffee in front of him all but untouched. His phone rested on the table next to it. Dang's not-so-subtle offer echoed in his mind. He didn't regret the choice to not help Dang, even if it meant not having police help to find Lianne.

At the sound of voices, he looked up to see the Dragons filtering into the coffee shop, laughing and messing around. Two of the younger ones went over to Winston while the others just sort of hung around.

The big one named Conroy came over to Noah and slapped him on the shoulder, a gesture of camaraderie. "Noah, my man, you're about to have your fuckin' mind blown," he said, a huge smile on his face.

"I am?"

"You sure as fuck are! You're about to have Mama Fo's dim sum, man!"

Noah chuckled. "I've had dim sum before."

Conroy crossed his muscled arms over his chest. "You ever had dim sum in Shangbu before? Didn't think so. You ain't had real dim sum, then. Ain't that right, Wei?"

Noah, who hadn't seen Wei come in with the others, nearly jumped when Wei appeared next to him, voicing his agreement.

"I can come too, right?" Winston asked. "Since white boy here—" He winked at Noah. "—is going, that means it isn't Dragons only."

"It's fuckin dim sum, man, not a strategy meeting." Conroy punched Winston in the shoulder like a big brother would. The younger man rubbed the spot to soothe the pain, scowling overdramatically.

"It looks like it's going to rain outside," Noah realized, looking out the big window. Clouds had come in quickly, hiding the sun, and everything had taken on a gray tone.

"No surprise, it's the rainy season," Winston said with a shrug.

"Yeah, but Wei and I are on a motorcycle, and I didn't bring a jacket."

Conroy slung his arm over Noah's shoulder, drawing him in against him. "Don't worry, my man, you and Wei can hitch a ride to Mama Fo's with me." Noah wriggled to escape Conroy's hold. Such tactile behavior was unfamiliar to him, having never been friends with a lot of guys. "You'll have to ride in the back, though; I already promised Steel the front."

Conroy topped off the physicality by ruffling Noah's hair before releasing him. "Let's get going, bitches."

Conroy's car sat out front, a green Corvette, sleek and shiny as if it had just got a coat of paint. Noah figured Conroy must be one of those guys who was constantly washing his car. Conroy got behind the wheel—on the right side instead of the left, Noah noticed; the influence of British colonialism, no doubt—and Steel, one of the young men who hung with Winston, got in on the other side. Wei climbed in the backseat behind Conroy, and Noah got in the other side. He started to pull the door closed, but Winston caught it.

"I'm riding with you guys," he said. "Walker's car smells like cat piss. Scoot over."

Noah did as commanded to allow the taller guy in. He didn't realize how little space the car had—or at least how much space the two men on either side of him took up. His right leg pressed against Wei's, the constant pressure stirring his blood as his touches always did. Every time Wei or Noah moved their arms, they brushed together as well.

Noah couldn't imagine a more awkward situation to be in at that moment. He was a grown man sandwiched into the middle seat, achingly erect because of tiny touches from a man who drove him crazy and officially in the company of "known gangsters."

His life had become so strange in such a short amount of time. The men chatted amongst themselves as they drove, but Noah sat in surprisingly comfortable silence, allowing their banter to pass over him without really hearing any of it. All he was aware of was the rock of the car, the beat of his heart, and the heat of Wei's presence at his side.

Perhaps we are in a position to help one another, whispered Dang's voice in his mind. What kind of deal would that be, though? One shouldn't feel like they were entering into a deal with the devil when they were dealing with the police. Then again, the police shouldn't be trading services—it was their job to protect civilians at all times, not only when they were going to be getting something out of it.

At least with the Dragons there was no duplicity; Wei and the others, they made no qualms about who they were. You got exactly what you saw. As surprising as it might seem, Noah would pick them over Dang any day.

As the conversations went on, Noah glanced up into the rearview mirror and saw Steel looking back at him. It surprised him at first, but he soon realized it wasn't Noah he was looking at but Winston. No one else was paying attention to it, and Noah wondered what it could mean. After a moment, Steel realized Noah was watching and quickly turned his eyes back to the road.

Maybe there was something going on there? Noah wanted to ask Wei about that later, but it was none of his business, no matter how curious he was.

By the time the car pulled into the small parking lot of a tiny hole-in-the-wall place, rain had splattered the windshield in big, heavy drops. They hurried to the door, heads ducked against the rain. Wei held the door open for each of them. The dour-faced man from earlier, Walker, and the other young man who'd talked to Winston in the coffee shop soon joined them. Three minutes later, four others arrived for a complete group of twelve.

"Are they going to be able to seat all of us?" Noah asked Winston.

Steel snorted. "Do you know who you're here with?"

"Ease off, Steel," Winston chided, nudging the other guy with his elbow. "He's not from around here."

"You got that right."

Noah bristled a bit. "What kind of name is Steel?"

"It's a nickname I got in bed," Steel replied cheekily.

"Because you have to knock someone out with a steel bar to get any?" Noah threw back without thought.

Winston coughed in an apparent attempt to not laugh. Steel's eyes widened for a moment, and Noah wondered if he'd made an enemy in the Dragons—well, a second one; Walker seemed to be his enemy already—but then Steel laughed and held out his fist for a fist bump, which Noah returned gratefully. "I walked right into that, I guess. I'm Steel. You got a damn quick mind there."

"I'm Noah."

"Hey, we got a table," Conroy called back to them, and they followed him to a large round table in the center of the room, big enough to fit each of them. Wei motioned Noah over to a chair on his right. Next to Noah was Winston and Steel. On Wei's left was Conroy and Tony, Chris and the others, and Walker sat directly across from Wei at the table.

A waitress quickly brought bottles of beer and traditional Chinese rice alcohol before they could call for it. She paused momentarily to exchange a pleasant greeting with Wei.

"They'll bring around carts with the options on them," Wei explained.

Noah made an exaggerated face of realization. "Oooh, is *that* how it works?"

Wei made an affronted face. "Okay, be that way. See if I translate the dishes for you, then."

Noah laughed, touching his arm apologetically. He didn't know what made him do it, touching Wei in such a familiar way; it just seemed like a natural thing to do. "I'm sorry, I'm sorry. Please don't let me eat anything weird."

Wei shrugged noncommittally, his eyes twinkling.

Noah turned as Winston handed him a bottle of beer with a smirk on his face. "What?"

Winston shook his head while Steel mimicked Noah's laugh, and he blushed, wondering if he really sounded as overly flirty as the other man was making it seem. *God, I hope not.* He wanted to sink under the table and hide. His embarrassment must have shown on his face, because Winston laughed, not unkindly.

"Hey, Winston, stop laughing like an idiot and pour the *yum cha*," Conroy called across the table. Winston gathered his composure and turned to a cart that had been pulled up beside him. He distributed cups, Steel rising to help him get them around faster.

"Is this normal?" Noah asked Wei as Winston poured the pale green tea into Wei's cup. Wei tapped the crook of his slightly bent middle and index fingers of his right hand on the table as Winston did it.

"The tea? Very much. In Hong Kong you can't have dim sum without *yum cha*; the two are interconnected. It's not the same in Taiwan or the Mainland, but it's the tradition here."

"I've never had tea with dim sum in America," Noah murmured, regretting the playful way he had made fun of Wei just trying to guide him through the experience. Maybe he didn't know as much as he thought he did.

Noah watched Winston make the rotation around the table, and each time the person he poured for made the same gesture Wei had with their middle and index finger. When Winston came to him, last, he too did it.

"He catches on quick," commented Conroy, who saw it.

"I'm not stupid," Noah retorted, hiding how much the comment pleased him. He practically glowed after Wei patted his leg gently.

Wei named the dishes for Noah as they appeared—*har gau*, shrimp dumplings; *siu mei*, the steamed pork buns Noah loved (he ate five of them); the pork buns like he had for lunch yesterday, Wei called them *char siu pau*; there were even bowls of *congee*, rice porridge—Noah didn't touch that.

"What's that one?" Noah pointed to one coming closer.

"*Feng jow*," Wei replied.

"Phoenix claw," Winston translated with a chuckle.

"Oh? Phoenix claw? What is it really?"

"Phoenix claw is what it translates to, but it's actually chicken feet."

"They're good for your skin," Tony said.

"In that case," said Conroy, taking three or four from the passing cart and placing them all on Wei's plate. "You need to eat as many as they got."

"Fuck you," Wei laughed, but he picked one up and bit into it. Noah cringed at the sound and the way he just chewed the bone and everything. "The way they're cooked makes the bones really soft," Wei explained after seeing Noah's face. "They're good—here, try one."

Wei extended one toward Noah, who eyed it as if it were something dangerous. Wei shook it insistently, and Noah finally took it, biting a small piece of it. It was strange to feel the bones breaking beneath his teeth, but it tasted fine.

"How is it?" Wei asked, eyebrow raised in curiosity.

"Surprisingly good," Noah answered, taking a bigger bite.

"I think this white boy has some Asian inside him," Conroy said, raising his beer in a salute to him.

"He definitely *wants* an Asian inside him," Steel murmured. Winston snickered childishly. Both boys laughed louder when they saw that Noah had heard and was now blushing red.

They were there for nearly two hours when the dessert cart came on its way, filled with traditional egg tarts. Everyone at the table was really enjoying themselves, even Walker. The atmosphere was light and cheerful. They included Noah in their conversations and jokes—he found himself bonding surprisingly quickly with Winston and Steel. He felt...comfortable, like he belonged there. He was even able to set aside his worries and concerns for that brief amount of time.

They were just about to pay and leave when the door opened and three men in designer suits and dark sunglasses came into the restaurant and made a beeline for their table. The change in everyone was remarkable, almost like magic. Looking around the table, Noah saw that the faces had become cold, guarded. The air carried the subtle smell of danger.

"Who are they?" Noah asked Winston softly, but the other man held up a hand for him to be quiet.

The three men came to stand at the side of the table behind Steel and Winston, facing Wei. The man on the left glanced at Noah for the briefest moment, and fear lanced through Noah's mind. Without thinking, he reached back and took Wei's hand under the table.

"Mr. Tseng." The man in the middle bowed his head ever so slightly.

"What are Vipers doing in Dragon territory?" Wei's voice was cold and harsh in a way Noah hadn't heard before, and it chilled him almost as much as the other man's look had.

"We come with a message from our boss, Leo Tong," the man replied, keeping his voice respectful despite the derision in Wei's tone.

"Leo Tong? I have no idea who that is." Wei turned to look at Conroy, who shrugged. He didn't know, either, apparently.

"He recently gained power over the North Point territory. Mr. Tong would like to meet with you to discuss a business proposition."

"I can't think of any sort of business I would have with the Vipers."

"I cannot say more, sir, but Mr. Tong promises it will be a very lucrative proposition for you. He would like to set up a meeting to discuss this with you." The man produced a card from his pocket and handed it to Wei. We didn't even look at it, just passed it to Tony.

"Is that all?"

"Yes, sir." The man's voice was placid, emotionless, but Noah glanced at his hands and saw he was clenching them tightly, the veins bulging.

"Good. Smile, Chris, make sure our visitors get back to their own territory safely. *Without* any stops."

Chris and the dour-faced man rose, eyes hard, and the three men, sensing the dismissal, departed, the two Dragons behind him.

"Who were there?" Noah asked, surprised to find his voice shaking.

"Members of the Twisted Vipers," Wei answered grimly. He squeezed Noah's hand tightly for a moment before releasing it. "They're the triad in charge of the Quarry Bay and North Point district. They've been growing pretty steadily along our borders recently."

"Are they dangerous?" Noah asked.

Conroy reached across the table and patted Noah's hand like he was comforting a girl. "Don't worry, you're safe with us. Those *puk gai* aren't going to fuck with us—they're dumbasses, but not suicidal."

"*Puk gai*?" Noah's tongue stumbled over the strange, foreign words, and he knew he butchered the tones. The others around the table laughed. "What is so funny?"

"The first Chinese we hear you speak is a swear, that's what. It means something along the lines of 'asshole' or 'bastard'—"

"Or 'shithead,'" Winston added. He seemed to enjoy teaching a foreigner dirty Cantonese.

"Are you going to meet with this Tong fucker?" Conroy asked, bringing everyone's attention back to their recently departed visitors.

"Might be best if I did, if only to see who is in charge next door."

"I didn't know that old Zhou lost power," Tony commented thoughtfully. "I guarantee you he didn't just step aside. Zhou loved being in charge. This Leo Tong took control by force."

"Is it a trap?" Noah asked, panic rising at the thought. He was even less happy with this, considering how it would distract them from Lianne.

"It's always possible. That's why we will set it up somewhere advantageous for us. More likely he wants to get a look at me, too." He shook his head. "You don't need to worry about any of this. Conroy, give your keys to Winston. Winston, you take Noah and Steel to my place. You know the code, right?" Winston nodded. "Good. You and Steel stay there until I get back. Conroy, call this Leo Tong and set it up."

Conroy glared at Winston as he dropped his keys into the younger man's hands. "You get one speck of dust on my baby and you're dead meat, Chang."

27

Noah protested several times that he didn't need a babysitter, but everyone ignored him. He kept trying anyway. He leaned into the space between the two front seats where Winston and Steel sat. "Come on, I'm sure you guys don't want to be stuck watching me all night."

"Irrelevant," Steel said, legs stretched out in front of him, hands loosely joined on his stomach. "What Winston and I want doesn't matter one bit right now. You heard Wei—that was his 'I'm the boss' voice, and it wasn't a request."

"So because he told you to, you're going to babysit the foreigner."

"Precisely," said Winston and Steel in unison.

Noah grunted crossly, pressing his back against the seat. In reality he wasn't resentful of the company—he didn't think he could sit in Wei's apartment alone. He didn't like that Wei forced these people to keep him company, though. Why would he want to spend that much time with people who were just being forced to be there?

By the time Winston came to a stop at the apartment building Wei lived in, Noah was in a foul mood. He climbed out of the car, slamming the door behind him. He did not wait for Winston and Steel, just marched toward the building.

When he entered, he found Inspector Hong coming out of the elevator. Both stopped and looked at each other in surprise. Noah recovered first.

"What are you doing here, Inspector?"

"I heard you were in with the Dragons, and I figured you'd be here. I wanted to give you a warning."

Noah raised his eyebrows. "A warning, huh? How kind of you."

"Listen to me. This is serious. Whatever else you see on the outside, however noble they act, the Dragons—especially Wei Tseng—they're dangerous. You don't know what they're capable of."

"Oh, and you do?"

"*Yes*, I—" Hong stiffened as footsteps approached. Noah glanced and saw Winston and Steel coming in behind him. Both walked carefully up to them, studying the inspector as if he were as dangerous as the Vipers who had come to them in the bar, or some bug they wanted to squash.

"What the fuck are you doing here?" Winston demanded, cold hate burning in his eyes.

Hong didn't answer. He walked by them. Before he reached the door, he turned around, catching and holding Noah's gaze. "Be careful, Mr. Potter. It can be seductive, the world of the Dragons. That glamor makes it hard to see it for what it really is. Do you really think they can be trusted?" His eyes flicked to first Steel and then Winston—something swam in his eyes then, but Noah didn't know what it was—before he exited the building.

Steel let out a string of Chinese that sounded like curses based on his tone.

Winston turned to Noah, eyes blazing angrily. "What did he say to you, Noah?"

Noah shook his head, still thinking over what the inspector said. What exactly did he know about the Dragons? "It was nothing, really."

"Bullshit! So what, you spying for the fucking cops?" Winston advanced on Noah, but Steel grasped his shoulder, pulling him back roughly. "What? He just met with a fucking traitor right in front of—"

"Right in front of Wei's apartment," Steel finished for him impatiently. "Do you really think the cops would be dumb enough—" Winston muttered something at that, but Steel went on over him. "—to meet with their spy in front of the home of the *head* of the Dragons?"

"Well, when you put it that way," Winston muttered, but Steel was ignoring him. Instead, he turned back to Noah. "You need to tell us what he said to you, Noah."

"He told me to be careful, that you guys are dangerous," Noah said impatiently.

"And that's all?"

"That's all."

"You need to not talk to him again," Steel said brusquely, leading the way to the elevator.

"Excuse me? Where the hell do you get off telling me who I can and can't talk to?"

"He's a cop! Nothing good is going to come from talking to him. Besides, it's going to piss Wei off if he hears you've been chatting it up with Allen Hong."

"Why would I care if I piss Wei off?" Noah scoffed, though even as he said it, he knew he *did* in fact care.

"Well, if you get him mad he's much less likely to give you the D," Steel said bluntly.

Damn my fair skin, Noah thought, knowing it would give away the lie as soon as he spoke it. "I don't know what you mean."

Steel made a lewd face. "You know, the D? Dick? Cock? What I'm saying is I don't know if Wei is going to want to fuck you if you piss him off."

Noah felt as if his face was going to melt off, he had no doubt his ears were bright red as well. He couldn't believe that this guy was so openly talking about someone else's sex life—a sex life that didn't even exist. Thank god there was no one else with them in the elevator.

"That's, I mean, who says I want to, to, you know?"

"Your eyes every time Wei walks by," Steel said, enjoying his discomfort.

"Not to mention the huge bulge you had going on in the car on the way to dim sum," Winston added, dashing Noah's assumption that no one had noticed in the car. And if Winston had noticed, then Wei probably did, too. Shit. Talk about embarrassing.

"I don't know what you're talking about," Noah said, turning his nose up and exiting the elevator.

"Sure you don't." Steel and Winston snickered behind him. It didn't feel good being the focus of their mocking, but at least they'd moved on from Inspector Hong's visit. Winston stepped to the door, pressed in the code, and opened it. "You know, I should just give you the code now," he commented as Noah passed him.

"Why is that?" Noah asked as he removed his shoes.

"You're going to be over here all the time anyway."

"Yeah," said Steel, slapping Noah on the ass as he passed him. "I hear Wei has a pretty big sexual appetite."

Noah groaned. "You two are ridiculous."

"We're what?" Steel asked with a barely suppressed smile. "I didn't hear that clearly."

"Ri. Dic—"

"See, Winston, this man can't stop talking about dick. He wants it bad." Both younger men collapsed into laughter.

"You know, you're not as funny as I think you think you are," Noah quipped, annoyed.

"Aw, man, Wei doesn't have any snacks?" Winston complained after opening the refrigerator.

"We just ate lunch, and you're complaining about snacks?"

"Winston is always hungry," Steel explained, flopping down on the couch and turning on the television. "No one knows how Constance keeps the shop open with him eating everything."

"*Hou sei la lei,*" Winston called from the kitchen.

Noah sat down on the couch, trying to keep as much space for himself as possible. Steel had stretched out, legs wide, and was sitting in the middle. "You two have known each other a long time, huh?"

"Pretty much forever," Steel said. "Winston kept me out of trouble. I used to do some stupid shit when I was younger."

"When you were younger?" Winston teased, sitting down on his other side and then clawing the remote out of Steel's hand. "You saying you don't do stupid shit now?"

"Fine. *Stupider* shit."

Noah shook his head, amused at their antics. They maybe wouldn't get invited to any high-society shindigs—hell, it seemed that was true for all the Dragons—but they were good guys, and they were being friendly with him. They could have been resentful of the babysitting assignment, but instead, they seemed perfectly at ease, as if they were just friends hanging out.

Without really thinking about it, Noah pulled his phone out of his pocket and dialed Lianne's number. His thumb hovered over the red "end call" symbol on his screen, ready to hit it as soon as the automated message kicked in. He was so used to it instantly going to voice mail that he very nearly pressed end before he realized he didn't hear the automated message but ringing.

He sat there in disbelief, hands suddenly trembling as he listened. Two, three times, four times, and then the automated message. What had happened? Every other time he'd called, it had gone straight to voice mail, like her phone was off. But this time...

"It rang." His voice was shaking, barely audible, and Steel next to him looked over to see what he meant. "It rang. Her phone rang before going to voice mail! It's never done that!"

"Slow down, white boy, what do you mean?"

"Here, listen." Noah dialed the number again, hitting speaker phone, waiting for that wonderful sound of a ringing phone—

"Your call has been forwarded to an automated voice message system."

"What? No! No, no, no. It rang! Really, it rang. It didn't go straight to voice mail last time. It didn't!" Whatever barriers Noah had erected in his mind to keep his constant fear and panic at bay, they were rapidly crumbling, unable to bear the weight of this disappointment he could not put into words. "It rang," he repeated, throat thick, eyes burning as he fought to hold back tears, a battle he was quickly losing.

Winston and Steel looked on, uncertain what to do, as Noah dialed the number again—straight to voice mail—and again—straight to voice mail. "Yo, man, it's all right," Steel said awkwardly, moving as if he were going to touch him, but Noah jerked away.

He felt suddenly sick with shame. How could he break down in front of these...these *gangsters*? Noah had worked so hard to never show weakness, and yet here he was, about to cry and freaking out over a voice mail in front of two guys he didn't really know.

He climbed unsteadily to his feet, ignoring the other two guys, and hurried to the relative safety of the bathroom, pushing the door closed behind him. He tried to lock it but couldn't figure out how, so he gave up, slumping against the door in defeat. Once safely concealed from the others, he wrapped his arms around his knees and quietly cried.

28

The meeting didn't take long to set up. It would be held in Wei's territory at a fairly large body shop the Dragons owned, close enough to Viper territory for Tong to agree while still completely in Wei's control. It kept the Dragons in a position of power, which Wei wanted. He needed to maintain the image of strength by any means necessary; it was the only thing that kept the other smaller gangs from testing him in ways that would get innocent people hurt.

"I think we're wastin' our time, boss," Conroy said as the two of them, accompanied by Tony, entered the body shop parking lot. It was surrounded by a tall and sturdy chain-link fence and had the only one entrance; Tong would not be able to sneak men in behind the Dragons' backs. Just in case, though, Wei had a few men around back, keeping an eye out for any tricks that might get pulled. One could never be too careful.

"We don't have much choice, Conroy," Wei said impatiently, getting out of the car. He'd explained this to the other man twice since leaving the restaurant. "He stepped forward to meet with me. If I reject this meeting, it makes it look like I'm scared of the Vipers. We can't have that happen, Conroy, you know that. There's no telling what this Tong guy might do."

The afternoon sun was beating down on them. In this part of the city there were few trees and the taller buildings were in the distance, leaving them free of their shade. Wei wiped a hand across his brow, mopping up the sheen of sweat blooming on his forehead. He was outwardly calm, but inside he was beyond tense. He hated needing to meet with rival gangs, hated the show it required of him. His persona as leader of the Dragons was cold and cruel, which was necessary in the world he was operating in, but it took its toll on him each time he had to slip into it.

"How much longer until he gets here?"

Tony checked his watch. "The meeting is at three, so he should be here in the next ten minutes."

"Okay, make sure everybody is in place. No one gets in with weapons, Tony, are we clear? I mean nothing—not even fucking fingernail clippers. And only Tong and two others come inside."

"Got it."

Certain his orders would be followed, Wei walked inside with Conroy and Chris. If he was going to limit the amount of men Tong could bring in, he would have to do the same; it was the proper etiquette. He wanted to say fuck etiquette, but he couldn't. He was trapped in his role—a role he'd fought for, knowing the consequences. It was better this way; the streets were safe and people could carry on with their lives as they pleased.

Everyone except him.

The inside of the garage was blessedly cool with no windows to allow in the heat of the sun. There were a few cars inside but no workers; when setting up the meeting, Wei had sent them home for the day. The fewer innocents around the better, just in case things went wrong.

Chris found the keys to the office in his pocket and unlocked the door, holding it open for Wei. It was a cramped space, mostly dominated by a large wooden desk and three three-drawer metal filing cabinets. Invoices and receipts were all over the place, but Wei didn't bother straightening up. He knew the man who ran the shop for him liked the chaos and would be unable to find anything if something got moved. It wouldn't make for the best impression, but Wei didn't care. He didn't need the *place* to impress Tong. Besides, he was certain Tong would understand not wanting to bring a rival gang member any deeper into their territory than necessary.

In their world, trust was lethal.

His mind turned to Noah as he took a seat behind the desk. He'd only known him for a very short period of time, but he seeped so easily into Wei's thoughts. Part of him wanted to just dismiss it as lust—and there was no denying that he lusted after the other man, yearned to bury himself in the warmth of his body—but that was only part of it. Lust was nothing new to him; he was a man, after all. He'd never felt such an intense desire to protect some stranger before. Somehow Noah had slipped under his guard, found a crack in his defenses, and now he was there in his mind. And maybe in his heart.

"Tony says they're here, Wei," Chris said from the door.

Wei nodded his understanding. *Okay*, he thought. *Showtime.*

He adopted the stony, cold look he used in these circumstances, dwelling on thoughts that made him angry enough to have that cold fury he was famous for reach his eyes. The exercise would leave him mentally exhausted once finished, but it was the price Wei paid—willingly—for peace in the Eastern District.

Tony came into the room, followed by one of the two men who'd come to the restaurant to deliver the message. The second man through the door was no doubt Leo Tong. He was tall and scarecrow thin, his suit hanging off him. He was young, perhaps only a few years older than Wei, his eyes surprisingly pale and his black hair parted down the center to hang on either side of his head. Next came the other man who'd been in the restaurant. Chris closed the door behind them, waiting on the other side to ensure they had no interruptions.

"Mr. Tseng, we meet at last." Leo Tong's eyes glanced around the office, but his face showed nothing of his thoughts.

Wei did not rise to greet him—he was in his own territory, he didn't need to. "Mr. Tong. Have a seat."

Tong folded his long body into the one other chair in the room, his men staying back near the door, hands crossed in front of them, eyes sharp. Wei paid them no heed. Tony and Conroy would deal with them if necessary. He stayed focused on Tong.

"I guess congratulations are in order, yeah? My people tell me you recently became a redpole for the Twisted Vipers."

Tong inclined his head, affirming it. "You might say we're neighbors."

"Let's hope we can be peaceful neighbors." The implied warning did not go unnoticed by Tong; one didn't rise to his position—especially taking down a crafty bastard like Zhou—without being smart.

"Peaceful neighbors, yes. That's why I requested this meeting—so we could take a step toward becoming better neighbors. The best neighbors are able to help each other, after all. Wouldn't you agree?"

"Get to the point," Wei grunted. He didn't want to sit here listening to this man's double talk all day; he was a Twisted Viper—that alone was enough information for Wei. You didn't invite a snake into your home, and you certainly didn't trust it not to bite you when you turned your back.

Tong's smile faltered somewhat; it was clear he was expecting a friendlier reception, though Wei couldn't imagine why. He had a reputation for being completely unfriendly toward the other gangs; Tong had to have known that before coming here.

"The point is that I think it is time we go from just occupying adjacent territories. Imagine what could be accomplished if the Dragons entered into a business arrangement with the Twisted Vipers?"

"Not fuckin' likely," Conroy muttered at Wei's side. A quick glare from Wei shut him up.

"Think about how beneficial it would be," Tong went on, pretending Conroy hadn't spoken. "What's better than a mutually lucrative deal?"

"Well, that would depend entirely on the type of arrangement you had in mind," Wei said, drumming his fingers on the desk. It was just a casual gesture, one calculated to make him seem impatient, to put Tong on edge. Judging by the look in the Twisted Viper's eyes, it was working. He was at that moment wondering if he'd miscalculated in coming here; Wei could see it in his eyes. Wei intended to show him he had.

"I've come across a new supply of opium—good, quality stuff from the New Territories. If I can get it to the streets here, I'll make a fortune. The problem is getting it from there to here."

"North Point harbor not doin' it for you?"

Tong sighed, spreading his hands in a gesture that said *what can you do?* "The police in North Point have become quite keen on stopping my operations since I took power. They've tightened their hold on the harbor—I'm having a hard time getting anything in or out right now."

"And so you come here." Wei knew where this was going, and he didn't like it.

"The Dragons have Quarry Bay," Tong explained. "From what I hear, you also have a much better understanding with Eastern District police than we have over in North Point. So you let my people bring the goods over through Quarry Bay, we transport it back to North Point, and you get a cut of the profit—thirty-five percent."

It was a damn good proposal, Wei knew; if it had been some other gang he was meeting with it probably would have been too good to resist. Thirty-five percent from an opium profit? That could be an astronomical number.

"You're new in charge, right, Mr. Tong? How much do you know about me? If you'd done good research, you'd know I don't deal in drugs here."

Tong's smile slipped into a frown. "I'd heard you keep drugs off the streets here. But that won't be any problem—product's going right to Viper territory, and I'll make sure none of it seeps through to your side. Just the cash."

"I don't need your cash," Wei said dismissively. "You're gonna have to come to some arrangement with the cops or figure out some way to get it in under their noses—not gonna have opium comin' in through Quarry Bay. Last thing I need is to fuck up this peace I got with the cops here. You're on your own."

"Are you sure? This is a lot of money you're turning down."

"I'm sure." Wei rose, signaling the meeting's end.

Leo Tong sighed as he too stood. He had this expression, like a teacher disappointed in a student who hadn't learned their lesson properly. "You have my contact information if you change your mind. I hope we can come to some sort of arrangement."

"My boys will escort you back to your territory." Tony opened the door, ushering them out into the garage itself. Wei saw he'd come with four additional men—that was it. How trusting of him. Wei figured if he had been meeting with any other gang, he wouldn't have been so short on men.

Wei, Tony, Chris, and Conroy walked Leo Tong back to his car. Once he was in and the doors closed, the window rolled down and he leaned out. "I'm really sorry we couldn't come to an agreement, Mr. Tseng."

"That was a giant waste of fuckin' time," Conroy spat once the two cars drove off, followed by Wei's men behind them. "Can't believe he was crazy enough to think we'd go for that shit."

"I doubt he expected us to," Tony said thoughtfully.

"So he's just wastin' our time for shits and giggles?" Conroy raged.

"Not for shits and giggles, no." Wei realized where Tony was going with his thoughts. "He was sizing me up. I'm sure his story was true enough, and if we'd taken the deal, great, but if not, he could at least get a look at me." It was the only reason Wei could think of that the Twisted Viper lieutenant would come this far with Wei's reputation being what it was.

Conroy glowered darkly. "Well, I hope the fucker got the message that we ain't to be fucked with!"

Wei felt a heavy weight settling around his shoulders. "Me too," he said. For the entire district's sake.

29

Leo Tong's expression hardened as soon as the car was in motion. He let out a snarl and banged his fist hard against the window. His men fidgeted, wary of his wrath, but he didn't pay them any attention.

Who the *fuck* did that Wei Tseng *ga tsan* think he was? Tong knew the reputation of the Dragons' leader, but didn't think the man would be stupid enough to turn down a deal as good as the one Tong had brought to him. In a city like Hong Kong, opium would bring in hundreds of thousands, if not *millions*—thirty-five percent of that had been a more than a generous offer. Why did Wei Tseng turn him down? There was no profit in keeping their relationship hostile.

Ming, who'd been in the meeting with him, drove, glancing at Tong in the mirror, apprehension on his face. "Boss, what are we gonna do now? That shipment's coming in soon, and we ain't got anywhere to send it. If Johnny—"

"Shut the fuck up, Ming," Tong scowled, kneeing the seat in front of him hard. "I'm not fucking worried about Johnny Hwang." A lie, and a bold one at that. Things might be all right with the leader of the Twisted Vipers for now, but that was temporary. He'd gotten his territory by convincing Johnny he'd be able to bring in much more than the revenue old Zhou had and promising quick results. Tong already had the plan worked out in his head. He was seeing a little more, what with the drugs he carefully leaked into the Eastern District—careful enough not to draw the attention of either the Dragons or his own boss, who didn't want a conflict with the Dragons for some reason—and the videos, but not yet enough to justify Johnny making him a redpole.

The plan relied on the opium coming from China through a supplier already lined up. Now he needed a way in. The police in his territory had an understanding with Zhou; they didn't extend Tong the same courtesy—retribution for offing Zhou, no doubt.

Ming had risen to the top with Tong, and he was smart enough to know that if Tong went down because of this matter, he would too.

Probably against his better judgment, he persisted. "If Tseng doesn't let us use Quarry Bay—"

"We'll get Quarry Bay, for shit's sake, no matter what that *puk gai* says. This time we were offering the easy way. Looks like the Dragons want to go the difficult route." Tong sneered as he spoke. He itched for a chance to take that smug bastard down a peg or two.

"We can't start any trouble with them, boss." Tong heard real fear in Ming's voice. "Johnny made it clear we can't—"

Tong scoffed, cutting him off. "Don't worry. I'm not going to pull anything stupid with Johnny watching me this close. We don't need to outright challenge the Dragons for Quarry Bay. We only need to keep them distracted long enough to sneak our shipment through and get it into our territory. The money from the first shipment should satisfy Johnny for a while. We'll use some of it to grease the pig fuckers here, and then we're good as gold. We'll have so much shit running through that Johnny won't give a fuck what we do. Then we'll slide that shit right into the Eastern District and watch it destroy the Dragons from the fucking inside. Don't you fucking worry. The Dragons' time is almost over. Soon, I'll be running the Eastern District, too. We'll see who the fuck is in charge."

A man had to have big dreams, and Tong had the biggest. He saw a change in the triads of Hong Kong—hell, maybe of the Mainland itself. If he could consolidate the island, he might have a chance at challenging the Black Lotus—but one step at a time. He couldn't get too far ahead of himself or everything would fall apart around his ears. His moves had to be plotted carefully.

He considered for a moment, looking out the window and watching as the cars Tseng had sent to ensure they made it home broke off when they reached the edge of Viper territory. Perhaps it was time to move things along.

Mind made up, he dug out his phone and dialed a number. It only rang once before being answered—that was the kind of promptness he expected. "Tell Chen to make the drop. He'll know what it means." He hung up, fully confident his orders would be followed. Time to see what Wei Tseng was made of.

30

The atmosphere in his apartment was morose when Wei and Conroy entered. Steel and Winston sat on the couch, the television on but neither of them watching it, engaged in a quiet conversation. They both looked up guiltily when the two Dragons walked in.

"What did you *puk gai* do to my car?" Conroy demanded. Wei could see the anger that blazed behind his eyes when he saw their faces.

"Nothing, nothing! I swear! It's perfectly fine and parked in the parking garage."

"It better be perfectly fine! Remember what I said, not one damn speck of dust!"

"Jesus, Conroy, you treat that car like it's your lover. I'm pretty sure your dick ain't big enough to satisfy it, you know that, right?"

Conroy snarled and lunged toward Steel, who cringed back, immediately apologizing for his bad joke.

Wei looked around. "Where's Noah?"

"In the bathroom," Winston said hesitantly.

"Where he's been for an hour," Steel added. Winston elbowed him hard.

Wei rounded on them, eyes fierce. "An *hour*? What the hell happened?"

"I don't know! Everything was fine—I mean Allen was here—" Steel cringed at Wei's answering, almost animalistic growl.

"That *sei yan tau* came here? What the hell for?"

"Came to warn Noah about us or something," Steel said dismissively. "That's not what—"

Anger bubbled hotly inside Wei's chest. "So that's why Noah's in the bathroom?"

Winston shook his head, glaring at Steel. "No. That didn't bother him. He was fine, and then he started freaking out about this voice mail, talking about how it rang, but it didn't..." He trailed off. "It was all very confusing."

Wei heaved a sigh and made his way to the bathroom, uncertain how to proceed. He knocked on the door hesitantly. *Why the fuck am I being so bashful in my own apartment?* He wondered, but his instincts told him this wasn't the time to be assertive.

"Noah, are you in there?"

There was a short moment of silence before an answer came. "Please go away."

"Is everything okay? What's wrong?"

"I just want to be alone." The sorrow in the younger man's voice pulled at Wei's heartstrings in ways very few things had in a long time, since Steven. But that was dangerous territory, a road he did not want to start down, not now. He didn't have enough alcohol in the house.

"You want to be alone in my bathroom?"

He heard a sniffle. "Yes."

"I'm coming in," Wei announced calmly, grabbing the door. He opened it gently at first in case Noah sat against it, but when it swung freely, he opened it wider and slipped inside. Noah leaned against the glass shower wall, head buried in his arms. Wei glanced out at the others—Conroy shrugged; naturally he would be no help in this situation—and then shut the door.

They were now alone in the darkness.

"You didn't even turn on the light?"

Noah let out a sound that was a cross between a laugh and a sob. "I didn't think about it when I came in. Once I was in, it felt silly to go back out to turn it on. Besides, it helps me forget that I'm crying in a bathroom."

Wei felt around in the darkness, making sure the lid on the toilet was down before he sat on it. "What happened?"

"You're going to think I'm stupid."

"No, I won't. You have my word."

Going slow and seeming to fight back tears, Noah explained the circumstances about the way he'd dialed his sister's number, the constant direct-to-voice mails, and the sudden ringing. "I didn't imagine it. It rang. It really rang."

"I believe you." Wei reached out carefully—he could not see, and the first thing he touched was Noah's head. He felt the other man flinch at his touch and almost pulled his hand away, but then Noah relaxed. Wei gently stroked his silky hair. "You're under a lot of stress, Noah. It's okay to break down like this."

"Oh come on—you must think I'm a baby. I mean, look at me: sitting on a bathroom floor, crying."

"No, I don't think you're a baby," Wei said firmly. He slid off the toilet seat, hand moving from Noah's head to his shoulder, gripping it firmly. "Anyone would have these emotions, going through what you're going through. Don't ever feel like less of a man for grieving for your sister.

"When my sister...when Mei died, I fell apart. It was—*I* was a mess. I couldn't get my emotions under control. Constance and A...and her brother...they finally helped me start the grieving process. You don't have to be ashamed of these tears, Noah. Not a single person out there or in the Dragons will judge you for them."

For a moment the only sound in the bathroom was their ragged breathing, the noises of the room beyond the closed door drifting in. Unexpectedly, Wei felt a hand on his right cheek, followed by the soft pressure of lips on his left.

"Thank you," Noah whispered.

He had no idea the fire the feel of his lips had awoken—hormones raged through Wei's body, every fiber of his being burning to take the other man, kiss him, comfort him, *own* him. But he would not take advantage of someone in this emotional state—that was *not* the kind of person Wei was. When Noah came to his bed, and he *would*, Wei thought fiercely, it would be from happiness and desire, not a need for comfort.

"I know what you need," Wei said, somewhat hoarsely. *My dick*, was the first thought that came to his mind, but he pushed his carnal mind aside. He needed to cheer Noah up, and he had a good idea how to do it.

Someone knocked suddenly at the door. Noah jumped and his forehead struck Wei's. "Yo, man, hurry up and get your boyfriend out of the bathroom," Conroy called. "I need to take a major piss!"

"Come on," Wei said, feeling for and taking Noah's hand and standing, pulling the smaller man to his feet easily. He released the hand before he opened the door; the last thing he wanted to do was subject Noah to the goading of the other men at the moment.

"All right, guys, I know exactly how to raise Noah's spirits."

"Oh, so you want us to go so you can get to it?" Steel asked teasingly, pointing toward the door with his index fingers.

"Shut up, Steel. What Noah needs is to see the *ye shi*."

Winston and Steel beamed at that idea, and even Conroy looked pleased.

"What's a *ye shi*?" Noah asked. He even got the tones of the word down; Wei was impressed.

"You'll see," Wei said, shooting the others a look that plainly told them not to spoil the surprise.

Conroy clapped his hands together in anticipation. "All right, I'm down, but first I need in the bathroom. I wasn't lying about needing to take a piss."

31

No matter how many times he asked, none of the Dragons would answer Noah's question about where they were going, so he gave up trying. *I'm starting to think these guys all have selective hearing.*

They piled into Conroy's Corvette once more—this time Winston had shotgun. Steel started to climb in after Wei but then stopped, letting Noah take the middle. As Noah moved past him, Steel gave him a little wink. Noah rolled his eyes.

The sun was setting as they started down the street, the glow of the summer sun replaced slowly by the vibrant neon lights of Hong Kong. The others were quiet in the car. Wei was staring out the passenger-side window, mind clearly elsewhere. Noah wondered how his meeting with the other gang leader had gone. Probably fine, he reasoned; they wouldn't be riding off to god knew where if it had gone badly.

Or perhaps they would. The truth was, Noah knew next to nothing about this world—he couldn't properly judge anything about it. He'd gotten the impression from those around him that there was a very real, palpable danger around these Dragons, but he wasn't afraid. If he were being honest with himself, he was a little excited. This was so different from the world he'd known, and that difference was almost as seductive as the man sitting next to him.

Wei glanced at Noah and smiled. It was all Noah could do to force himself to smile back before casually turning his face away instead of giving himself whiplash turning to face the front.

Memory of the feel of Wei's cheek in his hand and then against his lips as he gave him a kiss came coursing back through Noah. The warmth of the other man's skin, the way his stubble scratched against Noah's hand and face, his brain had catalogued every millisecond of that short exchange. He could feel it even now, as real as if he were still doing it.

He couldn't say what had driven him to it; impulse and emotional weakness. Wei was there for him in a very emotional time, and it had seemed like the right thing to do. He was really glad the light had been off so Wei could not see his face turn into a tomato.

He needed to learn to control his blushing if he was going to spend much more time around these people.

"When we get to the *ye shi*," Wei said, drawing Noah out of his reverie, "make sure you stay with us. Trust me, you don't want to get separated from us there."

"Is someone going to tell me what this *ye shi* is, or are you just going to leave me in the dark until we get there?" Noah demanded.

"It's way more fun when you got no idea," Conroy replied. He saw Noah's pouty look in the rearview mirror and shook his head. "That look don't work on me, yo. You might wanna stick to makin' them puppy dog eyes at Wei."

Noah huffed indignantly, crossing his arms over his chest, but he could not help but smile. Conroy's devil-may-care air and lack of filter when he spoke was refreshing and entertaining, even when directed at him.

Conroy brought the car to a stop at the curb behind a line of other cars, and Noah's curiosity grew. There was nothing around but a few shops and restaurants on either side of the street. *This* was where they were going? Doors opened on all sides of the car in answer to his question.

Noah was the last one out of the car. He didn't bother trying to hide his confusion. "You thought I would get lost here?" He scanned the streets on either side—there were people going about, but not in numbers large enough to obscure anything. "I don't think that will be a problem."

"We're not there yet." Wei and Conroy shared a grin, and they set off down the sidewalk. Noah didn't know if it was his imagination, but it seemed like they walked in a formation of sorts. Steel and Winston fell in on either side behind him, with Wei slightly ahead of him and to his right and Conroy straight ahead.

Noah heard a noise, then, one he couldn't place. It reminded him of the wind in trees, but there were no tress to speak of and no wind, either. The scents of food came to him as well, though those might have just been coming from the few restaurants that dotted the street they walked down.

At the end of the block, Noah saw a large number of people coming from the other direction, all of them turning down the same street. The noise had become loud and recognizable: the sounds of hundreds of voices as people milled about.

A *ye shi* was a night market.

Stalls of all sorts lined the street they turned down—knock-off clothing, pirated DVDs and CDs, jewelry, a large variety of street foods. There were carts with fish caught in the nearby Quarry Bay and vegetables and fruits laid out on display. The vendors called out loudly, a cacophony of Cantonese and the occasional English rising above the drone of the people going about their business.

It was incredible—so alive, so vibrant, so quintessentially Hong Kong.

"I thought you'd like it," Wei said, leaning close to Noah to be heard. He seemed pleased with Noah's enjoyment. "Remember, stay close."

The five of them started through the market, pausing every now and then for Noah to look at something on display or to laugh at the good-natured heckling the vendors were using to draw attention to their wares. At a fruit vendor's stall, Noah paused, eying a large round fruit, yellow-green in color with pineapple-esque spikes.

"Is that durian?"

"Don't even think about buying that," Wei said firmly, grabbing Noah's hand and dragging him away from the stall. "No way is that coming into my apartment."

"Does it really smell as bad as they say?" Noah asked, every nerve ending in his body hyperaware of Wei's hand around his—the callouses, the warmth of it, the surprisingly gentle way he gripped it.

"Yes." Wei released Noah's hand. "If you want to find out for yourself, you'll have to do it somewhere else—and find somewhere else to stay."

There was so much to see in the market that Noah could easily see himself wasting hours just meandering along either side, checking out the available wares. He stopped next to one of the pirated DVD stalls and glanced at the titles. There were many from the States and Mainland China, some of them quite recent. There was also a section where there were no cover images, only an "X-rated" indicator. Noah looked at some of these with amusement.

"Looking for ways to hone your skills before getting dirty with Wei?" Winston asked when he saw what Noah was looking at. He gave Noah a lecherous look and picked up a DVD called *Anal Addicts*. "This might help you."

Noah elbowed him in the side. "Shut up."

Noah walked away from the booth, Winston trailing behind him. Noah wondered if Wei had assigned Winston to keep an eye on him in the crowd. "Maybe you don't need any honing," Winston went on. "Have you already mastered those skills?"

"Mastered what skills?" Steel asked as they caught up with the others.

"Ignore him," said Noah firmly. He wanted to put a lid on that conversation before things got embarrassing with Wei in earshot. Ignoring Winston's snickering, he quickened his pace to walk beside Wei.

The other man seemed a little different than he had at other times, more relaxed. In this environment, he didn't appear to be the leader of the Dragons, responsible for the safety of the district; he was just a guy enjoying a night at the night market. It was nice to see him that way.

As they passed various stalls, people called out to Wei and the others in friendly greeting. Everyone there seemed to know him and have respect for him. Vendors at food stands offered him part of their wares, insisting on feeding him. He took it all in great stride.

Noah stood back and watched as a vendor fed Wei a fish ball on a stick. "The people really like him, don't they?"

Conroy, standing next to Noah, nodded. "He's a great leader. He keeps them safe, protects these places. And he does it for free. Many gangs demand protection money from the shop owners in their territory, but not us. We protect them because it's the right thing to do. Sometimes they give us lunch, sometimes little gifts, sometimes just smiles."

Noah watched the lady beam as Wei ate the snack she gave him. His opinion about this complicated man continued to shift. There was way more to Wei Tseng than met the eye.

Wei rejoined them with what remained of the skewered snack. Noah thought he saw a subtle, silent exchange pass between Wei and Conroy, and then Conroy moved to look at something at a nearby stall.

Wei offered the final fish ball on his skewer to Noah. Noah eyed it suspiciously. "It's good, just try it."

Noah started to reach for the skewer, but it became clear Wei was intent on holding it so he sighed and leaned in to take a bite. It smelled of fish—naturally—and some sort of seasoning he couldn't identify. He carefully took a small bite and chewed. He hadn't expected to like it, and he was not disappointed. The taste was very foreign to his palette and the texture was almost spongy. Noah was a texture person, and that turned him off immediately.

Noah's expression said exactly how he felt about it, and Wei laughed, a rich, melodious baritone sound that thrummed through Noah and right to his cock. He was erect in record time. *God, I hope Winston doesn't notice.* The last thing he needed was to encourage *more* heckling from the younger man.

"You don't like it? Fine, it's more for me." Wei made a show of pulling the fish ball from the skewer with his teeth, even adding a little animal growl. "I don't see how you don't like this. It's awesome."

"Perhaps Conroy was wrong and there's not that much Asian in me, after all."

"Not yet, anyway," Wei said, eyes twinkling. Noah couldn't tell if he was intending it to sound as sexual as it did, or if he was oblivious to the double entendre of the sentence. "Give me a little time, and you'll have plenty of Asian inside you."

Noah turned red from the scalp of his head all the way down to his toenails. There was *no* way he hadn't meant that sexually. He would have had to be an idiot to miss that innuendo, and Wei Tseng was definitely no idiot.

But was he actually interested or was he simply being flirty to be flirty? Noah couldn't tell. Winston and Steel's cryptic sexual commentary was also difficult to decipher; guys their age did that sort of thing all the time, so it could have been gentle teasing or else they were privy to information Noah didn't know. It was damn confusing.

"This way," Wei said, reaching down and grabbing Noah's elbow, guiding him along a small side street about halfway down the main road of the market. It was poorly lit compared to the main road, and there were few people traveling it. On all sides were buildings with signs Noah couldn't read.

"If you were trying to find a secluded to spot to kill me, I think you succeeded," Noah said with a somewhat nervous laugh. He knew he had nothing to fear from these guys, but the survival instinct ingrained in him by evolution was not so easily calmed; his panic was starting to rise, and he was getting the urge to run back into the nice well-lit market street.

"I could have just done that in my apartment," Wei teased. "Come on, there's somewhere we need to go; our last stop for the night." The alley came to a dead end with a building right at its end, a tall gray concrete monstrosity with a big sign he couldn't make out.

"Okay," said Noah, unimpressed, "why are we here?"

Wei grinned. "You said you wanted a bath."

32

"I've never been inside a public bath." Noah followed Wei and the others inside, unsure what to expect. "Is it going to be like, just a bunch of tubs and stuff?"

"You'll see," Conroy said, clapping him on the back with a rough affection. The others were taking pleasure in his confusion. It was a novelty for them; they were all born and raised in Hong Kong, and the city had precious few surprises or new experiences for them. With Noah around, they could see Hong Kong through an outsider's eyes.

"You're not body conscious, are you?" Steel asked as Noah placed his shoes inside one of the small wooden lockers that resembled a PO box. "No problems being naked around anyone?" He glanced specifically at Wei when he said that.

"I played sports, so no," Noah answered shortly. The truth was he *did* feel some amount of anxiety about this part. He'd been fantasizing about Wei ever since the moment he saw him, basically, and to finally see his naked body in all its glory might just be too much for him, especially since his body had somehow become convinced he was a teenager with raging hormones once more. Factor into that the fact that he'd be seeing Conroy, Winston, and Steel naked, as well—not to mention probably many other strangers—and he was definitely starting to feel body conscious.

Please don't get a boner, he prayed as he took the towel the attendant offered and followed Wei through a curtained off doorway marked "Men."

They came into a short hallway that turned and opened out into a wide room. Rows of lockers took up the majority of the space. Right next to the door was a desk where a wizened old man sat—they gave him their receipts and continued past. The sound of large amounts of running water came to Noah as they passed a fogged-up glass door on their way to the lockers. There was a television on the back wall, playing an old kung-fu movie.

Noah found the number on the locker that matched the number on his key and set about undressing. He looked to his left where Winston was a few lockers down. The younger man had already cheerfully shucked his pants and shirt and was putting them in the locker. To his right was Wei, and a glance in that direction threatened to stir his blood once more; Wei's shirt was off, and he was pushing down the pants, revealing dark blue boxer-briefs that hugged his body perfectly.

I'm not going to make it through this.

"Come on, man, what's the hold up?" Steel called to Noah, who hadn't removed a single article of clothing. He and Winston, both already naked, were standing at the door to the baths, radiating impatience. As much as he knew he shouldn't, he couldn't help quick glances at the two naked guys. They were of similar height and build, though Winston had a bit more muscle on him. Both kept their pubic hair trimmed down, and in their flaccid state, Steel was bigger with hefty testicles behind his cock—not that that meant anything, some people were showers, and others were growers. Steel had a tribal-esque dragon tattoo on the calf of his left leg. Winston, as far as Noah could see, didn't have a dragon tattoo anywhere.

Noah quickly undressed. He reminded himself he'd been naked with guys a hundred times through sports and martial arts, and this was nothing different. But it *was* different; he knew the rules of the locker room world, but a public bath was foreign to him. He would have to hope he caught on quickly and that they weren't so different.

Securing his key around his wrist, Noah followed Winston and Steel into the bath. Immediately upon entering, he was faced with row after row of low showerheads, beneath each of which was a plastic stool and a big plastic bowl along with a bottle of shampoo and body wash. There were a few men in there, washing their hair or lathering their bodies with soap. Noah made sure his eyes never settled anywhere for too long.

Winston and Steel found where Conroy and Wei were—both already had their hair shampooed. They were at the far end of the row of showers, Conroy at the last one. Steel and Winston sat down, leaving the shower next to Wei purposefully open, Noah figured, giving him no choice but to take that spot.

Noah sat on the stool and reached out to turn the water on. The water was cold when it sprayed out, and he jumped up away from the water. The others laughed at him, and he sat down with a blush. When the water temperature was finally comfortable, he sat again.

Conroy, Wei, Steel, and Winston were joking with each other and talking as they washed, but Noah could not bring himself to participate. While he'd been in plenty of locker rooms, Americans tended to reserve joking around for clothed moments, not while they were lathering up.

Once they finished washing up, they followed the path out into a wide area filled with various tubs. To the left were two deep tubs, a sign in blue Chinese characters over them. Directly ahead was a long, shallow tub with handrails and another sign over it he didn't understand. Up a series of stairs above that one, he could make out a sign that said "Sauna." Directly to the right were two tubs filled with steaming water. He didn't need to know how to read the red Chinese characters over them to know they were hot.

The guys made a beeline for the nearest hot one. Conroy said something in Chinese as he put his feet in and climbed right back out and ran around in a small circle. Noah couldn't help but admire Conroy's physique. He was quite fit with lots of definition. The colorful dragon tattoo on his back highlighted the ripple of muscles and his cock hung low between his legs. Steel and Winston reacted similarly, getting in and getting back out as if they could not handle the temperature.

Wei just rolled his eyes and stepped into the pool. Noah's eyes roved over his muscular chest, which he'd already seen, tracing that happy trail down to his trimmed pubic bush and the cock that swayed there. It didn't hang as low as Conroy's but it seemed thick, the head hidden within the sheath of his foreskin. Noah watched as he slid into the water until it reached his neck.

"You guys are pussies." He leaned back, resting his head against the back of the tub.

Noah decided it would be better to get in the water now—he felt a stirring in his loins and hoped the heat of the water would calm it. He stuck a foot in and hissed at the intensity of the heat, but he did not stop. He stepped both feet firmly in and then forced himself to sit, ignoring the protest of his super-heated skin.

"Damn, man, the white guy has more balls than us," Conroy laughed. Not to be showed up by a foreigner, he stepped into the water and sat, grimacing. The other two joined them.

"See, it's not so bad," Conroy said at last. "Once your skin burns and you can't feel pain anymore, it's great."

"This is your first time in a public bath, right?" Wei said, looking at Noah. "So you don't have them in America?"

"I imagine there are a few around," said Noah, considering. "I haven't ever seen one, and they're definitely not common. Guys in America would find being naked in a tub with a bunch of other guys as weird."

"What's weird about it?" Steel asked, splashing hot water in Winston's face.

"Ah, *puk gai!*" Winston rose, attempting to push Steel's head under the water, both of them laughing.

"Yes, what on earth could be weird about this?" Noah chuckled.

"You should try more tubs," Wei announced suddenly, rising from the water. "Come on."

Noah got up to go, but the others remained. "I've gotten used to this one, so I'm just gonna chill here," said Conroy. "You two have fun." Steel started to get up to join them, but Conroy grabbed his arm and pulled him back down.

Wei led Noah to the long shallow tub and got in. The water was tepid but felt cold after the heat of the other tub. "This is an electric pool," Wei explained as Noah sat next to him. "This might sting a little bit."

"What? Sting? Why?" Noah demanded. Wei just smiled and reached up, pressing a button. Noah felt a sudden wave of pressure against his back, like needles against his skin. It was a weird sort of feeling, almost like a massage that stung. It actually put a lot of pressure on Noah, forcing him forward, and he had to reach down and hold on to the metal rails, his left hand brushing Wei's.

The contact sent more thrills through him than the electric massage. He turned his head, looking into Wei's eyes, searching for something. He didn't know if he found it, but there was *something*. Wei started to speak when a high-pitched squeal cut through the bathhouse. The moment was broken. Noah looked to find the source of the noise.

Steel had snuck and grabbed one of the plastic bowls, filled it with water, and dumped it on Winston while he lounged in the hot water. Winston scurried out of the water, chasing him and yelling at him in Chinese. He caught him and tried to wrestle him into the cold tub until Conroy yelled at them to knock it off, and they quieted down again.

When the electric massage finally stopped, Wei climbed out of the water and made his way up the stairs. Halfway up, Wei pointed at the sauna sign, eyebrow raised in a question. Noah shrugged and followed him. The sauna was not very big—a single rectangular room with one long wooden bench along one wall. Noah sat down, keeping a bit of space between himself and Wei, which was good because as he sat, Wei splayed his legs out, propping his hands on the back of the bench and letting his head lay back, eyes closed.

Noah took advantage of the opportunity to really enjoy the look of Wei's body. Sweat already beaded along his flesh, giving him a glistening look that only served to make him sexier. The happy trail he'd followed with his eyes before led right to his impressive manhood. His eyes continued their travel, taking in his muscled thighs, strong calves, and legs before returning to his cock.

Before he realized it, Noah's own cock was starting to stiffen, and he quickly closed his eyes, taking deep breaths and trying to think erection-killing thoughts. *Why didn't I bring one of those towels by the door?* He hadn't seen the others grab one so he didn't think he needed to.

He managed to get his body under control just as Wei opened his eyes and leaned forward, smiling at him. "How are you liking your first public bath experience so far?"

Goddamn but Wei's smile was beautiful; Noah couldn't help but smile back. He wished the Dragons leader would smile more. "I'm liking it a lot, actually. It's nice."

"Well, there's one more thing you need to experience for it to be authentic."

Noah had no idea what he could be talking about, but he was certainly curious enough to find out. "Okay, lead the way."

Wei led him out of the sauna and back down to the main floor. Conroy was still in the hot bath, head leaned back, looking as if he were asleep. Winston and Steel were both in the electric bath, still joking around. It seemed to be their constant state; Noah wondered what was motivating it, thinking back to the way he'd noticed Steel watching Winston in the mirror on the way to the restaurant.

Wei led him through a fogged glass door into an area with a massage table and its own showerhead. "What's all this?" Noah asked nervously.

"Skin scrub. It's a very common element of the public bath—they do it in Japan and Korea, too. Lay down on the table, face up." When Noah hesitated, Wei raised his eyebrows high. "Don't you trust me?"

It's not you I don't trust, Noah thought as he climbed onto the table and lay down face up. He glanced over and saw Wei take what looked like a glove from some sort from a box. Before he put it on, though, he took a towel and folded it, placing it over Noah's eyes to shield them from the harsh light right above the table.

"Do you know what you're doing?" Noah asked, fidgeting on the table. He heard the sound of the shower coming on before he felt the warm water suddenly being sprayed on his chest, crotch, and legs.

"I've done this before," Wei answered when he cut the water off. "I'm going to start now, okay?" Noah nodded. Wei took Noah's right hand and raised his arm, setting about scrubbing something over it quick and efficiently.

"You worked in a bathhouse?" Speaking was the best way for Noah to keep his fidgeting under control. It helped to hear Wei's voice, to know it was Wei doing this. The roughness of the scrub balanced the gentleness of Wei's hand perfectly to keep him from feeling too much pleasure.

"After my father died, yeah. I needed to raise money to take care of my sister, so I started doing this. It was pretty easy work, and it was all right pay. I could do it at night while I worked other jobs during the day."

Wei's methodical cleaning moved from arm to chest. Noah resisted a shudder every time the cloth scraped over his nipple. It was a pleasure-pain he found quite appealing. He couldn't help but wiggle as Wei's hand made its way down his chest and over his stomach. He really wanted to push Wei's hand away; he was ticklish, always had been, as embarrassing as it was.

Wei's hand moved down his inner thigh, and Noah tensed as the back of his hand brushed against his balls several times before working his way down his leg. It was brief but Noah could not hide the effects, even if he wanted to. Just that slight contact had been enough to plump him up to half-mast. There was no way Wei wouldn't notice it. He just grimaced and hoped this would be over as soon as possible.

Wei reversed his progress, up Noah's left leg. If he noticed the burgeoning erection—and how could he not have?—he made no indication of it. He moved across Noah's stomach again, gently nudging the stiffening cock to the side so he could thoroughly clean. Noah nearly moaned aloud, and his erection awoke fully. He was beet red and ready to die of humiliation by the time Wei took his left arm and scrubbed it.

"Okay," Wei said, placing his arm back on the table.

"I'm really sorry," Noah said quickly. He started to sit up but Wei's hand on his chest gently pushed him back down.

"Sorry for what?" Wei asked.

"Well, uh..." Noah made a gesture in the general direction of his crotch, and Wei chuckled.

"Do you think you're the first person to get an erection while getting a scrub? Don't be ridiculous. Now turn over so I can scrub your back." Noah did as instructed, turning over and letting the towel fall from his face. He actually gasped when he was nearly face-to-face with Wei's own fully erect cock. "See? Not the only one." Wei's voice had dropped an octave, but Noah didn't really notice. He was staring at the length in front of him. He'd been right in his assessment; it was quite thick around, average in length.

He looked up further, into Wei's face. The passion and lust on his face was plain even for Noah. Never breaking eye contact, Wei lowered himself down until they were face-to-face. His hand reached out, gently caressing Noah's cheek before sliding around to the back of his head.

Wei hovered there, their lips only inches apart. Noah couldn't breathe, couldn't do anything but look into the other man's eyes. At least until Wei's tongue darted out to wet his lips. That simple gesture pushed Noah over the edge, and he closed the distance, their lips finally meeting.

The kiss was surreal. Noah almost didn't believe it was happening, but it was. It was Wei's silky smooth lips that had captured his own. Now that Noah had closed that gap, Wei took control, the gentle, cupping hand now pulling Noah's lips harder against him. His tongue gained entrance to Noah's mouth, scraping over teeth and lips to entwine itself with Noah's. The entirety of Noah's world boiled down to two points: the point where their mouths met and his now copiously leaking cock.

What the hell am I doing? Noah wondered. He was in a public bathhouse, embarrassingly aroused, kissing arguably the most intensely attractive man he'd ever met, and all while his sister was missing? *What is* wrong *with me?* As suddenly as Noah began the kiss, he pulled away, pushing himself back on his hands and knees so rapidly he nearly went right off the back of the table. "I'm sorry," he kept repeating, reaching for the towel that had covered his eyes and using it to hide his erection. He repeated it one last time and then bolted from the enclosed space.

33

When Wei emerged back into the main room, Noah stood under one of the showers again, head cupped in his hands as the water beat down on him. Winston walked up to Wei, watching Noah, too. "What the hell did you do, Wei?"

Wei growled at him and stomped over to the hottest tub, submerging himself fully in it, hoping the scalding heat would drive away the strange ache in the pit of his stomach now. What *had* he done? Noah had kissed *him*. Noah had gotten the erection first, which naturally had triggered Wei's own.

Had he tried to take the kiss too far too fast? Whatever the cause, the mood had soured. *All I wanted to do was make him feel better, and I just keep making it worse.* Noah Potter was one complicated individual.

He'd almost managed to crack that shell—he'd gotten so close. Maybe that was it; Noah realized just as he did that Wei had almost gotten inside his defenses, so he'd shoved him away, like a self-preservation method.

Wei wasn't the only one who sensed the sour mood, either; everyone seemed to feel it. They all showered and made their way back to Conroy's car. This time Wei rode shotgun next to Conroy.

"Drop me by Constance's," he instructed Conroy as he closed the car door. "I need to get my bike and get it back home."

"You're the boss."

The drive was quiet with the exception of Conroy's terrible taste in music—he was big into Japanese male idol groups and had their songs playing nonstop when driving. It was enough to drive a person mad. Normally Wei hated it, but today he didn't even really hear it; it went in one ear and out the other without his brain processing it in between.

His mind was focused on what to do with Noah. He watched Noah in the side mirror, seated behind him. Noah stared into his lap, no light in his face, no life. He was like a husk compared to how he had been when Wei first saw him. *What's going through his mind?* Wei wondered. How dark were the thoughts that had dimmed the effervescent glow in his eyes? The thought that he might have had something to do with it ate away at Wei.

They were nearly at the coffee shop when Conroy's phone rang. He frowned when he looked at the screen. "It's Haylin's mother," he told Wei. Haylin was the first girl to go missing and then turn up dead. In some ways, her discovery had been the hardest because it was the first time in the five years Wei had been in control of the territory that anything truly bad had happened, the first time something showed that the Dragons could not protect their own people. The first time Wei appeared weak to the people who looked to him to protect them. If she was calling again, it would be nothing good.

Conroy spoke to her in soothing tones, but Wei heard the woman's voice where he sat. Something was definitely wrong. "What?" he demanded when Conroy hung up the phone.

"She said she got something at her house. She's fuckin' hysterical man. I don't know what it is, but she was saying she needs us there now. Sounds urgent."

Wei thought for a moment, eyes once more on Noah through the mirror. It would take too much precious time to get Noah back to his place, and if it was truly an emergency, he needed to get to Haylin's mother.

"Get us there," he said at last. Conroy didn't argue.

Haylin's mother didn't live far from where they were, and Conroy was able to get them there within ten minutes. The woman lived in one of the more rundown tenements in the district, near Quarry Bay. The streets here were dirty, closer to the image of Hong Kong so commonly portrayed in movies.

They got out of the car in front of the apartment. Conroy looked as grim as Wei felt. Neither of them wanted to be here again. Looking at the stoop leading up to the door, Wei remembered arriving that night, in the pouring rain, to find Haylin's mother crumpled on those stairs, sobbing. Just the memory of it threatened to tear Wei's heart to pieces.

He wanted to tell Winston and Noah to stay in the car—it was Dragons' business after all—but he didn't know how safe they would be out here. That fact alone troubled him. He shouldn't have to have any concern about their safety in his territory. But if something else had happened here, he wanted to keep them close. Wanted to keep *Noah* close.

"You two stay quiet inside, got it?" Wei pointed to the two of them. His gaze lingered on Winston, communicating quite clearly without speaking: *I mean it*. Winston nodded his understanding. Noah did as well, his gaze never rising from the sidewalk. Figuring that was the only reply he'd be getting from Noah, Wei turned and led the way inside.

Once inside, the air became close and stale, reeking of the mingled scent of food, sweat, and cigarette smoke. The hallway of the old complex lacked air conditioning. Several tenants had opened their doors to fight off the heat and tempt in a nonexistent breeze as they cooked. A crowd of people gathered in the hallway as they entered. Most of them knew Wei, by reputation if not directly, and they all watched the newcomers with some interest—especially the foreigner with the leader of the Dragons.

Haylin's mother had an apartment on the second floor. As they ascended the beat-up stairs, the heat seemed to intensify. Wei found himself sweating like he was back in the sauna at the bathhouse. Halfway up the stairs, he made out the sound of a woman sobbing. Haylin's mother, Mrs. Li, no doubt.

Wei hurried.

An older man met him at the door. Haylin's uncle, if Wei remembered right. The uncle had a face sun-baked from his job as a fisherman off of Quarry Bay, lined with premature old age. He'd led a hard life, Wei guessed, though he didn't know the details. Life was hard for a lot of people in this area of the city. The man said nothing, just pushed the door open. His eyes were vacant, hollow, like he'd checked out and operated on autopilot. How much more must one family go through?

The apartment was dark, only a blue glow from the television illuminating the room. The furniture was old and rundown, the couch torn in several places, the coffee table in front of it had a few magazines slid beneath one of the legs to keep it balanced. Incense and alcohol hung thick in the air. Mrs. Li sat on the couch, limp, head thrown back as violent sobs wracked her body.

Wei could not fathom what she was going through, losing a daughter, but he empathized to a degree after the loss of his sister. It had nearly destroyed him. What had it done to her?

Wei walked over to her, sitting on the couch next to her. He took her hand—it was cold to the touch—and gave it a squeeze. "Mrs. Li, I'm here," he gently said to her in Cantonese. "What's happened?"

Mrs. Li raised her hand and pointed limply at the television. "Sonofabitch," Conroy hissed and Wei turned to the television to see what Conroy was looking at. A close-up of Haylin's face, pale and sweaty, filled the screen. Her eyes were dark and hollow, as if she weren't entirely awake, her cheeks gaunt. The image was from a paused video,

"We got a package at the door," Mrs. Li's brother explained from the doorway. "We didn't see who brought it, only saw the package on the ground. Inside was that." He pointed to the television and then a rectangular case on top of the off-brand DVD player attached to the television. The case was one you might buy anywhere, the cover of it was simple, just a printed piece of paper with Haylin's name written on it in block capital letters.

"I'm going to need to see the video, Mrs. Li," Wei said gently. He saw the remote on the other side of her and reached across to take it. Mrs. Li did not acknowledge his words as he pointed the remote at the DVD player. His hand shook. He didn't know what he would find on this video, but he had a few ideas and none of them good.

He hit play on the remote.

The sounds of sex filled the room: the moans of an at the moment unseen male, the slap of flesh against flesh. The camera stayed focused on Haylin's face. She moaned, too, but it was strange, heavy, more the sound of someone having a bad dream than someone enjoying sex.

"She's obviously drugged," Conroy murmured, echoing Wei's thoughts.

The camera panned out to show an action shot—a naked man, his face not shown, thrusting into Haylin's naked body. Haylin's uncle made a choked noise and turned away. "Yeah," muttered a deep-voiced male, probably the one holding the camera. "Fuck that hot little *hai*. Get in there deep."

"Oh my god." Noah had gone pale watching the video, eyes wide with horror. Winston placed a comforting hand on his shoulder, his eyes just as horrified.

Mrs. Li sobbed louder, and Wei hit stop. The sound of the DVD seemed to echo still in the apartment, and Wei wondered if it would ever stop. "I'm sorry, Mrs. Li. I'm so sorry." He turned to Steel. "Take the DVD." As Steel did as instructed, Wei assured Mrs. Li they would find the bastards responsible—the same assurances he'd made before; they rang hollow and weak in the face of this aftermath.

Knowing there was little else to be done and hating himself for it, Wei led the others out. At the door, Haylin's uncle grabbed Wei by the wrist. His eyes were red and bloodshot. "Why? Why couldn't you protect her?"

Steel gently dislodged the man's hand. "He did the best he could, *sinsaang*."

Wei turned his face away, an ache in his chest. *Did I?* He certainly didn't feel like he had. As far as he was concerned, he'd failed in the grossest possible way. Eyes cast down, he made his way outside.

As soon as they were in the car, he punched the dashboard in rage. Conroy's eyes widened, but he refrained from saying anything. It might have been his baby getting punched, but it was the boss doing it, and so he kept it zipped.

"Now this *lan ga tsan* is fucking with the families? Haven't they been through enough? Call a goddamn meeting, Conroy."

"Not tonight, boss. You're tired as fuck. Let it wait till the morning."

Wei growled but nodded. "I want Dragons watching the home of every victim, you understand me? Twenty-four-fucking-seven. Somebody dropped that damn DVD off. If they sent one here, you can bet they'll send one to the other families. I don't want them to have to see that, understand?"

Conroy nodded. They drove to Wei's apartment, detour to the coffee shop entirely forgotten. They sat in silence until they pulled in front of the apartment.

"I don't understand what's going on, boss." Steel's face was stony, but the strain in his voice and the way he crossed his arms over his chest— not in defiance but in a huddle—indicated how shaken he was. "So somebody is taking these girls and what, drugging them to film some porn? Why dump them after such a short time then?"

"Must have been hard to keep someone for too long," Wei said grimly. "Even if whoever did this kept them constantly drugged, they would need to be fed and would've had the chance of causing some trouble. They probably kept them and got as much use as possible out of them and then gave them the OD and dumped—"

"These are *people* you're talking about, for fuck's sake!" Noah shouted suddenly, his voice ringing in the car. There were tears on his cheeks, and his eyes were blazing. "They weren't *things*, and you're sitting here talking about them so callously. They had families. They had people who loved them!"

"We know that," Conroy said evenly, but Noah, it appeared, had reached his limit. He bounded out of the car and made his way for the apartment building at a near-run.

34

Noah didn't wait for anyone else. He hit Wei's floor in the elevator, tears blurring his vision. The face of that girl on the DVD blazed into his mind, etched there, no matter how hard he tried to push it away. And again and again, the question that beat against him, threatening to break through his emotional shields: *is that what happened to Lianne?* Was it at that very moment taking place? Was she out there somewhere, hidden, drugged out of her mind, and being used as some prop in a sick and twisted black market fetish video?

Oh god. Noah stumbled out of the elevator and collapsed against the wall, stomach heaving, threatening to rebel. His breath came in short gasps, not bringing enough oxygen into his body to pump through his blood. He ducked his head between his legs and struggled to control his breathing, eyes squeezed shut.

The blood pumped through his ears so loudly he did not hear the elevator *ding*, did not hear Wei call his name, didn't know Wei was there until he felt the strong hands on his arms, smelled that scent he would forever associate with the Dragons' leader.

"Breathe," Wei kept saying in his ear. "Just breathe, Noah."

Noah didn't know how long he sat there in the hallway, head ducked down, but finally he regained control of his rebellious body, and his breathing returned to normal, if somewhat ragged. He tried to stand but found that his legs were too wobbly to do so. Before he could slump back to the ground, Wei caught his elbow and then lifted him up into his arms, much the way a groom would his bride at the threshold. Noah didn't even bother protesting; he didn't have the energy, and if he were honest with himself, it felt good to be cradled against Wei's strong chest, feeling his warmth and surrounded by his scent. He leaned his head against the other man's shoulder, eyes closed.

Noah heard Wei input the code to the door and then open it. He opened his eyes and started to say that he was okay, but the look on Wei's face stopped him. He was silent as Wei carried him to the bed and deposited him gently on it before sitting next to him. Wei hadn't bothered to turn on any lights; he knew his own apartment well enough to get around without them.

Wei's voice was rough when he spoke. "I'm sorry. I shouldn't have taken you along on that—you didn't need to see what you've seen."

"I keep thinking...is that what's happening to Lianne? If her disappearance *is* connected to all of this, then it has to be, right? Looking at the girl on that video, I just wonder if I do manage to find her and she is by some miracle alive, how much damage will she have suffered? Will she even be my sister?" Noah shook his head bitterly. "Some brother I am, right?"

Wei shook his head. "I wish I could answer that, but I don't know. All of this, it's my fault, you know? Mr. Li was right to blame me."

"He was talking through his grief," Noah said, surprised by this sudden show of weakness. "None of this could possibly be your fault."

"I'm supposed to protect these people," he argued vehemently. "I'm supposed to keep them safe. If I can't do that, then I'm no better than the Nine Stars or the Twisted Vipers or the Black Lotus."

Noah sat there on the bed, studying Wei's profile etched in the pale light of the moon coming in through the window in the main section of the apartment. He could barely make out any features, but he could see the pain written all over his face nonetheless.

Noah slowly reached over, taking Wei's hand in his own and squeezing it softly. "You're way better than them, Wei. Based on what you told me, you're a saint compared to them. No matter what, you have the best intentions of these people at heart. I saw you, the way these people matter to you. They have someone who genuinely cares looking out for them, and that's something you can't put a value on."

Wei lifted Noah's hand to his lips and placed a gentle kiss on it. A simple gesture that set Noah's heart to fluttering and his blood pumping. Ashamed of his reaction, he tugged his hand roughly from Wei's grasp.

Wei heaved a long-suffering sigh. "Why do you do that? You initiate contact and then you shove me away. You kissed me in the bathhouse, and then here, when you took my hand. What's wrong? I know you're attracted to me, Noah. And I know you know I'm attracted to you, too."

"That's the problem," Noah groaned. "I'm getting all fired up like some hormonal teenager when my sister is in god knows what sort of hell. What is wrong with me?"

"You're *human*, Noah. There's nothing wrong with that. Humans want comfort and affection, especially when things are bad. Wouldn't it be better to have someone you can turn to for support?"

"I feel like I'm being selfish even thinking about that right now."

"Selfish? Really? Look at me, Noah." Noah hesitantly turned his face to Wei as the other man reached over and turned on a small lamp on the nightstand so Noah could see the intensity on his face. "You traveled around the world to find Lianne. You put yourself in danger—knowingly, I might add. You've put her above everything else. I can't think of many people who would fly to a foreign country and hunt down their loved one, even getting involved with a gang to do it. You really think that's being selfish?"

Wei closed the distance between them carefully, as if he were approaching an easily startled animal. "You shouldn't go through this alone, you know. You don't have to, either. If you want me to, if you'll let me, I'll be right here for you."

"But why?" Noah whispered. "I mean, I get helping me find Lianne—if it's connected to what's going on in your territory, that benefits you. For that, things between us just need to be platonic, no need to go any further. What do you get out of...this?" Noah gestured between the two of them.

"What do I get?" Wei leaned in closer until his lips were right beside Noah's ear. Noah trembled as he felt Wei's breath on his ear and neck, the sensation spreading until it felt like Wei was breathing all around him, within him. Noah closed his eyes, his breath once again coming quicker, though this time it wasn't because of a panic attack but because of how much he wanted the other man. "I get you."

Wei's lip gently caressed Noah's lobe, the teeth coming to nibble on the sensitive flesh, and Noah whimpered. "You have no idea how much I want you," Wei went on, lips ghosting now along Noah's neck.

"Oh, I think I do," Noah panted, the memory of Wei's turgid cock in the bathhouse surfacing in his mind.

Wei chuckled, lips still pressed against Noah's neck, sending vibrations through him. "Yeah, I guess you do, huh? Just like I know how much *you* want me." His kisses came along Noah's jawline, stopping just short of his lips. "You do want me, right?"

What kind of question was that? There wasn't any part of Noah that *didn't* want the other man, and that was part of the problem, wasn't it?

He couldn't believe how quickly he'd found himself caught up in his feelings for Wei. It had been what, forty-eight hours? Such a short time span, and yet those feelings were there and they were powerful. That was what terrified him at this point.

But he did, and no amount of sulking or wishing would change that, nor could he lie to himself, much less to another person; he was a terrible liar. "Yes," he answered at last, voice catching in his throat. "But I'm not sure if it's a good thing."

Wei gently caressed Noah's cheek with the knuckles of his left hand. Noah sighed and leaned into the touch. "When I came out to my father, I was terrified. I told him, and I told him I was sorry, and I knew it was wrong, but I couldn't help it. My father took me by the shoulders, his face stern, and I was convinced he would yell at me, curse and tell me to get out of his house. Instead, he looked me dead in the eyes and he said, 'Son, there's nothing wrong with you. When you find love, it won't be evil or wrong or disgusting or whatever other people might tell you, because it is *love*, and love can only be a good thing.'"

Noah smiled at those words, opening his eyes and looking into Wei's. "Your father sounds like he was an amazing man."

"He was."

"Like his son," Noah added, closing the distance between them once more with a kiss.

Wei, maybe fearing Noah would pull back again, took control of the kiss, keeping it slow and gentle.

Noah's arms came up around his neck, and Wei pressed him forward until he was lying half on top of the other man. Wei's heartbeat thudded against his own—he was happy to see it was moving just as fast as his. He moaned softly into the kiss, arms moving to caress the muscles of Wei's arms, stroking the warm skin. Wei shifted, then, bringing his full body over Noah, settling between his hips.

Noah's face reddened, and he broke the kiss as Wei's erection pressed hard against his own. Almost without thinking, he pushed his lower body upward, increasing the friction between them. Wei grunted, running one hand up and down Noah's side, slipping beneath the fabric of his shirt on an upward slide and tracing across the skin of his stomach and chest, leaving a trail of goose bumps in his wake. Noah's back arched when Wei took his left nipple between finger and thumb and gave it an experimental tug.

"Your body is so sensitive," Wei observed, pulling the nipple harder and eliciting a whimper from Noah. "So responsive." He ran his hand down Noah's stomach, watching the body writhe in the wake of his hand.

Noah lay there, panting, looking up at the other man, eyes hooded in desire. Wei was teasing him—he didn't want to be teased, not right then. He wanted to be taken, to be owned. To express this desire, he took hold of Wei's hips and pulled the other man hard against him.

Wei raised an eyebrow, managing to make such a simple look hugely erotic. "Something you want, Noah?"

"Yes," Noah said impatiently. He ground up against Wei, but Wei leaned back so that he could not get the friction he desired.

"What do you want?" Noah glared up at him. "I'm not a mind reader, you know."

"Damn it, Wei! I want *you.*"

Wei grinned cockily. "Why didn't you just say so?"

Noah watched Wei as he reared back on his heels, pulling his shirt over his head and quickly discarding it before he did the same. Wei made an appreciative noise as Noah exposed himself, reaching down now to tweak both nipples simultaneously, clearly enjoying the way Noah wriggled beneath him.

Just when Noah thought he could not handle any more sensation on his hypersensitive nipples, Wei released them only to take the left one in his mouth, tongue swirling around it, sending fireworks through his body to burst before his eyes. He gasped, grabbing the bedsheets beneath him and clenching them tightly in his fists as Wei alternated between smooth, gentle licks and a firmer application of teeth.

Wei finally pulled away from the reddened nub and looked up into Noah's face. "Sensitive, huh?" He kissed and licked his way across Noah's chest, leaving tingling nerve endings in his wake until he reached the right nipple and gave it the same treatment.

Noah tossed his head back and forth, releasing the sheets to grasp Wei's hair in his hands. Part of him wanted to push the other man off his chest, the other part wanted to pull him harder against him, to encourage him to keep going and never stop. He'd never had a lover spend enough time on his nipples to really know how incredibly sensitive they were, but now that he was uncovering it, he just wanted more. It was a blissful, pleasurable torture.

Wei reared up over Noah, then, eyes dark with desire. He grabbed the front of Noah's pants, undoing the button and sliding the zipper down expertly. He took them on either side and tugged, dragging the fabric off his body with one smooth motion, leaving him in nothing but socks and tight-fitting bikini briefs.

Wei's eyes went right to Noah's cock straining against the front of his underwear, the full height of his arousal made evident by the dark stain spreading from the tip. Noah lay there, body tense, waiting to see what Wei would do.

Wei returned his lips to Noah's nipple, his hand reaching down to fondle Noah's cock at the same time, applying just enough pressure to be maddening but not enough to drive him toward climax.

"Wei, please," Noah whimpered, biting his lip. He thrust his hips upward to get more pressure.

"Please what?" Wei asked, tongue lazily circling the stiff nub of Noah's nipple.

"More!"

"As you wish." Wei grasped Noah's erection firmly through his underwear and began to pump it up and down. Wei watched Noah's face, cheeks flush, eyes glazed over with pleasure. He grabbed the waistband of the bikini briefs and tugged them down, letting Noah's erection swing free. He tossed the underwear aside and took Noah fully in his hand, nothing but the feel of skin on skin. Noah moaned loudly, his cock throbbing with his heartbeat.

Wei returned his lips to Noah's nipple, his hand setting a steady pace and his grip alternating between tight and loose, Noah's precome coating his fingers and acting as a natural lube.

Flesh to flesh, it did not take long before Noah's hips were bucking, and he grunted. That sensation built, familiar but this time more intense than normal, barrelling rapidly toward his climax. "Stop, stop, I'm going to come!"

"I don't think you really want me to stop." Wei didn't let up, but in fact quickened his pace, his free hand coming up to cup Noah's balls, which had drawn up tightly against his body. Noah made an incoherent sound, and his whole body went rigid, his cock thickening even more, and he coated his stomach, chest, and Wei's hand with a copious amount of thick come.

Noah lay there, panting, occasional shudders still coursing through his body.

"Feel better?" Wei asked, laying down beside him and propping himself up on his not-covered hand.

Noah opened his eyes and looked shyly up at Wei. "Much better," he answered. "Though I think I could use a shower."

Wei laughed. He started to get up, but Noah raised his head enough to kiss Wei softly. "Show me the shower?"

"You know where it is."

Noah grabbed Wei's clean hand and tugged him. "I'm not showering alone."

"I see." Wei was on his feet immediately, leading the way.

Once in the bathroom, Wei activated the shower taps while stripping off his own clothes. Noah heard him let out a sigh of relief when he freed his cock from the tight confines of his clothes.

Noah let out an appreciative noise, stepping under the hot shower spray, motioning for Wei to join him. Noah placed his hands on Wei's chest, exploring the firm muscles of his pecs, admiring the feel of them. He brushed his thumbs along Wei's nipples the way the other man had done for him. He kissed the strong chest muscles, the stiff nipples, but that was not his main target.

He let his lips blaze a trail down Wei's stomach, following the faint trail of hair lower to his prize. He could smell Wei's manliness this close to his cock, an intoxicating aroma that made his cock stir even though he'd came minutes earlier. He took the thick length in hand, stroking the veiny flesh and enjoying the way Wei's breathing changed from his touch. Looking up into Wei's eyes, he leaned farther down, the water running down his back and face as he let his tongue taste the flesh of Wei's balls.

Wei moaned loudly, stance widening as he leaned back against the wall. Noah quickly sucked both orbs into his mouth, enjoying the taste— uniquely Wei. Noah released the other man's balls from his mouth and ran his tongue up the length of his cock to the head, enclosing it in his mouth, teasing it with the tip of his tongue.

He remained like that for a moment until Wei, impatient, starting trying to thrust his hips. Noah used both hands to hold Wei in place, wanting to do this at his own pace. "Fucker," Wei breathed, eyes and voice full of desire. Noah smiled as much as he could around Wei's thickness and began to work it in and out of his mouth, the wet heat and suction setting Wei's legs to shaking. Wei moaned and muttered something in Cantonese that sounded encouraging. Noah glanced up to see Wei's head thrown back, his eyes shut, relishing the pleasure he was receiving.

Noah redoubled his efforts, taking as much of the thick length in as he could, using his hand to stroke the length as he removed it from his mouth only to plunge back down again. He kept to this pace, tongue swirling the head on every upward stroke. He could read Wei's body language, saw he would not last much longer. As he thought that, Wei let out a loud moan and pulled himself free of Noah's mouth, stroking as his cock spurted several ropes of come on Noah's chest and the shower floor.

"Feel good?" Noah asked. In answer, Wei grabbed him under the arms, pulling him to his feet and kissing him deeply, sensuously, the kiss no less powerful now that their lust had been spent.

"Felt fucking amazing." The two finished the shower slowly, lathering the other's hair and backs, pausing for the occasional minutes-long kiss. They dried off, both feeling the blissful contentment of a post-orgasmic glow.

They did not bother dressing as Noah slid into Wei's bed. "Where are you going?" Noah asked Wei's retreating back.

"To the couch."

"You're going to sleep out there?" Noah asked incredulously.

"What? No. I'm getting my pillow. You think after the best blow job of my life I'm going to sleep on the couch?"

Noah laughed. "Okay, maybe not." He lay back on the bed, feeling surprisingly content after venting all that sexual energy. While thoughts of Lianne were never far from his mind, he was able to relax, at least a little bit.

Wei returned after a moment, tossing the pillow onto the bed. "Scoot over," he said, looking down at Noah. "I always sleep on the right side."

Noah rolled his eyes but did as requested. Wei turned off the light and slid into the bed, wrapping Noah in his arms and pulling him tightly against him, cradling his smaller body.

"The best blow job of your life, huh?" Noah asked after a few moments of silence.

Wei simply squeezed him tight and gave a grunted, "Go to sleep."

35

Wei awoke the next morning, body curled around Noah's. He sported an almost painful case of morning wood grinding against Noah's ass, throbbing, urging him to bury it deep into the other man's body, own him completely at last. His left arm, beneath Noah, had fallen asleep. He shifted to move it, trying not to wake Noah, but the younger man stirred, thankfully rolling off his arm.

"What time is it?" Noah asked, burrowing under the covers to shield his face from the light in the room.

Wei turned and checked the clock on the night table beneath the lamp. "Nine thirty," he answered. He was painfully aware of how naked he was—and how naked Noah was, as well.

But he had no time for that. He humped himself against Noah's backside a few times, luxuriating in the pleasurable torture he was imparting on himself. As much as he wanted to obey his body, he had a lot of things to do today, starting with the little gift someone left on Mrs. Li's doorstep. He needed to talk to a few people, to set some things up, not to mention plans that needed to be laid for the surveillance of K.

"Somewhere you need to be?" Noah surmised as Wei rolled out of bed. His eyes went to Wei's cock, but he did not otherwise acknowledge Wei's naked state.

Wei nodded. "Unfortunately, yes."

Noah smiled a little. "Why unfortunately?"

"Because I've got a hot naked man in my bed who I haven't even had the chance to thoroughly fuck yet and I have to go out and take care of my responsibilities."

Noah laughed, stretching out luxuriously. The motion reminded Wei of a cat. The difference between this morning and the previous night was startling. So much of the tension he'd been carrying around had drained from him. Of course orgasms relaxed you, but it went beyond that. Finally getting a good night's sleep had a part to play, Wei guessed. It was amazing what a night of uninterrupted rest could do for you.

"I'm sure you've got a few minutes," Noah teased.

Wei turned his body, leaning forward so that he was directly over Noah, looking him in the eyes. "Trust me, I'll need more than a few minutes." He captured Noah's lips in a demanding but chaste kiss. "Much more."

Wei rose and made his way to his dresser, donning a pair of black form-fitting, trunk-style underwear and digging around for other clothes to wear that day. Noah sat up in bed, drawing his knees to his chest beneath the blanket and wrapping his arms around them as he watched Wei move about the room. Wei could feel the weight of his gaze as he dressed in a pair of baggy jeans and a blue V-neck T-shirt.

"Where are you going so early?" Noah asked, sounding tentative. He wasn't sure Wei would answer, then. He almost didn't, honestly. He had Dragons' business, and just because he'd taken Noah to his bed didn't make the man a Dragon. But Noah had a stake in this, too—the very reason Wei had originally sought to bring him in. Noah's sister could be an invaluable connection to whatever the hell was going on in his territory. On top of that, Wei desperately wanted to help him find her. No good would come of shutting him out now.

"With this DVD I'm going to be able to prove that these deaths weren't simple overdoses—these are murders. Even Allen Hong will see that."

"Do you think you can get police support from this?"

Wei shrugged. "Not going to hold my breath, but I've got to give it a shot. Besides—even if I don't, I can rub this in Hong's face, show him he's wrong. He's not the great protector he thinks he is."

"There's a story there." A statement, not a question, and Wei didn't want to go into that—it was history, unpleasant history.

"There is. But I'm not going to tell it now—and it's not entirely my story to tell. Maybe one day."

"What do you expect me to do exactly? Just stay here and patter around your apartment?"

Wei grinned. "It *could* use a little cleaning." He ducked the pillow Noah threw his way. "I figured you would want to rest a little. Around noon someone will come to take you to the coffee shop. There's a lot to be discussed."

"Am I actually going to be involved in the talks this time?" Noah asked. "Or am I going to have to sit in the corner while the adults take care of business?" The comment lacked ire or malice, but it still stung Wei a bit.

"It's complicated. You—"

"Are not a Dragon, I get it," Noah said. "But it's not just your people in this—my sister is, too."

Wei nodded. "I know. That's why you're going to be involved from here on out, don't worry. I'll see you at the coffee shop." This part was awkward; *something* had happened the previous night, but they hadn't resolved it, not really. It hung in the air, unspoken, waiting to be addressed.

Noah smiled a little, nodding. The look in his eyes saying that he, too, felt it, but that bridge could be crossed later. But what was on the other side?

36

On his way down to collect his bike, which Conroy had thankfully arranged to have returned the night before, Wei sent a message to Allen Hong, instructing him to meet him at the old place. He had no doubt he would come. Hong would give Wei that much, at least.

The old place was Jourdan's Lookout, a small neighborhood near Tai Tam nestled in a rundown area. It looked like time had forgotten it as Hong Kong had progressed, leaving it the way it had been before even the signing over. His sister had been born in this neighborhood. It was here that his father had died, after working so hard to get his family to safety.

It was impossible for him to go there without his mind conjuring up the dangerous streets of Kowloon, territory of the Red Sun, where he'd grown up. In Kowloon, he'd seen his father struggle to eke out a living to care for him and his mother. He had struggled for years, but he'd gotten them out, taken them to the island, where he hoped they'd be safer.

Eventually it had killed him.

Half the houses in the neighborhood were empty, the families either moving on to new homes or the owners having died off. The place Wei grew up stood empty and had been that way for five years. Wei pulled his bike to a stop in front of the house, but instead of going inside, he took the path through the side yard. He hadn't stepped into that house since the day after his sister died. He never would again. There weren't many individual houses on the island, with space being such a commodity, but the home—his home—harked back to a different era.

The path was small, running between the house and the shoulder-height wall dividing the property from the neighbor's. Trash and refuse littered the ground, but Wei paid it no heed. The path opened into a backyard of sorts, a small, cramped space surrounded on three sides by the wall and the house on the fourth.

Allen Hong sat on the single stone step that rose toward the elevated wooden porch. He looked up at Wei's approach, rising to his feet.

"It's been nearly four years since you asked me to come here," Hong said in greeting. "Feels strange, standing here again. There are ghosts here, almost like the past is watching us."

"If the past *is* watching, do you think the ghosts approve of the choices we've made?" Wei's voice carried a challenge, one issued every time they met.

"There's no way to know, is there?" Hong's voice was soft, a whisper.

"If you doubt, isn't that answer enough?"

A scoff. "You telling me you don't doubt the years since we washed the Eastern District in blood?"

"It needed to be done." Hong remained silent, and it rankled Wei. "You thought so too, once."

"I still think so," Hong said at last. "That's not where we differ—you know that. We both just have different definitions of *protect*."

"And loyalty." Wei regretted the words the moment they passed his lips, but they were out there. Hong stiffened, eyes hardening and lips tightening.

"When you asked me to meet you here, I figured you had something important to talk about, so go on."

Just like that, the door to their past slammed shut, and they once again became Dragon and Inspector, so-called criminal and the law. That worked better for them, anyway. "I've got new evidence for you on the overdose cases, specifically Haylin Li. Her mom received a tape from some *puk gai*—a sex tape. Looks like someone drugged her, raped her on camera, and then dumped the body."

"A video makes it hard to tell consent," said Hong. As always, he seemed to pick his words carefully.

"Don't give me that—she was almost unconscious, drugged out of her mind. No way she gave consent." Wei saw in Hong's eyes he knew that. Why was it so hard for him to do his damn job?

"You think there's a rape video ring going on and these girls are the targets?"

"They all disappeared after frequenting the same place," Wei pointed out. "All turned up overdosed on the same drug. Add in the foreigner who disappeared—"

"You're dragging him into this, aren't you?" Hong demanded, changing the subject abruptly. "You've taken him under your wing, and now what? What is the end result of that?"

Wei narrowed his eyes. He didn't want Noah getting brought up in all of this, not in their history. "I will help him find out what happened to his sister—more than I can say for the police."

"He's going to get tied up with the Dragons. Do you think that's safe?"

"That's none of your business."

"You're going to get him killed, Wei—"

"*I said it's none of your business!*" Wei took a step toward Hong, rage pumping through him like adrenaline before he got control of himself. "I just wanted to let you know how wonderful your police department's investigative skills have been."

"Where is this video?" Hong kept his voice neutral, but he was clearly wary now that he'd woken Wei's anger—it showed in the tense coil of his muscles, the hard set of his jaw.

"I'll get a copy made and sent to your apartment. I won't send it to the precinct." Wei started for the path.

"Wei, you said they were at the same place before going missing. What place?"

Wei paused but did not look back. "That I'm not going to tell you."

"I can have you arrested for obstructing justice."

"That would require an investigation to be active, Inspector, and last I heard, your department ruled these accidental overdoses."

Wei returned to his bike. He stared at the empty windows of the house, gazing vacantly at the world around them, and felt a profound sadness settle over him. Hong was right, he decided. There were ghosts there. Too damn many of them.

37

Noah wasn't sure what to do with himself once Wei left. He lay in Wei's bed for a while, enjoying its softness, but once the warmth left over from Wei's body faded, it lost its luster.

He rose and went through his clothes and dressed. He saw that Wei had a washing machine in the apartment, so he tossed his dirty clothes in there to keep himself busy. He was somewhat hungry but remembered that Wei had nothing in the way of food and resigned himself to waiting until they got to the coffee shop.

Noah's phone rang as he was transferring the clothes from the washer to the small dryer. He froze for a moment, damp shirt clutched tightly in his fists, remembering the previous night, the call to Lianne's phone. He hadn't so much as looked at the thing since then and almost couldn't bring himself to do it now.

But what if it *was* Lianne again? What if she was in trouble and trying to get a hold of him? He couldn't take that chance—not again; the last time he'd ignored her call, she'd gone missing in Hong Kong.

It took him a moment to find it on the couch where he'd left it the night before. When he looked at the number, his stomach sank. It wasn't Lianne, but his father. They had not so much as spoken since Noah had departed for Hong Kong. The man didn't seem the slightest bit invested in whether or not his only daughter was alive.

"Hello, Richard." Noah greeted him tersely. He hadn't called him father to his face in a very long time, longer than he could actually remember. "So good of you to finally call."

"Glib as always, I see." Richard Alvin Potter's voice was brusque and hard, the voice of a man far too used to giving orders and not comfortable conversing with others as if they were human beings and not just creatures there to do his bidding. "Have you managed to actually accomplish anything yet, or are you just wasting time?"

"I've only been here a few days," Noah reminded him, irritated.

"If you haven't found her in a few days, then she doesn't want to be found," Richard said. As if it were that simple. The man didn't know the first thing about his children. "She'll turn up eventually when she's gotten bored of wherever she's ended up. Probably jetted off somewhere else on a whim."

Noah snorted. "You know damn well that's not true; you have access to her bank records, so you'd know if she purchased a plane ticket." He hesitated then, not sure how much he should reveal to his father about what was going on in Hong Kong. "There's a lot going on here. I think...I think Lianne got into some trouble."

Richard let out a dry laugh. "When is that girl not in trouble? I think you've wasted enough time chasing her flights of fancy. You need to come home and think about the responsibilities you've put off for too long. It's time for you to take up your proper place as a Potter."

That was it? A complete dismissal of any concern about Lianne and an instruction to come home? Noah didn't know why he let it surprise him; this was exactly what he should expect from the man who coldly deposited them in the care of nannies and housekeepers after the death of their mother.

"You might not give a damn about Lianne, but she's my sister, and I'm not leaving until I find her or find out what happened to her." Noah hung the phone up, having reached his limit of Richard Potter for the day. Hell, for the *month* more like.

He was still brooding over the call when the doorbell rang, startling him. A moment later, he heard the door beep and open and Tony entered. The man looked a bit older than the other Dragons he'd seen, maybe closer to forty. His face was a bit too sharp to be handsome, but he was attractive. His nose sat unevenly on his face, broken in the past, his eyes shrewd—he had a brain in that head, Noah could see that plainly. Slight frame and average height, but Tony was not a man to underestimate.

"So you're my chauffeur today, huh?" Noah asked lightly, checking to make sure he had everything of importance—not that there was much, just his wallet and phone and picture of Lianne. Tony just grunted. "A man of many words, I see. Well, I'm ready."

Tony led him down to the lobby and out to where a silver sedan was waiting. It was a much more low-key vehicle than what Conroy drove, that was for sure. Noah started to climb into the passenger seat and then stopped when he realized he was actually about to get behind the wheel. *Stupid European-style cars*, he thought to himself, refusing to look at Tony as he crossed around to the other side and got in.

They drove in silence for a few minutes, not even the radio to act as background noise. It was unnerving. Noah glanced at Tony and decided to see how responsive the other man might be to some of his questions. "So, Tony, right? Mind if I ask you a few questions?" The look he received seemed to say *Shoot*, so he did. "From what I've gathered, the Dragons have a huge territory in their control, right?"

"The Nine Stars had the second-largest portion of the island, so yeah."

"How is it you keep order here? I've only seen like eleven or twelve people. There's no way a gang that size could control such a large area."

"You've only seen Wei's lieutenants. There are plenty of lower ranks—we call them soldiers—that you'll probably never see because they report to us lieutenants."

That made sense, given the size of the district from what Noah could tell. "So how big of an operation is it?"

Tony shook his head. "That's not something I'm just going to tell you, even if Wei has taken an interest in you." It was clear he would not change his mind on that matter.

"You don't trust me, do you?"

"Trust is a luxury that people who do what I do can't afford. People who trust don't live long." He spoke in a voice of absolute authority on the matter, like he knew from personal experience. Remembering what Wei told him about the war with the Nine Stars, Noah thought it was possible. Still, it frustrated him to be dismissed so easily.

"Wei trusts me." It came out petulantly, a child saying *but Mom lets me do it*.

"That's his prerogative. He also wants in your pants, if he hasn't gotten in them already. Also his prerogative. Sometimes the dick can outthink the brain. The rest of us, we still need to be convinced."

"Fair enough." Noah couldn't really expect them to trust him just like that. He thought once more of the phone call he got from Dang, the request to spy for him. *I told him no*, he reminded himself. But then he didn't tell them about it, now did he? That was the behavior of a guilty person, whether he was actually guilty or not.

They were silent for a few more minutes until at last they reached the coffee shop. "Has Wei made it back?" Noah asked as he exited the car. Tony shook his head. *I wonder if he's like this with everyone, or if he just really doesn't like me?*

Inside the coffee shop, Winston greeted him. Winston was wiping down a table, dressed in a gray apron that read "Coffee by Constance" in green lettering. He looked like there was nothing else he wanted to do less. Constance was behind the counter. She smiled kindly at Noah when he came in.

"Hungry?" Noah nodded shyly. "I'll get you a panini. Sit tight."

Noah took a seat at the table Winston was cleaning. The younger man gave him the once-over and grinned. "You and the boss have fun last night?" The question lacked the intensity Noah had gotten used to from Winston; it was almost gentle, an obvious effort to distract him from his dark thoughts.

"You were with us in the night market and the bath." Noah purposefully disseminated, knowing damn well what Winston meant. He refused to look away from Winston's amused gaze, refused to give him the satisfaction of a blush.

"I'll spell it out then: did the boss fuck you blind last night?"

"No, he didn't." It was the truth, so that helped. It was still jarring to have the question put to him so bluntly, even if he was expecting it.

Winston narrowed his eyes, like he was not sure whether or not to believe him. "You sure? *Something* had to happen, the way the boss was eying your ass last night. I was sure he'd have tapped that. Not that I blame him—you got a sweet bubble ass, looks like it's begging to be dicked down."

"Winston, don't be vulgar in my shop," Constance chided as she returned with a delicious looking ham and cheese panini and a healthy serving of French fries. "Here you go. There's ketchup if you need it."

Noah didn't like ketchup much, so he shook his head. "This is great. Thanks."

Winston took a seat at the table across from him as he ate, watching him intently. There was obviously something he was waiting to say. "Can I help you?"

"Did the boss say anything to you about where he was going this morning?" Winston asked it casually enough, but Noah could tell he really wanted to hear the answer.

"What, he didn't tell any of you?" That surprised Noah, who had the impression that Wei kept the others in the loop.

"He doesn't need to explain himself to us," replied Winston with a shrug. "I figured you, though, he might have told."

"If he didn't tell any of the Dragons, what makes you think he told me?"

"You have a different relationship with him than the rest of us do." Winston made it clear with a lewd wiggle of his tongue exactly what he meant by *relationship*.

Noah shook his head. "I don't know what you think but there's no 'relationship' to speak of." Was there? They'd fooled around one time, that was it. But, the truth was, Noah knew his feelings were more than just sexual, and he could tell Wei's were, too. Maybe that was wishful thinking on his part, though.

"There's something between the two of you," Winston insisted, as if he could hear the dialogue taking place in Noah's mind. "Whatever it is, it's different from what the rest of us have. Did he tell you or not?"

Noah ate a few fries and sighed. "He said he was going to see Inspector Hong."

Winston made a sound deep in his throat that Noah had never heard before, a sound that could be of nothing but disgust. He remembered the look of hatred on Winston's face when he saw Hong the previous day at the apartment. None of the other Dragons had that hatred. Emotion like that couldn't be felt for a stranger; their connection had to be deeper than that.

"Why would he need to go see that *puk gai*?"

"Winston, how many times do I have to tell you not to say—"

"Not to say what, the truth?" Winston was on his feet, face white with anger. "He's an asshole, Mom, and I can't understand how you keep defending him!"

"You know it's not that simple," Constance said, but Winston was in no mood to listen. He shook his head and stormed out through the kitchen, doors slamming behind him. Constance closed her eyes against whatever emotion she must have been feeling, and Noah felt like an intruder in a very personal moment.

"I shouldn't have said anything," he said at last. "I didn't think..." He trailed off, unsure what else to say.

"It's all right," Constance assured him, her voice sad. "Allen Hong is a sensitive matter for the Dragons."

"I've noticed."

"For Winston, it's more personal than the rest. You see, Allen is my brother."

Noah's eyes widened in shock. "So Winston's uncle. What happened? You don't have to tell me," he added quickly, realizing his curiosity had gotten the best of him and he might have crossed a line with a woman he barely knew. "I understand if you don't want to."

She leaned forward on the counter, propping her chin up with her right hand. "It's an old wound for me, but for Winston, it's still raw. You see, Allen was once part of Wei's inner circle—that's how I got brought in originally."

The surprises just kept coming. "So the inspector was a Dragon?"

"No. He was there during the formative years, during the war with the Nine Stars. He fought for this territory as hard as any of the others did, except maybe Wei. Our parents had a small business, and when the Nine Stars demanded protection money they couldn't pay, the Nine Stars set it on fire. Ruined my parents, devastated them. That was when Allen found Wei and what led me to them as well."

"When did it change?" Noah asked, voice soft. He felt as if a strange curtain had fallen over the shop, separating them from the outside world.

"It changed gradually, I guess," Constance mused, eyes slightly glazed as if she stared back through the mists of time. "The violence of the war— and it was definitely a war, have no doubt—left him jaded. He started to think that there had to be other ways to protect people, ways that weren't so violent. He grew to hate the bloodshed, the necessity of it."

"So he became a cop." It made sense, the need to protect driving one to law enforcement. Ideally it would be a world of less bloodshed, less murder.

"Right. Now, that didn't sit too well with Wei because the cops had been so unhelpful during the battle with the Nine Stars—they made it worse more often than they did any good. A lot of them were on the Nine Stars' payroll. Made it really hard to trust one of them." Constance's eyes turned sad. "I remember the day he told us he was joining. Wei's reaction...it was like he'd been betrayed by a brother, and in a way, he had."

"And Winston?"

Constance sighed. "He couldn't understand the reason. He hates the police, and not without reason. His father was also a member of the fight, but some dirty cops arrested him. There were some Nine Star *puk gai* planted there by the dirty cops—they attacked him. He died."

"I'm really sorry, Constance." Noah didn't know what else to say; was there anything else? There weren't any words that could ease the sort of pain that must have brought; any attempt would just fall flat.

"That was a long time ago," she said dismissively, but the wetness in her eyes told Noah all he needed to know. She still felt the loss, no matter how long ago she said it was.

"The point is the only thing Winston can see is that Allen chose to work for the people who set his father up and caused his death. He doesn't see the intentions Allen had. It's most disappointing because Winston and Allen were so close before that—especially after his father died. Winston lost a good man to look up to. Thankfully, the Dragons are also good men. They've kept a rein on Winston's wild side, given him focus, purpose. I owe a lot to them."

Constance tilted her head sideways, listening to something. Just like that, the strange spell that had descended during the story broke, and the coffee shop returned to normal. "Wei's here."

Noah quickly turned to look out the window as Wei dismounted his motorcycle. He'd gotten so caught up in Constance's story he hadn't heard the bike's approach. He was a little annoyed to find he was almost craning his neck to watch Wei enter the coffee shop, acting like a lovesick teenager. He clamped down on the flutter in his stomach as Wei entered and gave him a glancing smile.

Constance came around the counter to meet him, an unspoken question on her face.

"He's doing fine, Constance," Wei said gently. Noah saw that when he spoke to Constance of her brother, he lacked the disgust that was usually there. Probably out of respect for her relationship with him. Constance looked relieved to hear it. "Is everyone here?"

Constance nodded. "Mostly. Walker hasn't shown up yet, but he should be here soon."

Wei nodded. "Tell him to hurry up when he gets here. Don't let him get dessert first." Constance chuckled and nodded. "Let's go, Noah."

Noah followed Wei through the kitchen and up to their gathering place above the shop. He tried to gauge Wei's mood as they went, but it was difficult. His face was expressionless, and while his shoulders seemed tense, Noah couldn't tell if it was unusual or not.

Winston was sitting at the top of the metal stairs just as he had been when Noah exited the last meeting. He looked up as they approached, the anger not fully released from his face, and when he spoke, Noah detected a tinge of bitterness. "At the kiddie table with me again today?"

"You're in luck, Winston," Wei said, clapping the young man hard on the shoulder. "You're both invited to the grownup table today."

Winston jumped to his feet and hurried to open the door for Noah and Wei, the anger evaporating from his face. Noah wondered if the decision was a way of clearing up Winston's feelings or if Wei had intended his presence all along.

Inside the room, Noah saw most of the others were there. Steel, Conroy, and Chris were sitting around the poker table playing a hand. The others engaged each other in conversations, a television Noah hadn't seen on his first visit blaring out some music show. As soon as Wei came in, someone shut off the television, and everyone turned their attention to him.

Winston, chest swollen with pride, went to the poker table and sat down next to Steel.

Wei cleared his throat. "We're just going to get started. Walker can be filled in when he gets here. You have the DVD, Noah?" Noah stared blankly for a moment, surprised to be addressed so quickly, and then pulled out the DVD Wei asked him to bring, handing it over.

"Someone delivered this to Haylin Li's mother last night." Wei held the DVD aloft, the gesture reminding Noah of one of those old-time revivalist preachers with a Bible. "I'll spare you the details, just know that this is proof that these girls were kidnapped, drugged, and forced into making porn. Girls from *my* territory." He tossed the DVD to Tony, who caught it as if he'd been expecting the toss the whole time.

"I want to find the fuckers responsible for this," Wei went on, voice hardening. "I want to show them that no one fucks with my people without consequences." The men gathered there, Wei's lieutenants, his closest allies, let out sounds of agreement, filled with as much rage as Wei clearly felt. Noah could not understand it—he hadn't experienced the lives they had, wasn't a part of the battle for this area, but he could appreciate the dedication they all had for their cause.

Noah remembered what Dang said—no better than the other thugs—and shook his head. No, that wasn't true at all. They were much better than the others. They didn't rule by violence, only used it to protect. It wasn't a matter of *the lesser of two evils*. In that moment, he knew these were the good guys, plain and simple. Nothing would ever convince him otherwise.

"How are we going to do that, boss?" Conroy asked.

"We know the common link these girls all have—the only one we've been able to find. There is something going on at K—I want to know what. I asked you to look into the employees; what do we have?"

The guy everyone called Smile straightened, glancing at Noah uncertainly. Reading the look, Wei cleared his throat. "Listen, everyone. Noah is as involved in this as we are, and I'm not sending him away. We clear?" Everyone just nodded their understanding, though Noah could see a few people might not approve of Wei's decision. Wei's acceptance of him meant a lot—even if it did come from the fact that there was *something* going on between them. "What did you find out, Smile?"

"Nothing seems out of the ordinary. All the employees check out," Smile said. "Most of them have worked at K for a long time."

"What about the bouncer?" Chris asked.

"Georges hired the bouncer you're talking about—a man named Vaughn—two months ago. No red flags or complaints from any customers about him."

"Guy was a dick," Wei muttered.

"Anything on a guy with a scar on his cheek?" Noah asked, unable to stop himself. Wei might accept his presence at the meetings, but that didn't mean his intrusion into Dragon affairs would be accepted. He should have just kept his mouth shut.

"The guy the coat check girl described as being with your sister?" Wei asked. Noah nodded.

"No one's said anything about a guy with a scar," Smile said.

"We got anyone checking the security cameras in the club?" Steel asked.

"We don't have enough info about what happened to get any use from the cameras," Tony explained. "We don't have any idea exactly when the girls went missing."

"That's not entirely true," Winston interjected, as uncertain about speaking out in the meeting as Noah. "You got that voice mail from your sister on your phone, right, Noah?"

Noah nodded, a smile blooming on his face. "I do—date stamp and everything."

"Even if we do narrow the day down, it still gives us hours and hours of footage to look at," Tony warned.

"It's better than nothing," Wei said after considering for a moment. "Tony, you and Chris get those tapes and look them over. Keep an eye out for the foreign girl and anyone she might leave with."

"What about the rest of us?" Conroy asked.

"We're going to be staking out K real closely," Wei said. "Not too many on the inside—I don't want whoever it is to notice us and get spooked. Some of the less recognizable will be on the inside—Smile, Steel, Winston, that means you guys. The others will be watching the parking lot and the doors. Anything look suspicious, we act. The real work starts tonight, people. I don't want another girl going missing on my watch. Everybody get ready. Club opens at eight, and we're going to be there from dusk till dawn."

Noah guessed that was everyone's dismissal; people broke into small groups and discussed what was to come. Tony and Chris left for K to get started reviewing the footage, stopping to have a quiet conversation with Wei beforehand.

As soon as they left, Noah approached Wei. "I hope you don't expect me to just sit around here and wait for you guys to come up with something. That's not going to happen. I won't sit on my hands while I should be helping find out what happened to my sister."

Wei chuckled. "I figured you would say that. That's why I brought Winston in. I want him to keep an eye on you in the club. If something happens, I'm giving Winston strict instructions to get you the hell out of there."

Noah rolled his eyes at Wei's overprotectiveness. "What's going to happen in the middle of a crowded club?"

"Don't jinx it."

38

K was somewhat alive at eight o'clock, a testament to its popularity. While by no means full, at least twenty people were already inside just after opening. Noah and Winston claimed table space while they could, drinks in their hands in the hopes of looking inconspicuous. They were young, right about the age of K's regular crowd, which helped.

Noah was feeling antsy. He'd been in there before asking questions, so he knew there was a risk this Vaughn guy would remember him, which might tip him off that something was wrong, but he couldn't let this go down without being there himself. If they managed to find Lianne or even find a lead that would eventually take him to her, he had to know right away. He didn't want to hear secondhand news, didn't want to risk that something might be withheld from him, for whatever reason.

He didn't want to admit it even to himself, but Noah was nervous, too. There was a tension in the air he hadn't experienced the last time he was there, a tension born from the knowledge that any moment now, he might finally *know* something, instead of being surrounded by constant questions and his own suppositions.

Of the twenty other people in the bar, nine had gone up to the VIP area. They seemed to be a group consisting entirely of girls. Noah reminded himself to keep an eye out for one of them leaving the club with a man, just in case. It was unlikely that whoever was behind this would target a group, but you never knew. The others were together in groups of two or three. At the far side of the bar, a group of men in business suits were clearly having some sort of event after work.

He wished Wei was there, but the leader of the Dragons was pretty high profile here; all of the employees—with the exception of Vaughn, it seemed—knew who he was, and so did plenty of people. Instead he, Conroy, Tony, and most of the other members were outside in the parking lot, parked around it in a spattering pattern that would allow them to keep a good eye pretty much anywhere throughout it.

"It's gonna be a long night," Winston muttered next to Noah. Noah nodded in agreement, glancing at Winston from the corner of his eye.

Winston cleaned up nicely. He was now wearing a V-neck shirt of pale red, which showed off the nice body he'd honed from years of mechanical work and workouts with the Dragons. He had a pair of slim-cut, dark-wash jeans that rode low on his hips, and his shirt rode up high enough to reveal his stomach, the small trail of hair, and the tops of his boxers as was the style. He had styled his hair into tall, stiff spikes. He would have fit right in in any club in America.

Noah didn't have as much experience clubbing as his sister, but he knew enough to know that he'd blend in if he just kept his phone out constantly. It sat on the table in front of him, within quick reach of his hands, next to his drink.

"Go easy on the drinks," Noah warned as Winston took a deep chug from his beer. "It would be better if we split up as little as possible. Not to mention we definitely shouldn't be getting drunk."

"God, you sound like my mom." Winston rolled his eyes but sat his beer down. "'Keep your eyes open,'" he said in a really good imitation of his mother's voice. "'Don't let yourself get distracted. Don't drink too much. Don't forget Wei is counting on you.' Like I needed that reminder. Wei basically beat it in my head before he would let me out of the coffee shop."

Noah remembered Wei holding Winston back as everyone was piling out into their cars to get ready, sending Noah on ahead. He'd spoken to him briefly, and then they'd emerged, neither of them talking about it. "What did he say to you, anyway?"

"Oh, just the usual. 'If you let him out of your goddamn sight, I'm going to have to explain to your mother why you have several broken limbs.'" Winston chuckled dryly. "He's really nervous about you being in here and him being out there. I've never seen him so worried about someone before."

Noah didn't say anything to that—what could he say? The dynamic between him and Wei was complicated, to say the least, more so because they hadn't talked about it. It hung between them, felt but unspoken. He didn't know how much longer they could leave it like that, but there were a lot of things going on, and the state of their whatever it was came in at the bottom in terms of importance.

"You said you two haven't fucked yet," Winston went on, eyes trained on the crowd as he spoke. "But you've done *something*, right?"

"Shut up," Noah sighed. He didn't want to discuss his sex life with someone who was basically a stranger in the middle of a crowded club.

"We can't just sit here silently watching the room," Winston argued. "That will look weird as fuck. Might as well talk about something."

"You know what? You're right—we might as well talk about something. How's *your* sex life, Winston?"

Noah took great pleasure in the way Winston suddenly squirmed, attempting to stammer out some sort of witty reply. "It's—I mean— Just—*my* sex life isn't all that interesting. At the moment, I mean. I've had plenty of—well, you know. Plenty."

Noah's eyebrows rose almost into his hairline. "Are you a virgin, Winston Chang?"

Winston scowled, staring into his beer. "No, of course not. Look, let's talk about something else, okay?"

Noah grinned victoriously. "I will if you will."

A few more people began trickling into the club. Noah got his first sight of Smile leaning on the surface of the bar, head moving to the rhythm of the music and eyes sweeping the crowd. Even in the dim light of the club, Noah could see that Smile's expression was placid and blank. Did he ever show any expression?

Steel was constantly making circles of the club, a drink in his hand, as well. On one of his rounds, he stopped by their table for a moment, leaning in to speak to them. "Seen anything out of the ordinary?" Noah and Winston shook their heads. "Me either. Can't wait for this place to get packed. At least then there would be plenty of eye candy."

"Don't get distracted," Winston said, suddenly scowling. The shift in Winston's tone surprised Noah. What had brought that about? Steel felt the same—Noah could see the hurt in his eyes.

"I know my duty," he replied coolly. He pivoted on his heel and strode away from the table without looking back.

Glancing at Winston, Noah saw that his face was set in a frown as he watched Steel go. "What was that all about?"

"What was what all about?"

"*That*," Noah said, gesturing at Steel's retreating back.

"I just reminded him why we're here, that's all. I'd rather not have Wei pissed off at me, okay? This is the first thing he's ever trusted me with, and I'm going to do it right." There was more to it than that—Noah could read it on Winston's face—but the younger man wasn't going to say anything more, and Noah wasn't going to force the matter. There were much bigger things for them to deal with in the long run. It was, though, another little oddity for him to mark down when it came to Winston and Steel.

Despite what Winston said, his mood grew increasingly dark as the evening progressed. All he would do was sit there at their table and scowl whenever he saw Steel walk by. Steel, though, was doing his best to fit in, socializing and spending time every now and then on the dance floor. Maybe it was a good thing that Winston reminded him of their purpose there. When he wasn't fitting in as an attendee of a club, Steel found his way casually to the bar next to Smile, where the two exchanged hushed words before he moved on.

Steel never made it back to their table that evening, didn't even look in their general direction. That only served to make Winston's mood worse.

"I'm going to the bar," Noah said finally, unable to handle sitting next to the glowering younger man.

"We're supposed to stay together," Winston protested.

"The bar is within eyesight, and Smile is there," Noah reasoned. "Besides, I can get a better view of the VIP area from over there." *And get away from your mood for a minute*, he thought privately.

When Winston offered no further protest to his plan, Noah slipped away toward the bar. It was a relief to be away from the negative air around Winston, even if only for a few moments.

At the bar, Noah took a barstool a few over from Smile, who's only acknowledgment of his presence was a glance from the corner of his eye. Settling back against the bar and drumming his fingers on it casually in time to the music, Noah looked back at the Winston and found him staring, jaw set like he was gritting his teeth, at Steel, who was at that moment engaged in conversation with a pretty girl in a low-cut top and skintight jeans.

What was the source of that anger? Was he jealous that Steel hadn't been saddled with the burden of Noah on Wei's orders and was thus free to talk to the pretty girls? Or was there something else going on between the two men?

Now's not the time to be worrying about anyone else's love life, he reminded himself. *I've got Lianne to think about. Not to mention my own love life.* He did his best to block that from his mind as well. Tonight he was putting his entire focus on Lianne. That was the reason he was in Hong Kong in the first place. Everything else was an afterthought.

Noah let his eyes scan the room, hoping he looked casual about it as he focused on faces, hoping to see the man the coat check girl described to him his first night there. The lighting and atmosphere of the club made it difficult to distinguish features, though. For all he knew, the guy could be in there right that moment and Noah wouldn't know until he was upon him.

He turned his attention to the VIP area, hoping to catch a glimpse of the faces milling about up there. A small part of him was still hopeful he would catch a glimpse of Lianne, but he knew that was just a wild delusion he simply could not bring himself to let go of. But now wasn't the time to entertain that sort of nonsense, not if he wanted to really see his sister again.

He was in his thoughts so much that he didn't notice the man who approached the bar on his right side, the side opposite of Smile, until he asked to pay his tab. His voice was a deep baritone, and it made Noah look over.

At first glance, he was just an average guy—typical Asian profile, clothes looking much like the clothes of everyone else in the club, an earring gleaming in his ear. Something made Noah look back a second time, though, and his heart stopped beating.

There, on his cheek, barely noticeable in the dimness of the club, was a pale scar. Noah only noticed it because the man was smiling, stretching the scar. *It's him.*

This was the man his sister was with the last time anyone saw her.

This was the man who could give him all the answers he wanted. It could all be over in mere moments. Not likely, really, but at least he would be a step closer than he was before. Noah glanced toward Winston, who wasn't looking in his direction at that moment, and then toward Smile.

He should get one of them, have them join him, but there wasn't time; the man with the scar was already weaving his way through the crowd, on his way out, off somewhere he'd not be able to find him again.

Noah couldn't miss this opportunity.

Noah didn't give it a second thought. He was away from the bar and right on the tail of the man. He had to crane his neck again and again to see around people, desperate not to lose him. Muttering quick apologies, he slid past people, hurrying his pace as he lost sight of the man.

Noah came into the long hallway that led to the front door, but the burly figure of a man blocked his path. He tried to step around him, but the man followed, stepping the same way. Noah thought it an accident, until he tried to step around the other way and the same thing happened.

It was by chance that Noah noticed the glint of light off of the blade of a knife moments before the man, a big, barrel-chested guy, took a swing at him. Noah cried out and stepped back, the blade cutting into the sleeve of his shirt and scoring a white-hot line across his upper arm.

Other people around him began to scream and hurry out of the way, but Noah ignored them, focusing entirely on this sudden obstacle in his way. Fury coursed through him, and the reason why was insane. He was not angry that he was suddenly being attacked, but that this man was preventing him from following the man with the scar.

He stepped back from another swipe of the knife and then quickly stepped forward and grabbed the assailant's knife-wielding hand and gave it a hard twist. The man cried out in pain and dropped the knife.

"Noah!" Winston's voice, full of alarm, came from behind him, but he ignored it. He drove his knee hard into his assailant's gut and shoved him away. The man stumbled but kept his feet, barely. Noah lashed out with his foot, catching him just above his ankle and driving him to his knees. He followed that up with a hard kick to the chest, sending the man sprawling onto his back.

"Holy *fuck*," Winston gaped in disbelief. He noticed the blood on Noah's shirt and grimaced. "Wei is gonna *kill* me."

Noah ignored him, hurrying past the fallen guy and out into the balmy night, but the man with the scar was nowhere in sight. He'd lost his chance.

39

The Dragons searched the parking lot, but the man with the scar didn't turn up anywhere. The Dragons waiting outside in cars hadn't really noticed anyone walking by, but they didn't have time to do a really thorough check.

Wei, who was absolutely *livid*, sent Winston and Chris to his apartment with Noah, despite his protests. He'd also called Constance to get there with her emergency kit. With Noah being a foreigner and on Dang's radar, they couldn't afford to take him to a hospital at the moment, and it didn't seem too serious.

Yet. It remained to be seen how bad it would be after Wei was through with him.

Wei didn't even want to *look* at Winston at that moment; it was only his respect for Constance and his uncle-like affection that kept him from beating the young man to a pulp. He'd been given simple, *simple* instructions, and yet he'd fucked it up. That's what he got for trusting something important to someone other than one of his Dragons.

The whole incident could potentially lead to trouble with the local cops. The last thing Wei needed was the place shut down because of violence. He put the rest of the Dragons on crowd control, trying to find the people who saw what had happened and making sure they said the right things to the police if they showed up.

With that handled, he, Conroy, and Tony grabbed Noah's assailant and drug his ass upstairs to a room Georges kept around if Wei needed to meet with anybody while at the club. Wei was really fighting his baser instincts with this guy. He'd attacked Noah—he'd fucked with someone under his protection—and all Wei wanted to do was teach him that no one fucks with what belongs to Wei Tseng.

Wei felt Conroy's concern, and could guess what he was thinking: Wei was in a dangerous place. Wei felt the tightness in his jaw as he clenched his teeth, knew fury burned behind his eyes, was aware of the veins bulging in his arm as he clenched his fists so tightly he thought his palms might bleed. Wei was close to losing it, and someone would have to keep control of him once he did. Conroy was no doubt at that moment regretting that that someone would be him.

Once they got the attacker secured in the room, Conroy took Wei's shoulder and led him out, pulling the door shut behind him and leaving Tony with the man. "You see the condition this dude is in? Be careful not to piss that one off, boss." Wei didn't react to Conroy's attempt at humor and started into the room, but Conroy stopped him.

"*What*?" Wei demanded sharply.

Conroy raised an eyebrow at Wei's tone but let it pass without comment. "I just wanna say somethin' real fast. Look, I know you're pissed—for good reason—but if you wanna get anything useful out of this *puk gai*, you gotta keep your cool. He can't tell us shit if he's got a broken jaw." Conroy studied Wei's face, gauging his anger. "Or, you know, if he's dead."

Wei gave a single curt nod to show his understanding, and he and Conroy reentered the room. Tony had the man sitting on a chair. He was a bulky guy, probably seventy kilos or so. His neck was thick, his arms flabby, but with muscle beneath the fat. The guy had to be twice Noah's size, and yet Noah had taken him down with little fuss, by all accounts. Wei was impressed.

But Noah shouldn't have had to in the first place.

"He's said some interesting things while you were out of the room, boss," Tony said, eyes on their "guest." "Go on and tell them."

"I got no idea what's goin' on," the man said immediately, eyes wide with fear. He was smart enough to realize just how deep in the shit he was, then. "Some dude approached me in the toilet and offered me a thousand dollars if I took the knife he had and attacked some *gweilo* here."

"You a hit man or something?" Conroy asked, arms crossed over his chest.

The man shook his head emphatically. "Naw, man! I just figured some skinny little *gweilo*—"

Wei crossed the room then in two steps, punching the man in the stomach while holding his shoulder so he didn't tumble out of the chair. He wanted to punch him in his face, but that was a bad idea. Movies might make it look reasonable, but Wei was quite experienced and knew better; a guy like this probably had a jaw like a brick wall.

"My boss *really* doesn't like that word," Conroy commented from the door where he still stood.

"Sorry! Sorry!" the man managed to croak out through his pain.

"Let me get this straight." Wei spoke for the first time, and the man, sensing the gravity of his situation, looked up at the leader of the Dragons. "Someone approaches you in the fucking toilet and offers you a thousand goddamn dollars to stab someone you don't know and you fucking do it?"

A look of desperation came into the man's eyes. "I was desperate, man. I know it was stupid, but a thousand dollars? Do you know how much food that could buy?"

"He means how much heroin," Tony scoffed, pointing to the track marks on the man's big arms. The man didn't even bother to look ashamed. Tony dug into his pocket and pulled out a thick roll of money and tossed it to Wei. "A thousand Hong Kong dollars, like he said."

Wei crouched down until he was at eye level with the guy. When he spoke, his voice was deadly quiet, like the sound of a blade on velvet. "Who the fuck was it that paid you to do this?"

"I don't know! He didn't say his name, and I didn't ask. Never saw him before in my life."

Wei was quickly losing patience. "Okay, then, what did he fucking look like?"

The man shrugged helplessly. "Just looked like a normal dude. Dark clothes, earring. He had a scar on his cheek, like he'd been in a knife fight or something."

"Sonofabitch." Wei stood up abruptly and turned to Tony. "Make sure this fat fuck knows what's going to happen to him the next time he fucks around in my territory." Tony looked like he wanted to say something but stopped himself and nodded.

"What about my money?" cried the man as Wei started for the door.

"Consider it your payment to the Dragons for causing trouble."

Wei and Conroy stepped outside, closing the door firmly behind them.

"The bastard must have recognized Noah somehow," he said to Conroy. "If he ducked into the bathroom to pay this dude to attack Noah, he probably didn't leave before it happened. He might still be in the club. I want this *sei bat po*, Conroy. I want him real bad."

"Ah, Monsieur Tseng?" Georges stood at the end of the hall, looking less than thrilled to have to interrupt Wei at the moment. He was carrying a thin shipping box. "Zis came for you earlier today."

Wei took the offered box, and Georges scurried back to his office as if afraid that Wei would turn his anger on him next. The box bore a simple label, clearly a fake return address, preprinted so to not even include handwriting. Wei didn't have a good feeling about it.

"What's that?" Conroy asked, looking down at the box as if he could discern what was inside with X-ray vision or something.

"Let's find out."

Wei opened the box. Inside he found a piece of computer paper with a message printed on it and the same generic DVD case they'd seen at Haylin's home. Conroy cursed vehemently in Cantonese. Wei shared his sentiments.

"What does the letter say?" Conroy asked.

"'Wei Tseng, I thought you might like a little preview,'" Wei read aloud. "'Enjoy this taste of what's to come. Do you think the family will like it?'" He crumpled the piece of paper up in his fist, knuckles white, his vision nearly blinded by rage.

Wei turned the DVD case over. Someone had written a name along the side, in the same block letters as Haylin's.

"Shit."

40

He watched Wei Tseng return from upstairs from a safe, unnoticeable place. Not that the Dragons would recognize him. Ming had gone with Leo Tong to the meeting with Wei, but he hadn't. He could still act as Leo's eyes and ears in the Eastern District.

Still, he was cautious. While the Dragons hadn't seen his face, the *gweilo* sure had. He'd survived this long in the Twisted Vipers by making sensible choices. Sure he wasn't climbing the ranks any time soon, but he was surviving, and there was something to be said for that. He was fine staying right where he was. The higher the rank, the shorter the lifespan it seemed to him.

Judging from the look on the Dragon's face, he'd received his present. Good. That was another perfect step forward in the boss's plans.

He didn't look up when someone joined him in the private room; didn't need to. He could smell the pungent aftershave of his company and knew who he was. Everybody called him Scar—a nickname he hated, but that Zhou had started when he was in charge. Story was Scar mouthed off to Zhou when he shouldn't have. In response, the old bastard swung the handy butterfly knife he kept on him at all times too fast to be noticed, leaving the scar along the man's cheek. "Next time," Zhou had said, "I'll cut out your tongue." From then on, he was called Scar and nothing else. Even after Zhou's ouster, everyone kept it up.

"It was stupid to send that guy with the knife," he said. Scar just grunted. "Tseng is already pissed. From what we can tell, he's got the hots for the *sei gei lou*."

A shrug was his answer. "What do I care?"

"Wei Tseng is dangerous, man. You know his history as well as I do."

Scar scoffed. "Things change, obviously. Does that look like the ruthless man who took down a triad to you? He's weak, gone soft. Especially if he's become so emotional over a bunch of whores and two fucking *gweilo*. I'm not intimidated by him."

He didn't think Scar was right, but he didn't say anything. He wasn't stupid enough to go off and antagonize someone who might fly off the handle.

"Give it time," Scar said, patting him on the back. "Soon we won't be slinking around in the dark here. We're going to run this place real soon, all of it, and every triad will know that the Twisted Vipers are meant to be feared. He's the only thing that stands in our way, and he won't be a problem much longer."

41

"Ouch!" Noah cringed under Constance's ministrations.

"Stop pulling away," she chided, taking a firm grip on his wrist and holding his arm still while she dabbed alcohol on the knife cut. It was no longer bleeding and upon inspection, was a very thin, shallow cut. It still burned like hell when alcohol was applied, though. "It's not too bad. I don't think you'll have a scar."

"You seem to know a lot about first aid," Noah commented.

"I was a nursing student until I left university. Got plenty of practice, though, patching up the boys during the war with the Nine Stars." A crease appeared along her forehead, like it always did when she brought up that time period. There were a lot of painful memories there beyond what she'd shared with him, he guessed. Whatever they were, they were hers, and he would let her keep them.

He looked around the apartment to distract himself from the pain of the alcohol dabs. Chris was looking out the window at nothing in particular, just watching the view judging by the angle of his head.

Winston was sulking at the table in the kitchen area, shoulders hunched and hands tightened into fists. Guilt lanced through Noah, as burning as the alcohol applied to his wounds. Winston was beating himself up pretty hard, even though it wasn't his fault. Noah remembered Wei's expression, the look of disgust on his face when he looked at Winston before banishing him to the apartment.

All his fault. He'd let his eagerness for some answers get the better of him, and he'd acted, not even once considering the consequences Winston might face if something bad happened—like it did.

Done with the antiseptic, Constance wrapped a bandage around Noah's bicep, the stinging of the material against his injury drawing a hiss from him before he clamped his lips shut. He could handle a bandage.

"That should do it," Constance said at last, straightening. "For the physical injuries, at least." Her eyes traveled to Winston, and the guilt drove deeper into Noah's chest.

"I'm so sorry," Noah started, but Constance raised her hand to quiet him.

"You don't understand everything about the world you've walked into here, I get that. What you have to really know here is that you're no longer a single individual. You've gotten yourself tangled up with a group, one that functions very tightly that way. Members of the group can't simply go off and take action on their own. There are very real consequences when they do. Part of it is about authority—Wei is the boss, and it has to look that way, or he, and by extension the Dragons, look weak."

Noah nodded, though that was still a concept that was hard for him to grasp. He'd never had to unwaveringly obey someone before, never been in a situation or environment where survival was dependent on it. Humans didn't operate with alphas, not anymore. Not in the world he was from, at least. But he'd stepped into a new world, at first by necessity, but he'd chosen to stay, he'd chosen to become involved. It was time he started learning to operate in this new place he'd put himself.

"That's just one small aspect of it, though," Constance continued, her tone and expression making it clear that Noah needed to hear this next part. "The other, and far more important, aspect is that they *trust* each other. They know they have support no matter what situation they find themselves in. Their bond isn't just boss and subordinates, but friends, family. They have to know that they are safe putting their faith in someone."

"I understand," Noah said quietly.

He got up from the chair Constance had sat him in, bending his arm to test out the pain—nothing too bad; he could handle it. He crossed to the refrigerator in the kitchen, pulling out two bottles of Tsingtao and putting one down in front of Winston before taking the seat next to him.

"I'm really sorry I took off on my own like that. It was stupid."

Winston made a grunt, though whether it was of acknowledgment, assent, or dissent Noah did not know. Hell, maybe it was a *go the fuck away* grunt.

"I should have kept a better eye on you," Winston said. "I shouldn't have taken my eyes off the bar when you went over there. I just... I thought you were right next to Smile, so if anything..." He shook his head. "No, not passing the buck on this one. This was all me."

Noah opened his beer and took a swig. "You didn't make me go off after that guy."

"No, but Wei was expecting you would do something like that. That's why he had me watch you in the first place." That piece of information raised Noah's eyebrows. So Wei had anticipated that, huh? Seemed like Wei might have a better understanding of Noah than he first thought. Impressive.

Figuring that nothing he wanted to say would be capable of breaking through the funk that'd settled over the younger man, Noah was content to just sit there, drinking his beer in silence. Chris remained at the window, unmoving, almost like a statue. Constance busied herself in the kitchen, muttering to herself when she saw the state of Wei's pantry.

They were in much the same positions twenty minutes later when Wei returned home, followed closely by Conroy.

As soon as Wei was through the door, Noah was on his feet. "Wei, listen. Don't be mad at Winston—he didn't do anything wrong. I was the stupid one who—"

"Noah—"

"—wandered off on my own and didn't even try to get help from anybody. If there's anyone—"

"Listen, Noah—"

"No, just hold on. If there's anyone you should be mad at it's—"

"For Christ's sake, Noah!" Wei shouted, and Noah fell silent, shock stealing the words from him. He couldn't remember the last time someone had raised their voice to him like that—certainly not since he'd become an adult. Everyone else in the room was also gaping at Wei, evidently as surprised as Noah.

Anger stirred inside of him, then. Just who the hell did this guy think he was? Noah was *not* going to be shouted at like an unruly child.

Wei, apparently seeing the storm brewing behind Noah's bright blue eyes, reached out and grasped his shoulders firmly. One of those hands was clutching a DVD case. When he spoke, his voice was soft. "Noah, listen."

Noah's turned his head and focused on the hand with the DVD case. "What's that?"

"Just wait—"

Noah shook Wei's hands off his shoulder, reaching for the box. "I said what's that?" When Wei didn't answer, Noah attempted to snatch the

DVD case out of his hand. Wei's reflexes were sharp, and he was able to yank the case out of Noah's reach, using his size to his advantage.

"*Listen*, damn it. This was delivered to Georges at K. It came with a letter."

"What name is on the case?" Noah's voice had gone harsh, leaden, no trace of the foreigner who'd been standing there moments before. He was asking a question he already knew the answer to, but he needed to see or hear it.

"We haven't seen it yet," Wei said, a hint of something like desperation in his voice.

"What. Name. Is. On. The. Case?" Blood pounded in Noah's ears, then, and it took every ounce of willpower he had to remain standing, his knees threatening to go weak.

"Boss." Conroy said it gently, nodding his head toward Noah.

Wei muttered something in Cantonese that Noah didn't hear and then held the case out to Noah. As Noah took it he saw that Wei's hand trembled, and he felt suddenly nauseous.

Noah examined the DVD case, looking for the name, his fingers suddenly refusing to cooperate. He was afraid he would drop the thing, but he finally managed to maneuver it around and found the name on the side.

Lianne.

42

"Play it." Noah tossed the DVD back to Wei. His words were as cold and harsh as they were before, but those bright eyes were dim and empty, like he'd slammed shutters on them from the inside. He was building walls against what he thought they'd find on that tape.

Constance took a step forward, concern on her face. "Maybe it can wait until morning?"

Noah shook his head. "No. Play it. I need to see it. *Play it*," he nearly shouted when Wei made no move to follow his command. "Now, tomorrow, it's not going to change anything, so put it in."

Noah wouldn't back down on that. Wei wouldn't have either, if the roles were reversed. There was no point in delaying the inevitable. It would be much better to rip the band-aid off now and deal with it. If they tried to make him wait until morning, he wouldn't sleep; he'd just lie or pace the floor, tortured, thinking about what *might* be on the DVD.

Even knowing that horror awaited on the DVD, Wei knew the imagination could be so much worse.

Praying that what was on there didn't break Noah, Wei went to the DVD player and put the disc in, hesitating only a moment before pushing close on the tray button. A simple menu popped up, though there was no still from the video to mark it, only a black screen. Wei picked up the remote and walked over to where Noah stood.

He met Noah's eyes for a moment before placing the remote in his hand. The meaning in his look and the gesture was clear: it was entirely Noah's choice. He had the power to start it as well as the power to stop it. Wei stood right beside Noah, desperate to reach out and pull him into his arms or take his hands, but he sensed Noah didn't need that right now. Wei noticed that the others, Chris and Constance and Winston and Conroy, had come closer, as well.

For a moment, Wei thought Noah would be unable to do it, that his resolve had wavered, but then Noah pointed the remote at the DVD player and hit play.

The sounds they heard then were similar to the sounds Haylin made in her video, the barely conscious noises of someone who had no idea what was going on. Wei noted several voices in the background, but they were somehow distorted, and he couldn't distinguish anything particular about them; he couldn't even say for sure whether they were male or female. There was another sound in the background, too, a constant droning sound Wei couldn't easily place, though he was sure he'd heard it before.

The video was blurry and dark, though the occasional movement in and out of the frame told Wei that whoever was filming had the camera pointed down at the ground, and those were feet he was seeing coming and going into the scene.

The sounds of the moaning girl grew louder and then she was in the shot. All they could see of her was her legs and her naked lower half. Her legs were rigged up as if she were in a gynecologist's chair, her body obscenely opened. A mask-wearing figure entered the frame, something in his hand. Wei kept most of his attention on Noah, watching him for sign of weakness, any indication that he couldn't handle what was on the screen. How could he? Wei could barely handle it, and it wasn't his sister there on the screen.

"How awful," whispered Constance. No one else spoke, but Wei sensed movement behind him and guessed that Winston was comforting his mother.

"Show her face," Noah murmured next to Wei, so softly that at first Wei didn't hear him. Soon, though, he was repeating it like a mantra.

On the video, a male body stepped into the shot, naked from the waist down, stroking his erection. The body was thin and lean, with a tattoo of a Chinese character on his abdomen right above the base of his manhood. The camera stayed focused on that as he stepped closer to the girl.

"Show her face..." It was now more plea than mantra. Noah's entire body was rigid, tight with so much tension Wei didn't know how he didn't simply snap in two.

Finally the camera panned up the girl's body, but the video cut out before it reached her face. The video was meant to torture, Wei realized. Whoever sent it wanted Wei—no, not Wei; the video might be addressed to him, but it was meant for Noah—to see the sort of horrible things being done, hints with the label that it was Lianne in the video but never show her face. Someone was playing a psychological game.

The video started playing once more, surprising Wei. He didn't want to see it again, couldn't imagine why Noah would want to, especially if he had even the smallest inkling that this was happening or had happened to his sister.

Studying Noah's face, he saw that there was something manic in his eyes as he stared at the screen. He was searching for *something*, though Wei didn't know what. When the video ended once more, Noah hit play again. This time when he finished watching it, he let out a sigh of relief and tossed the remote onto the couch.

"It's not Lianne," he said at last, his eyes closed.

"Maybe it isn't," Winston agreed, though his voice sounded doubtful.

"I *know* it isn't. It's not her." There was iron conviction in Noah's voice, but Wei wondered where it came from and how necessary that conviction was for Noah's state of mind. Of course he needed it to not be his sister—no one in the world could blame him for that, either. If he needed for the girl in the video to not be Lianne, then that was fine with Wei. Whatever it took for him to hold it together.

"The video didn't show the girl's face," Chris argued. He wasn't trying to be unkind, but at that moment, Wei wanted to punch him. How could he not see how important this was for Noah?

"My sister has a tattoo just over her breast. My mother's initials. The girl in the video didn't have that tattoo. I'm one hundred percent positive it isn't her."

With those words, the tension seemed to bleed out from Noah's body. His legs became wobbly, and he started to collapse. Wei, seeing the danger, caught him effortlessly, holding him in a standing position and pulling him close to his body.

"Why did they put Lianne's name on the DVD then?" Winston asked. His face was pale from what he'd seen.

"To play with Noah's head," said Constance, echoing Wei's earlier thought. "The sick *puk gai* behind this are just toying with us now. They know we're looking for them—that's why they sent it to the club and not here to Wei's apartment. They must know we're not really any closer to finding them, either."

"This just means we've got to try harder, then," Wei said fiercely. "Conroy, see if you can find out who this girl is, okay? I want to know before her family receives a similar DVD. Everyone else, go home and get some rest. Tomorrow is going to be just as busy."

43

When everyone had left, Wei turned to Noah, who was standing behind the couch, supporting himself with both hands on the back of it. He was staring at the cushions as if they were the most interesting things he'd ever seen.

"You okay?" Dumb question, really, but it was the only thing Wei could think to say. Noah muttered a response, voice so soft Wei couldn't make out what he said. "What did you say?" Wei placed his hands on Noah's shoulders, giving them a gentle squeeze.

"I said I'm a terrible person." Noah gently pulled away from Wei's touch, but did not turn to face him.

Wei frowned, but gave Noah his space. He would not make the mistake of pushing things too fast between them; he could do things at Noah's pace. "How can you think you're a horrible person?"

"Watching that video, I was... I was happy that it wasn't Lianne in that video."

"Of course you were; she's your sister—"

Noah finally turned to Wei. His face was pale, his eyes red, like he was on the verge of tears. "I was happy that it was a different girl being tortured and raped, Wei. Happy that it wasn't Lianne, that it was someone else. That girl is someone's daughter or sister or girlfriend or best friend, and I was happy to see it was her being violated in the most horrible way I can imagine instead of my sister. How can I *not* be a bad person?"

"Being happy it's not your sister and being glad it's someone else are not the same thing," Wei insisted, gripping Noah's chin so he couldn't look away. "I've been around a lot of bad people, so believe me when I say you're definitely not one of them. The bad people are the ones in the video, the ones behind it all. And we're going to stop them. Together."

"I hope so," Noah murmured. "I really do."

Wei led Noah to bed, helping him under the blankets before sliding into it himself. He allowed Noah to get comfortable before settling in.

Considering the emotional stress Noah had experienced that day, Wei wasn't surprised when Noah fell asleep quickly.

Wei couldn't sleep, though. Every time he thought he might something jarred him back awake. Instead he just lay there, listening to the sound of Noah's breathing and the distant hum of the city below. Every now and then he glanced at the clock, marking the ticking of the hours.

Just after three in the morning, Noah jerked awake suddenly, flailing around on the bed.

"Hey, hey, hey," Wei gently coaxed him back into calmness. "It's okay."

"I had... I had a bad dream," Noah confessed, covering his eyes with his right hand. "In it Lianne kept asking me why I wasn't trying harder to find her. She thought I gave up on her."

"You're trying as hard as you can," Wei told him firmly. "You have to know that. You haven't given up, and I haven't either. We're not going to stop until we figure this out."

Wei placed a comforting hand on Noah's chest. He could feel the other man's heart racing beneath his touch. "Thank you," Noah whispered, the words barely audible.

"Any time."

Noah rolled onto his side, facing Wei, eyes seeking out Wei's in the dark.

Wei covered Noah's lips with his own, gently. His intention was to keep the kiss chaste, a way of showing support, nothing more. Noah, however, had other intentions. As soon as their lips touched, Noah sought to deepen the kiss, slipping his arms around Wei's neck and pulling his face down more, opening his lips to entice Wei's tongue in.

Wei resisted for a moment, pulling back. "I don't think this is a good idea." Noah grunted in frustration, pulling Wei back for more contact, only to have Wei pull away again. "I don't want to do something because you're in a vulnerable place and then have you regret it tomorrow."

Noah rolled his eyes. "I promise this isn't just me seeking comfort. Well, not just comfort. I've wanted this since you first stormed into the police office and confronted Hong and Dang. I don't know what it is about you, but you've been in my head ever since."

"I have that effect on people." Wei raised an eyebrow. "Are you sure about this?"

Noah grabbed Wei's hand and pressed it hard against the bulge of his erection in his jeans. "Does this feel like I'm sure?" Without realizing he was doing it, Wei gave the bulge a squeeze. Noah whimpered.

"I'd say that feels pretty sure," Wei said, his voice now down two octaves. He continued to squeeze, alternating the amount of pressure he put on it and using his free hand to draw Noah's mouth to his again. This time Wei accepted the invitation, his tongue slipping beyond the boundaries of Noah's lips to tease and dance around the other man's. Noah's hands clutched at Wei's strong back. The combination of Wei's massaging and the kiss was driving him wild, Wei could see.

He placed his body over Noah's, capturing his mouth once more as he ground his denim-clad erection against Noah's. One hand snaked up under Noah's shirt, caressing the smooth surface of his stomach before reaching the hard nubs of his nipples and giving them a not-so-gentle twist. Noah's back arched, and he gasped into Wei's mouth.

Wei broke the kiss long enough to pull Noah's shirt over his head and let his mouth descend on the nipple that wasn't between his fingers, catching it with his teeth and flicking his tongue against it. He smiled at the violent shiver that ran through Noah's body. "Feel good?"

"Yes!" The word came out as a long, slow hiss.

Wei released Noah's nipple from his fingers and slid the hand down to the button of Noah's jeans, deftly undoing it with just his thumb and index finger. The zipper followed next, and Wei slid his hand beneath the material, rubbing his palm roughly against the hot hardness of Noah's cock. There was already a rapidly spreading stain of wetness in the fabric stretched against the head. Noah rubbed his index finger against that wetness, looking up into Noah's hooded eyes.

"You really do want it bad, don't you?" Noah arched his hips in an attempt to wiggle out of his jeans in response. Wei decided to help him, sitting up and pulling the jeans off Noah's legs in one smooth motion. "You're so beautiful," Wei murmured, sliding his hands up Noah's legs and following the trail with his mouth.

"Don't tease me." Noah writhed in pleasure.

Wei nuzzled Noah's balls through his tight underwear with his nose, inhaling the scent of him. "If I don't take it slow, I won't be able to be gentle," Wei warned.

Noah propped himself up on his elbows, staring into Wei's eyes, lust swirling behind his hooded gaze. "I don't want you to be gentle."

Wei arched an eyebrow at that. "You say that now..."

Noah raised his hips, attempting to rub himself against Wei's crotch. "I know what I want, Wei Tseng."

Wei tugged his shirt over his head in response, fingers diving down to undo his belt so he could remove his pants, which were much, much too tight at the moment. "Get on your hands and knees."

Noah heard the command for what it was and rolled over immediately. Wei paused his own stripping to grab the waistband of Noah's underwear and tug them down, exposing the pale, unblemished globes of his ass. Wei made a noise of appreciation, placing several kisses on one cheek as he freed himself from the last articles of his clothing.

Unable to help himself, Wei's hand fell right to his erection, gripping it tightly and stroking it ever so slightly, not wanting to truly stimulate himself but needing the touch. His lips traveled along Noah's cheeks until he drew near his destination. Noah arched his back further, exposing that intimate place.

Wei settled into a comfortable position, his left hand gripping Noah's erection from behind as his tongue began a tentative and gentle exploration of the area around Noah's entrance. He let out a loud moan as Wei's wet tongue caressed him, alternating between soft touches and deep probes.

Wei's self-control was quickly in tatters, and he rose from his kneeling position behind Noah, opened the drawer of his bedside table, and withdrew a tube of lube and a condom. Noah wiggled his hips impatiently. Returning to his position, Wei applied a liberal amount of lube to Noah's ass, using his middle finger to smear it where he needed it. He circled his finger against Noah's puckered entrance, applying just enough pressure to tease but not enough to penetrate.

"Damn it, Wei, come o—" Noah's words died in a surprised gasp as Wei unexpectedly pressed his middle finger inside of Noah as deep as it could go. Wei moved that finger in and out, enjoying the way Noah's muscles contracted around it. He was tight. Wei's cock throbbed in anticipation. He still had some control, though, and he refused to take things too fast and hurt Noah. He would make sure Noah was ready before he gave him the ride of his life.

Wei's index finger joined his middle one, and he spread them apart every now and then. "I'm ready, damn it!" Noah panted.

"You are, are you?" Part of Wei wanted to keep teasing Noah, enjoying just how much the other man was pleading for him. That part was not in charge at the moment, though. Wei withdrew his fingers and tackled the condom wrapper, his fingers, now slippery with lube, having a hard time finding purchase. After a few tries, he finally got it open and rolled the latex down the length of his shaft.

When Wei squirted lube onto the head of his cock Noah reached his hand back between his legs and gripped Wei's shaft, rubbing the lube in for him. His touch was almost enough to make Wei explode right there, but he maintained control.

Damn, was Noah sexy.

Wei positioned himself properly behind Noah, head against his entrance, and pushed. It was Wei's turn to moan as he buried his length in the tight, hot sheath of Noah's body. Mere seconds in and he was in heaven.

Wei was sure Noah could feel every inch of him inside as he began to move his hips slowly, the speed of a man attempting not to lose it right then and there. Noah closed his eyes and luxuriated in the sensations. There was discomfort—it had been a while since he'd had sex—but there was also a pleasant fullness, which, when coupled with the knowledge it was Wei inside him, elevated the experience into pure pleasure.

"Are you okay?" Wei asked, leaning over Noah's back and dropping kisses along his shoulder. Noah's skin seemed to burn in the wake of his lips.

"I'm great," Noah said, thrusting his hips back against Wei to show that he was more than ready.

Wei tilted Noah's head to the side, capturing his lips in a searing hot kiss. As he did, he pulled nearly entirely out and thrust his entire length back in. Noah almost purred in response. Wei broke the kiss, strong, calloused hands gripping Noah's hips tightly. He was ready to begin in earnest.

"*Lei hou lin*," Wei moaned, caressing Noah's back. "You're so beautiful."

Wei began driving himself deep into Noah, his speed intense, his strokes deep and powerful. Noah lay there in visible ecstasy. His eyes, glazed over, stared, unseeing, at the wall, lost to the passion between them.

Wei's groans of pleasure seemed to spur Noah's own, and he was soon thrusting back to meet Wei's thrusts. The sounds and smells of their sex filled the room.Without warning, Noah's body tensed as he came, his muscles tightening like a vise around Wei.

The increase in pressure undid Wei quickly. He managed five more thrusts before his own orgasm overcame him.

Wei pulled out of Noah, removed the used condom, and tossed it onto the floor to be cleaned up later. He collapsed onto the bed, pulling Noah's body around to lay against him, unwilling to be out of physical contact with him.

"That was amazing," Noah said sleepily, hand across Wei's sweaty chest.

"About sums it up," Wei muttered. He was clinging to consciousness by a tenuous thread. Noah made staying awake more difficult by tracing his fingers around Wei's chest in light, gentle patterns.

Noah released a contented sigh and rolled onto his back. As soon as he did, he cringed, rolling right back against Wei. "Gross!"

Wei blinked his eyes rapidly, trying to force himself to stay awake. "What? What is it?"

"I made a mess and forgot about it. Until I rolled into it, anyway." He grimaced. "It's cold and sticky."

"Would you feel better if we took the sheet off the bed?"

"Yes."

"I hope you appreciate the things I do for you," Wei grumbled, turning on the light and stripping the sheet off the bed. He fetched a second set from the closet and put them on. "What do you think you're doing?" he demanded as Noah sat down on the edge of the bed.

"Going to bed...?"

"I don't think so." Wei bent down and picked up the dirty sheet from the floor and tossed it to Noah. "You made the mess; you put these in the wash."

Noah muttered complaints as he deposited the sheets in the dirty laundry and returned to the bedroom. "I assume I can get in bed now?"

"Actually," said Wei, who was already lying in bed, "could you turn off the light first? I can't reach it."

44

Steel and Winston are never going to leave me alone now. That was Noah's first thought upon waking up. They were remarkably good at reading him—no, it was more likely that he was just remarkably bad at concealing anything; he had no poker face.

Being wrapped in Wei's arms, though, he didn't care. Wei had become a rock for him to cling to in the chaos of his life. While everything around him was in a state of constant flux, Wei was a consistency he hadn't expected to find in Hong Kong. Wei was solid and dependable, offering strength when Noah needed it most. Wei might not think so, but Noah could see he was a good man.

Noah stared up at the ceiling, pale gray light barely entering the room through the heavy, closed curtains. He didn't bother looking at the clock on the bedside table; it was early, that was all he needed to know. Wei was still asleep beside him, his breathing deep and steady.

Was it possible for someone with a past as filled with horror and loss as Wei's was to sleep so soundly? Noah hoped so; that would mean there was hope for him on the other side of it all.

The other side of it all. Noah hadn't even thought about what the future would hold for him beyond this. He couldn't imagine anything past the looming shadow of Hong Kong and Lianne's disappearance. What would come next? He didn't *want* to think of that, he realized. Because that meant this would be over and whatever Lianne's fate was would become reality. He knew the chances of finding his sister unscathed, finding her at all, were slim. As long as she was missing, he could hold on to hope. As soon as they found her, that hope was gone, replaced by reality, and he recognized what that reality most likely was.

And then what? What came next? He would have to go back to America eventually. The thought brought an ache to his stomach that he didn't recognize. Why should he be sad to leave this place? What had Hong Kong been to him, but a place of fear and loss? This was the place that took his sister from him.

But it was also the place that had given him Wei.

"What's wrong?" The sound of Wei's sleep-rough voice gave Noah a start. "Sorry, didn't mean to scare you."

"It's okay. I didn't realize you were awake, that's all." Noah's voice sounded too loud to his own ears in the morning stillness. "I was just thinking about what comes next. After finding Lianne, I mean."

Wei took Noah's hand in his own, intertwining their fingers. "You can't focus on the future, Noah. What good does that do anyone? Keep your attention on the here and now. Think about what happens after we find your sister *after* we find your sister."

Noah turned his head to look into Wei's eyes. "Do you think we'll find her?"

Wei was silent for a moment before he answered. "*Wo bu zhidao.* I don't know. I really hope we do. I'm not going to lie to you, though, or tell you what I think you want to hear. If we *do* find her, and she is still alive, I don't think she'll be the same person she was. You've seen what these *puk gai* are doing. The chances they've spared her aren't very high."

Noah squeezed Wei's hand tightly. He'd thought the same thing. "I know. But I want answers. I want to know, one way or another, bad or good. I want to know."

Wei drew Noah in tight, doing his best to comfort him, knowing he couldn't offer more than his physical presence. "We'll find out. On my honor, we'll find out what happened to your sister. And we'll make the people who took her pay."

Noah nodded. Wei lay back on his pillow again, eyes closing. "You should go back to sleep. We've got another long night ahead of us."

"Right. Sorry I woke you up."

Still holding Noah's hand, Wei fell quickly back to sleep. Sleep eluded Noah, however, and he just lay there, staring at the ceiling as the glow of the morning slowly spread across it. He was grateful when Wei's alarm went off and they finally got up.

The day passed in a strange limbo of anticipation. Everyone was on edge, knowing what they would be doing that night. Winston didn't speak much as they all waited at Constance's. He kept his focus on his car, working on it right up until Wei told him he should get a shower and get changed. Winston's perceived failure the night before was clearly still on his mind. He didn't speak much to anyone and did his best to avoid Wei.

Noah wanted to talk to him and apologize, but he wasn't sure if his approach would be welcome and didn't want to force himself on Winston. He decided it was better to let Winston decide when they should talk.

The time came to lay out the plan for the night, and everyone once again gathered in the usual spot.

"I want to know every person going in and out of the club tonight," Wei said without preamble. "I've already called Georges and told him I was putting a Dragon at the door. That's you, Chris. Your main focus is finding the *puk gai* with the scar on his face. You find him, you let me know. I *really* want to have a nice long talk with the fucker.

"Since Chris is now on door duty, Winston, you're in the car with Johnny."

To say Winston's assignment displeased him would be an understatement. "You're benching me? I made one mistake, Wei—"

"This isn't a punishment," Wei said impatiently. "I need someone fast in the parking lot in case scar-face does turn up and tries to run. You're the fastest bastard I know, so it's gotta be you."

The explanation mollified Winston somewhat, but Noah wondered how much of it was true. He hoped Wei wasn't punishing Winston when the mistake was clearly his. He wouldn't try to intervene, though. He was not a Dragon, and he knew that some of the people there—like Walker, for instance—would not be happy to have Noah express his thoughts on anything involving the Dragons, even if he was somehow involved.

They laid out the plan, then; it was much the same as the previous day. Wei wanted to be inside to protect Noah, but Tony and Conroy reminded him he was too high-profile and they had a better chance at succeeding if Wei wasn't there.

He might have agreed to go along with it, but he definitely didn't like it.

Before Noah got out of the car at the club, Wei grabbed his hand. "If you see him in there again—or anything, for that matter—*don't go after him alone*. Tell one of the others."

"I will, I promise." Noah acted without thinking, planting a gentle kiss on Wei's lips. Wei caught the back of his neck before he could pull away, deepening the kiss for a few moments before releasing him.

"Be careful."

Noah joined the small line of people beginning to form outside of K; it was a Thursday evening, and they were hosting a live DJ and advertising two free drinks for ladies to entice a crowd. It seemed to have worked.

Noah barely glanced at Chris as he flashed his passport, his form of ID, and entered the club. Just inside the club, a wall of sound slammed into him, bass thumping so hard it reverberated in his teeth. Whoever this DJ was, he didn't appreciate treble very much.

At the table farthest from the dance floor, Walker sat with a woman Noah'd met earlier that day: Sandra, Walker's wife. She was half Portuguese and half Chinese, the ethnicities playing equal share in her appearance. She had beautiful eyes, dusky skin, and sensuous lips. Sandra seemed like a pretty nice woman, from what Noah could tell; he hadn't spoken to her much, because that would have put him within the radius of Walker, and he'd rather avoid that.

The free drinks brought in a lot of girls, all of them dressed provocatively in the stifling summer heat outside. That was one way in which Hong Kong and America were the same—summer provided an excuse to reveal as much skin as possible. The girls weren't the only ones, either; lots of the guys were wearing tank tops, and more than a few would come out of their shirts as the evening progressed. Noah wondered if any of these girls were now targets of the bastards behind the disappearances, if any of them were at that very moment in danger.

Did the men there know how lucky they were, that by the virtue of their sex they were most often spared the horrors and indignities that all women feared they themselves would one day face?

Steel appeared at Noah's side as if from nowhere and handed Noah a bottle of Budweiser. "You already look like you need a drink."

"I need like fifty," Noah confessed. Unfortunately he wouldn't be able to even have one. "Didn't Smile tell you if he saw you actually drinking tonight he'd shove the bottle up your—"

Steel made a *psshh* noise with his lips. "Smile? *Gong dzau tin ha mou dik, dzou dzau mou lan wai lik.*" Noah stared blankly at him until he explained. "He's all talk and no action."

Noah arched an eyebrow. "If you say so." Smile certainly didn't *seem* to be all talk and no action, but Steel knew him better.

"So…" Something in Steel's voice made Noah look at him, and he instantly regretted it. The younger man waggled his eyebrows suggestively. "You and Wei fucked last night, didn't you?" Noah looked away, pretending to take a sip from his beer to hide the heat rising to his cheeks. "You don't have to say yay or nay; it's obvious. The boss hasn't gotten any in a long time, so we could all tell."

Mortification coursed through Noah. He wasn't used to someone talking so casually—or so accurately—about his sex life. It would just be safer not to say anything; he didn't want to open his mouth and accidentally make the situation more awkward than it already was. *I wonder if Wei is getting this kind of crap from his men?*

"So, was it good?" Steel was unperturbed when Noah looked at him askance. "Who was top? I mean, I know everyone would just assume the boss was top, because he seems that way, but there are plenty of super masculine, dominant-seeming men who are total bottoms in the bedroom."

Noah had to bite back a snarky comment asking if he knew that from personal experience. "I'm going to go blend in at the bar." Leaving Steel to do whatever it was Steel did, Noah made his way to the bar, more to have a place to sit the bottle of beer down than for anything else; the air in the room was somewhat muggy, thanks to the fog machines, and the Budweiser was dripping condensation.

The bartender was the girl with the nose ring from his first visit there, and she recognized him. "You're here again? You must really like this place."

Noah shrugged noncommittally. "It's an all right place. Cheap, so that's good."

"Did you ever find that girl in the picture you were looking for?"

"Not yet. I'm still looking."

"I'm really sorry to hear that." Much to Noah's surprise, she sounded genuinely sorry. It was a nice feeling. "Can I get you anything else?"

Noah shook his head, turning around to examine the crowd. It was monotonous work, but he'd found the guy once already and would damn well do it again. He didn't care if he had to visit K every night for the next month. He would never drop it. Until they physically removed him from the country, he would not quit trying to find the man who knew what happened to his sister, who must be involved with whatever was going on.

A hand tapped impatiently at his shoulder, and Noah realized someone was standing next to him, saying "Excuse me" repeatedly. It was Vaughn, the bouncer for the VIP section.

"Sorry, I must have spaced out," Noah apologized.

"You're Noah Potter, right?" Vaughn's tone was brusque and businesslike; it said he had better things to do than talk to Noah, as far as he was concerned.

"Yes..." Noah stiffened. How did the bouncer know his name? He hadn't introduced himself in their very short interaction together.

"You've got a phone call in the office. I'll show you where it is." Vaughn started from the bar but stopped when he realized Noah was still in his seat. "What are you waiting for? I said you have a phone call."

"Who is it from?" Noah asked, unable to think of a single person that would call him in Hong Kong.

"Some dude named Hong. He said he had something to tell you about your sister. That's all he'd say to me. Now come on, I've only got a few minutes left in my break, and I don't want to waste any more of it than I have to on you."

Inspector Hong had something to tell him about his sister? The words had Noah's heart thumping a thousand beats per second. Was he finally about to have answers? He couldn't imagine another reason Hong would track him down in such a way.

Noah considered grabbing one of the Dragons, but figured their distaste for the inspector would lead them to discourage him from taking the call—Steel had basically told him to never speak to Hong again. But he needed to hear what Hong had to say, especially if it concerned Lianne. Wei would just have to understand.

Got a call from Hong. Said he has something to tell me about Lianne. Going to take it in the office. Noah quickly sent the text message to Wei and slid off the barstool. "Okay," he said to Vaughn. "Lead on."

They skirted the dance floor, sticking close to the wall to avoid the crowds as they made their way toward a door marked STAFF ONLY in English and Chinese characters. "The office is through there, straight down the hall, last door on the right." Vaughn opened the door and waved impatiently for Noah to go in.

"Thanks."

"Yeah, yeah." Vaughn didn't walk Noah any farther. As soon as Noah went into the hallway, he turned and walked away, presumably back to his post at the VIP section.

The hallway was dimly lit, evoking the image of horror movies in Noah's mind. He ignored the uneasy feeling, walking toward the glowing

"EXIT" sign at the end of the hallway. Posters of various bands and events in the club's history—themed nights, live performances, special concerts and the like—decorated the walls.

The last door on the right was partially open, and Noah stepped inside. He wondered if he'd misheard the instructions; the room wasn't an office, it was just a space being used for various storage purposes, mostly for additional bar furniture. There were couches covered in sheets, barstools and chairs stacked all around the room.

Because of his confusion, it took him a moment to realize he was not alone in the room. A lanky man stood against the wall on his right. Even in the low light, Noah recognized him. It was Short Hair from the noodle shop on his first day in Hong Kong.

"What...what are you doing here?" Noah asked. Instead of answering, Short Hair started toward him. Something wasn't right here. His every instinct screamed for him to run. He started to turn, bumping into something behind him. He turned and barely had time to register Long Hair's presence before something hard connected with the back of his head and he fell into blackness.

45

Though the sun was down, the night was still unpleasant, the air muggy and stifling. Even the noisy, crowded club seemed like it would be a nice refuge to Wei, sitting in Conroy's car. They didn't want to risk running the car's engine and drawing attention to their presence, so they were making due without the air conditioner. They had the windows rolled down a bit to tempt in a breeze.

"Fuckin' hate summer in this place," Conroy complained, wiping sweat from his face with a towel he'd brought with him. "There's only one good reason to be drenched in sweat and this sure as hell ain't it."

Wei grunted. Of course, he agreed with Conroy. If he had to be sweaty he'd much rather it be with Noah beneath him. Or on top of him. Or on all fours in front of him... He had to stop himself when he felt a stirring in his groin. That was dangerous territory to let his mind drift into; he didn't need the distraction when he should be keeping his eyes out for the motherfucker who sent someone after Noah with a knife.

"Speaking of hot and sweaty," Conroy said, and Wei grimaced, knowing what was about to come. "How was it to finally tap that white boy ass last night? Was it good and tight? He looks good and tight." Wei punched Conroy in the arm. "Ow. Sorry. You should take it as a compliment, man. So, was it good?" Wei smiled despite himself. "I see you smilin'. It was good, wasn't it?"

Wei chuckled. "Yeah, it was damn good."

"'Bout time you got some. I know you were tired of the nightly *da fei gei*." Conroy made a jerking off motion to emphasize his meaning.

"Do we *have* to talk about my sex life? When was the last time you got laid?"

Conroy grinned cockily. "Last night. Went to the karaoke bar near my place. Went to take a piss. One of the servers was in there. He took a good look at this—" Conroy pointed at his crotch, "—and I could see he wanted it. Went to one of the empty rooms and fucked there while everyone else was singing around us."

Wei shook his head. If someone else had told him that story, he wouldn't believe them, but Conroy had never been known to make up stories of sexual conquests; he simply didn't need to. His looks and endowment made it easy for him to have sex whenever he wanted. "You are one *ham sap lou*, Conroy." *Horny bastard.* Never did the expression apply more perfectly to a person than it did to Conroy.

Wei's phone vibrated and lit up on the dashboard, bringing the conversation to a blessed end. Wei picked up the phone and read Noah's message, his expression moving rapidly from a frown to a deep scowl.

"What's up?" Conroy asked, peering over to look at the message.

"Noah said that Hong called him at the club to tell him something about his sister."

Conroy sat back again, propping his hands up lazily on the steering wheel in front of him. "And you don't like the idea of him talkin' to Hong?"

"What do you think?"

"I think that if Hong can actually tell him something about his sister, it's not so bad. The man needs to hear something. Look," he added before Wei could speak, "I know you want to be his hero and help him find his sister, but we both know she's dead, boss. Maybe it's better for you that he hears that news from someone else."

Conroy was right. Wei had no doubts that Noah's search was going to end unhappily, either way it went. If her disappearance was at the hands of the same people taking these other girls, then she was likely already dead. If not, she was sold off into sex slavery somewhere on the Mainland.

That wasn't something he could bring himself to tell Noah. Besides, the longer Noah looked for his sister, the longer he was in Hong Kong, which meant the longer he was with Wei. *Way to be selfish, Tseng. You're a* len gai tsan. *A real fucking asshole.*

Car headlights illuminated the stretch of parking lot in front of them as a vehicle slowly made its way up the lane, looking for a parking space. Something about the car looked familiar to Wei, but he couldn't place it until the car was right in front of them. It was the Lincoln Town Car driven by Superintendent Dang.

The car came to a stop right in front of where they were parked, killing its engine. The driver's side door opened, and Dang's scarecrow-esque frame emerged from it.

"What's that piece of shit doing here?" Conroy scowled. The windows were down, and he knew Dang could hear but didn't bother keeping his voice down.

"Let me do the talking," Wei said, voice pitched low. "I mean it, Conroy."

"You're the boss."

Henry Dang sauntered over to the car, his movements almost effeminate. He made a show of peering in through the windshield, as if he didn't know exactly who was inside. Wei opened the car door and stepped out, rising to his full height, happy to see that Dang did look at least a bit intimidated by Wei's stature.

When Dang spoke, his voice was patronizingly polite. "Ah, Mr. Tseng, I thought that was you in the car."

"You knew damn well it was me, Dang. Let's not play games. It's too hot for that shit."

Dang's upper lip curled in disdain. "Very well, Mr. Tseng. I came by to see what it was you and your no good thugs were up to here. Hiding in cars in dark parking lots? Seems very untoward to me."

Wei crossed his arms across his chest. "Right. You expect me to believe that the high and mighty Superintendent Dang drove all the way out here in order to investigate reports of people sitting in their cars in front of a night club."

"I admit, I was curious to find out if the rumor about your frequenting this establishment of late were true. You know, Mr. Tseng, some might think that your prurient interests in the foreigner you've recently come into contact with is distracting you from looking out for the people you claim to wish to protect. Why, just this evening we received a tip about a meth lab being operated right under your nose. Don't worry, while you were here partying my men took care of it. I guess the people will know who really does more to protect this district, won't they?"

Wei didn't believe for one second that there was a meth operation going on under his nose. He and his men were too damn careful to let something like that happen. No, this was one of Dang's manipulative ploys, nothing more. "Fuck you, Dang."

Dang's eyes flashed dangerously, and his voice became frigid. "Be careful, Wei. I would hate to have to put you behind bars."

Wei turned his head to the side and spit in distaste. "For what, exactly? Last I checked it wasn't a crime to tell a dirty piece of shit to fuck off."

Fluorescent headlights briefly illuminated them as a white van like the kind used by utility companies sped by them in the parking lot. Dang's eyes followed it as it passed.

"You think you're invincible, Wei Tseng," Dang said, still watching the departing van. "One of these days, you'll find out that you're not. Have a good night."

"Dang, how do you do it?" Wei called as the superintendent opened the door to his car. Dang stopped and turned back to him. "How do you sleep, how do you go into work every day, knowing that you've betrayed the people who put their faith in you and your department?"

Something flashed behind Dang's eyes. "My conscience is clear."

Dang climbed into his car and drove off, and Wei got back into the car.

"It's gonna take weeks to get the smell of that *diu lan tsai* out of those clothes," Conroy complained, but Wei didn't pay him any attention.

He grabbed his phone and dialed Noah's number. No one answered. Wei wondered if he was still talking to Hong. That would be a *long* conversation. Instead he typed a message to Hong.

—*What exactly are you telling Noah about his sister*?

Wei's phone rang barely a minute later, Allen's name on the display. A sense of dread building steadily in his stomach, Wei answered. "Hong?"

"What are you talking about, Wei? I don't know anything about his sister."

Wei felt like ice water had been dumped over his head. "You didn't call him at the office at K?"

"No, Wei, I didn't. If I needed to get in touch with him, I'd call his cell phone, or you. I don't even know K's number. What's going on?"

Wei hung up on him, turning to Conroy. "We've got a problem."

46

Something hard and uncomfortable jarred the back of Noah's head repeatedly, drawing him back into painful consciousness. The first thing he noticed was the sound of rubber on pavement and the feeling of moving. He was in a vehicle of some kind. The back of his head ached, and he wondered what they hit him with to knock him unconscious.

The second thing he noticed was that duct tape bound his wrists together.

Noah's every instinct urged him to struggle, to shout, to put up some kind of a fight, but he resisted, forcing his heart rate to slow down at least a little, so he could think properly. He turned his head to examine his surroundings. He was in the back of a van, laying on a scratchy, beat-up rug that had seen much better days. There were no distinguishing features inside the van and no windows for him to see out of. He had no way of knowing how long he'd been unconscious, or where they were taking him. Fear left a bitter taste in his mouth

Would Wei be able to find him? The thought threatened to undo him as the panic he felt upon waking raced through his veins, shutting out every thought but the grim realization that he was going to die. For a moment he was afraid he would hyperventilate, but several minutes of deep breathing helped him regain some modicum of control. *Come on, Noah, get a grip. You're not some damsel in distress who has to wait for a hero to come save you. If Wei can't get to you, you'll just have to get out of this mess on your own.*

He lay there for a moment, simply breathing, until the pounding of his heart no longer filled his eardrums. He could hear soft voices coming from the front of the van, speaking in Cantonese. That would be no help to him, but he continued to listen just in case one of them decided to check on him.

Noah carefully brought his wrists up toward his face, doing his best not to make a sound, and began to work at the thick wrapping of duct tape with his teeth. He would be completely at the mercy of these people with his hands bound, and he could not allow that.

He managed to get a deep enough tear in the tape that he could force it wider by attempting to roll and expand his wrists. If he kept at it, he'd be able to break the tape. That was a comforting thought amidst this entire mess. Or it was at least enough to keep him from giving up. He knew his chances of getting out of this situation weren't great, if he went down, he would go down fighting.

With the tape loosened, there was nothing more he could do other than lay there and wait until they reached their destination. He lay with his head turned to the right so the sore place on the back of his head didn't press against the hard metal floorboard of the van beneath the thin rug. His thoughts turned to Wei. Did he even know that Noah was missing yet?

He should have gotten one of the Dragons to go with him. Twice he'd made that mistake. It didn't look like he'd get a chance at a third time.

The van made a sharp turn, then, causing Noah to slide across the floorboard, before it came to a jerking stop. For a moment Noah considered making a run for it once his captors opened the door, but he had no idea where he was, so there was little point to it. They had the advantage there; they would just hunt him down again. He could tell his iPhone was not on him just by the lack of its weight pressing against his thigh. Nor, it seemed, was his wallet. These bastards were thorough.

The back of the van opened, and two long shadows fell into the van. While Noah couldn't see their features against the backdrop of a bright streetlight, he could tell they were the same two men who'd accosted him at K. The same two men who he saw in the ramen shop. How long had they been following him? What were they even doing in that shop that day? There was no way they could have known Noah was arriving.

Noah forced himself into a sitting position, wincing as pain jolted through his head and his stomach threatened to rebel. He tried to meet the eyes of these men with an icy indifference, but that was difficult, considering all he wanted to do was lay back down.

"Manny, look," said one of them. "The *sei gei lou* is awake."

"Guess you didn't hit him hard enough, Ming."

"This way we don't have to carry him." The one with shorter hair—Manny—climbed into the van and grabbed Noah by the elbow, yanking him violently to his feet, not caring when he banged his head against the top of the van.

Noah nearly fell to the ground when he stepped out of the van; only Manny's hand on his elbow kept him on his feet. When he looked up and took in exactly where he was, he couldn't believe his eyes.

The van was parking in the empty parking lot in front of the noodle shop beneath Lianne's old apartment. The entire building was dark with the exception of one light coming through a window above. To Noah's surprise—and concern—police tape marked the door to the apartment and the restaurant.

What the hell happened here? Noah prayed no one had been hurt, because he didn't think he could forgive himself if they were. He knew without a doubt that this was all his fault.

"Fai di laa," Manny growled, shoving Noah toward the noodle shop, guiding him with one hand. Manny's fingers dug roughly into Noah's shoulder, but he refused to offer any sign of pain or discomfort. He wouldn't give these people the satisfaction.

They bypassed the noodle shop, going straight for the door that led into the apartment section of the building. Ming opened the door and then held up the police tape high enough for Noah to duck under it. Noah didn't move fast enough for Manny, who shoved him hard. Noah went sprawling to the ground just beyond the door, landing on his right side. A tremor of pain shot through his arm and shoulder.

Manny crouched over him, looking down on him with clear derision. "I said *fai di laa.*"

"Would help if I knew what that meant," Noah snapped. Noah registered no movement from Manny before the back of his hand struck the side of Noah's face with the loud slap of flesh on flesh.

"It means *hurry the fuck up,* you fucking faggot!"

Manny made to strike him again, but Ming caught his wrist. "Let's just fucking get him upstairs." Manny snarled a wordless reply and walked toward the stairs, dragging the toe of his boot over Noah's stomach as he did.

Ming pulled Noah to his feet. "Come on."

The two men led Noah to the top of the stairs. By the time they reached the second landing, Noah knew exactly where they were going. The door to Lianne's old room stood open, confirming his suspicions. Light poured into the hall from within. Noah could hear low voices speaking as well as another sound, one he'd heard before but couldn't place at that moment.

"We're back," Ming announced, stepping into the room, Noah on his heels.

Noah hadn't seen the room since the night someone—probably someone in the room at that moment—had trashed it. It was now remarkably different, very clean, the only furniture in the room the bed and the dresser. There were several lights like those used on the sets of movies set up, and a camera sat on a tripod. Atop the dresser was a television that hadn't been there before. It was currently playing one of those horrid videos.

Noah stared at it dumbly, his mind slow to process what it was seeing, not wanting to accept it. It was plain as day, though. The video was of Lianne. Tears sprang to Noah's eyes, blurring his vision. Beneath the tears, though, a fierce anger was growing. Noah's every muscle tensed.

There were several men in the room besides the two who'd brought him there. Most of them looked similar to Ming and Manny—no-good monsters, sloppily dressed, an undeservedly high amount of swagger. Two of them did not have that look, though. One, Noah recognized immediately: the guy with the scar on his cheek. The other wore a business suit and looked extremely out of place amongst the others.

Noah forced his eyes to focus on the man in the suit—he was without a doubt the one in charge here. No matter what sounds he heard coming from the television, he would *not* look at it. The man in the suit noticed Noah's purposeful ignoring of the television.

"Is the entertainment we're offering here not to your liking, Mr. Potter?" The man spread his arms in a welcoming gesture. "Allow me to introduce myself. I'm Leo Tong. These are my associates."

"You're Twisted Vipers," Noah said, remembering the meeting at the dim sum restaurant, the men who were working for the red pole who'd recently come to power.

Tong's lips stretched in a shadowy imitation of a normal person's smile. "You are particularly well-informed, Mr. Potter. Too bad that information will do you no good." Tong made a motion and Scar Face brought a portable TV dinner tray from behind them and sat it near the bed. Laid out on the tray were four hypodermic needles. A murky, amber-colored fluid filled each needle.

Though Noah had never seen heroin before, except in movies, it wasn't hard for him to guess what it was. Desperation took over as the weight of the situation truly settled over him. He shouted at the top of his lungs. "Help! Help me!"

To Noah's surprise, no one moved to silence him.

"You can scream all you want, Mr. Potter," Leo Tong said lazily. "There is no one nearby to hear you. You'll find that I have friends in high places who can take care of a great many things for me."

Friends in high places... Noah thought about the police tape around the place, and he realized Wei had been right. "How long has Dang been in your pocket, then?"

Tong clapped limply. "You're very bright, Mr. Potter. Let's get him more comfortable, shall we?"

Ming and Manny stepped up to either side of Noah, reaching for his shoulders, but Noah shook them off violently, elbowing Ming hard in the stomach as he did. Ming snarled, but Tong just laughed, sounding genuinely amused. Out of nowhere, though, his hand came out, backhanding Noah across the face.

"Oh, this is going to be fun."

47

Noah was in danger. That was the only thought in Wei's mind as he hurried through the doors of K, dragging Chris in with him. It took three minutes to have every Dragon in the club gathered at his side.

"Find Noah," was all the order he gave, and each of them went scurrying off. Even Sandra did not protest the sudden very public appearance of the Dragons. Wei was not one to be trifled with, especially when someone he cared about was in danger.

They searched every inch of the dance floor. Noah sent Conroy and Tony into the office and to search the employee areas, but there was no sign of him. *How the fuck did he just slip past me?* He could only blame himself. He'd somehow left an opening for something like this to happen.

Tony and Conroy approached Wei, shaking their heads at Wei's questioning look. "*Diu!*" Wei really wanted to punch something; it had been a long time since he'd felt so powerless. The rage built inside him was aimed in large part at himself for being unable to protect his own territory and the man he loved. He didn't know how he maintained his composure.

"No sign of him in the office."

"That's what I thought you'd say."

Conroy stepped in closer. "Boss, I've been thinking. Remember that van we saw roll out of here while you were talking to Dang?" Wei nodded. "What if they had Noah with them?"

It was a thought that had occurred to Wei as well, but he didn't want to think about it. If that was true, then Noah might already be dead.

No, he refused to think that. If he thought that now, then he'd already lost. He had to focus on the moment, on saving Noah, not on what might happen if he failed. He wouldn't fail.

"Get back into the fucking CCTV cameras again. Do whatever the fuck it takes to *find him.*"

Conroy and Tony went off without a question.

One of the bartenders on duty, a girl with brightly colored makeup, approached him. "Hey, Wei."

"Now's not a good time, An." He didn't bother trying to keep the frustration out of his voice. At the moment, he didn't give a rat's ass if he hurt her feelings. He kept his eyes searching the crowd, not looking at her.

"I heard you were looking for the foreign guy that's been coming here."

Wei turned his full focus on her, and she shied back from him a step. "What do you know?"

She shrugged, looking like she very much regretted approaching him. "Just...he was here at the bar not too long ago, but someone came and told him he had a phone call in the back."

Wei took her shoulders in his hands. He could feel her tense up, so he released her and softened his voice. "Do you remember who it was that told him about the call?"

An nodded. "It was Vaughn. The bouncer for the VIP section."

Sonofabitch. Chris was right.

Wei turned on his heel and made his way toward the VIP section, motioning and catching the attention of Winston, who was talking to some people nearby. "Get Conroy. Tell him it's the VIP bouncer." Winston hesitated for a moment, looking like he wanted to ask Wei a question but thought better of it.

Wei reached the VIP section, but the guy standing in front of it was different, not Vaughn. "Where did the normal guy go?" Wei demanded, but the guy just gave a dismissive snort and ignored him.

Anger flaring, Wei grabbed the bouncer by the front of his shirt and pulled him in close. When he spoke, his voice was like finely honed steel. "Listen to me, *puk gai*. I'm only going to ask one more fucking time, understand? I don't have time for your bullshit. Where. Is. Vaughn?"

The bouncer tried to pull himself free from Wei's grip, but Wei held on, and he relented. "He went to the bathroom, damn!"

Wei released him. He started to walk away when the guy muttered, "*Sei ga tsan*," behind his back. Without thinking twice Wei wheeled around and slammed his fist into the guy's stomach, doubling him over.

"You need to learn some fucking respect," he spat.

You don't have time for this shit, he reminded himself, and left the bouncer where he was. The crowd of people near him gave him a wide berth, which worked out pretty well for him in getting to the bathroom.

He hurried through the bathroom door, nearly hitting a man as he tried to leave. Wei ignored his annoyed cries in Cantonese. Vaughn was standing at the urinal, fly open, shirt held slightly up. He looked over to Wei as he came in, and his eyes widened in noticeable fear. He quickly tucked himself back into his pants, but not before Wei got a got look at his abdomen.

There was a tattoo there, a quite familiar one, a Chinese character he'd seen on the naked torso of the guy violating the girl in the video marked with Lianne's name. It all clicked together in Wei's head, and he rushed toward Vaughn, slamming him against the wall.

"What the fuck is your problem?" Vaughn cried, pushing Wei back. Wei's response was to kick him in the gut, slamming him back against the wall. Vaughn slid to the floor in pain.

Wei crouched over him. "Did you think nobody would figure out what you were doing, you sick bastard?"

"I don't know what you're—" Wei silence Vaughn's protest with a punch in the jaw.

"How many times, you sick fuck? How many times did you rape those poor girls? How. Many. Times?" He emphasized each word of the question with another punch. "Those girls were innocent, and you bastards took everything from them—*everything*! Now you think you're going to take Noah, too?"

"Wei!" Conroy's voice barely registered in the back of Wei's mind; the only thing real to him at that moment was the contact of his fist with the bouncer's face. "Damn it, Wei, what the fuck?"

Conroy grabbed Wei under his arms, hauling him back away from Vaughn. The bouncer's face was now a bloody lump; his left eye was swollen shut, a deep gash from Wei's knuckles just beneath it. His nose was at an odd angle, broken, his lips busted and bleeding. At least one of his teeth had come out and now rested in a pool of spit and blood beside him. He was clinging to consciousness, though just barely.

Wei shook Conroy off, chest heaving, adrenaline and anger pumping through his blood cells and infusing every inch of him with pent-up energy dying to be released. A glance at his fist told Wei that when the adrenaline faded, he was going to be hurting like a motherfucker; punching someone in the face is, in general, a bad idea, and doing it multiple times is understandably multiple times worse.

"This guy knows where Noah is, I guarantee it. I want to know where. Put a fucking out of order sign on the door."

Conroy watched Wei carefully, but Wei ignored his look of concern, his eyes locked on Vaughn's good eye. There was hatred there, but there was also real primal fear. Maybe he wasn't so fucking stupid after all.

"Once you put the sign on the door, go get Tony." Wei let a sick grin come over his face. "Tell him I have need of his particular talents."

Conroy didn't seem to want to leave Wei alone with Vaughn—it was likely he didn't trust Wei to control himself. Wei wasn't himself, and the others had noticed. He wasn't stupid enough to disobey, though. Wei wasn't talking to him as his friend right now; he was speaking as the boss, and it was a bad idea not to follow the boss's orders.

When Conroy was gone, Wei crouched down next to Vaughn, studying him like he was some sort of unpleasant new bug recently unearthed. "Are you scared? You should be. By the time Tony is through with you, you're going to spill your every dirty secret."

48

Noah's jaw ached from Leo Tong's backhand, but he ignored it, keeping his hate-filled gaze on the Viper's face. He kept reminding himself that these people *wanted* reactions out of him, and he needed to do his best to *not* give them anything.

"There's fire in you," Leo Tong said appreciatively. He turned from Noah, moving to the television and hitting one of its buttons. The image changed—mercifully—from Lianne's torment to display the bed before him, awkwardly framed by the camera's position.

"That just won't do at all. Let's see if we can get a better angle. I want this video to be shot beautifully. It's going to have a very special audience, after all." Scar Face took the camera and began adjusting its position, looking back to Tong every few seconds to see if he was happy with the placement.

Noah had seen portions of three of these videos, now; he knew what was in store for him if he didn't figure a way out of this mess. His mind was racing with options. He had few avenues of escape, really. Just the stairwell. He could try to get into the restaurant and call the police, but he wasn't even certain what the number for the police *was* in Hong Kong. He had precious few options, but he had to try *something*.

"I think that will work," Leo Tong said at last, examining the view of the bed from the camera lens. "We can keep the *gweilo*'s face in every frame. I'm sure Wei Tseng will appreciate seeing his face while we have our fun with him."

Noah scoffed. "So your goal is just to piss Wei off? That's dumb, in more ways than one."

Tong turned to Noah, his face patient and polite, though his eyes still reflected the promise of what was to come on that bed. "My goal is much more than pissing Wei off, Noah—may I call you Noah? You see, once the police receive this video, it will become quite clear what's going on. Wei Tseng and the Dragons have been abducting poor, innocent girls and torturing and raping them to make a profit on the videos they make.

The final nail in the coffin will be the death of the sympathetic foreigner here to find his sister, who is known to have been in the presence of Wei Tseng and his Dragons. The police will arrest Wei, the Dragons will crumble, and the Vipers will take over this territory, too. As a nice little side bonus, we'll also make some money selling the video. Not as much as we made from your sister's, I'm sure, but there *is* a market for seeing arrogant white men put in their place.

"Well," Tong clapped his hands once. "I think it's time to get started. I hope to spend quite a while on this one. Ming, why don't you give our star a little help relaxing? Not too much, now; I want him to really feel what we're going to do to him."

Ming moved to the tray of needles and picked one up. He carefully uncapped it as he walked over to Noah. Noah tensed, eyes on the needle. Just as Ming got within easy reach of him he swept out with his leg, knocking Ming's feet out from under him. He hit the ground with a loud curse, the needle rolling away.

Noah took advantage of the surprise, slamming his shoulder into Ming, knocking him unstable. He knew it was now or never; he made a dash for the door. Part of him didn't think he would make it through, but he did. He actually made it through the door. Now he just needed to make it outside.

A loud *bang* startled him and he felt the spray of wood particles against the back of his legs as the bullet struck the stairs just behind him. He froze, his heart thumping in his chest. He couldn't outrun a bullet, and he had no doubt these people would not hesitate to shoot him.

"You were wise to stop, Mr. Potter." Noah turned around slowly. Standing in the doorway, surrounded by a nimbus of light, Leo Tong held a gun pointed right at the center of Noah's chest. "It would be unfortunate to lose such a financial opportunity, but I'm not about to let another *gweilo* escape."

"Another?" Noah repeated, knowing it was too much to hope that it would mean what he hoped it meant.

"Don't get your hopes up. As you saw on the video, we got her back. It *is* incredible, though, that she gave my men the slip in the first place and got so far." Leo Tong dug into his pocket and pulled out a cell phone. Noah recognized it instantly as his sister's; it was a custom-made case, a photograph of the two of them. "And what did she do? Did she call the police? No, the *tsai gwai mui* called you, all the way in America!"

Leo Tong's derisive laughter made Noah want to climb the stairs and punch him right in his crooked mouth. He wouldn't make it two steps before Tong used the gun, though, so he restrained himself through massive effort.

"Now, Mr. Potter, you can come along quietly and maybe suffer a bit less, or you can struggle against us and suffer a lot more. Either way, you're going to end up on that bed and on our video."

I'd rather die. It was not a difficult choice that Tong was posing him: either get raped and then killed, or get shot and killed. If he made a run for it, Tong would shoot him. Getting shot to death or else bleeding out didn't really make the list of ways Noah wanted to die, but it was the best possible scenario.

He started to step backward, waiting for the opportune moment to drop down low and make a dash, but stopped when he heard a noise, growing louder all the time.

Leo Tong heard it, too. His jaw tensed and his brow furrowed as he tried to make it out. A few minutes passed, and there was no mistaking it: the roar of a car's engine, the squeal of tires speeding into the parking lot, joined by the sound of two more cars.

Noah turned toward the stairs, the glow of the halogen headlights filled the landing. For the first time since waking up in that van, Noah felt real, genuine hope blossoming in his chest.

While he wasn't paying attention, Leo Tong's arm came around his throat, jerking him back forcefully, the cold barrel of the gun pressing against the side of his head painfully. He struggled, flailing his legs, but Tong dragged him back into the room, tossing him hard to the ground.

"They fucking found us," Tong snarled to the others. "I want every one of those fuckers dead, do you hear me? *Dead!*"

Noah let out a rasping laughing at the look of sheer panic on Leo Tong's face. "Plan falling apart, is it?" Tong kicked him in the chest hard enough to knock the wind out of him.

"If you think you're getting out of here," Tong snarled, spittle flying from the corner of his mouth, "you're mistaken. The fucking Dragons might think they're here to rescue you, but they're just going to die instead. And then, then I'm going to make sure that every last moment you spend on this planet from here on out is filled with agony."

49

"Turn here," Wei instructed Conroy as they drew nearer to the noodle shop. Vaughn was too easy to break; one look at Tony and he was blubbering like a little bitch, spilling everything he knew about the operation. He didn't know where they'd taken Noah, but Dang's veiled hints had been enough to make Wei suspicious. He'd called Hong and gotten the location of the supposed meth lab. When he heard the address, he knew that was where he needed to go.

Conroy sped into the parking lot, not bothering to hide their approach; subtlety wasn't his strong suit. The cars driven by Tony and Chris, both full of Dragons, arrived right behind them.

Wei grabbed the gun from the dashboard. It felt familiar in his hand, and it was a familiarity he hated. He hadn't carried the gun more than five times in the five years since the war with the Nine Stars came to an end; he hadn't needed to. While he wished it wouldn't come to a gun fight, he wasn't naïve, and neither were the rest of the Dragons. Moral qualms aside, he would do what was necessary to protect his territory— and more importantly, to protect Noah.

If he had to fight a thousand wars to protect him, he would.

Taking a deep, steadying breath, Wei gripped the gun tightly and stepped out of the car. "Be careful with your bullets," he warned the Dragons. Each of them was carrying a handgun, as well. "We don't know where they've got Noah. We don't need him hit in the crossfire. And no killing unless you absolutely have to. Aim to incapacitate."

The Dragons nodded their understanding just as the door to the apartment section of the building burst open and five Twisted Viper thugs came out, their own guns at the ready. The Dragons all took shelter behind the cars as the Vipers opened with the first volley, the bullets striking the ground and the cars.

"Do you know how much this car fucking costs?" Conroy shouted angrily. He rose up quickly, an expert shot striking one of the Vipers in the right shoulder, effectively knocking him out of the fight.

The other four tried to keep up a pretty steady volley of bullets, but they didn't time themselves well, and their reloading often came in sync, giving the Dragons ample time to pick their targets.

To Wei's right, Chris started out of his crouch to take a shot, only to drop back down as a bullet whizzed by where his head once was. "Don't be an idiot, idiot," Walker scowled. He pivoted upward, a clean shot nailing the Viper who'd shot at Chris.

The Vipers truly were terrible shots; Wei prayed that there were no innocent bystanders caught in their reckless crossfire.

The firefight was over in less than five minutes. The Dragons had experience in this department in their street war with the Nine Stars, and Wei insisted they each regularly practice at a place he had set up as a gun range. Wei was pleased to see that none of his Dragons were injured.

"All right, secure the outside—no one else gets in," Wei instructed. "Call Constance and get her here. Then call an ambulance for the Vipers. Have more Dragons on standby, in case the Vipers have more backup on the way." He paused for a moment, deliberating. "And call Hong."

Conroy frowned but nodded. "Yo, boss. Do you want me to go with you?"

Wei shook his head. "No, you take care of things out here. I'll handle the inside on my own." He clasped Conroy's hand tightly. Wei was sure Conroy knew how much Wei was relying on him. He wouldn't let Wei down. He never had, never would.

Conroy set off to secure the parking lot, and Wei made his way through the door left open by the now-injured Vipers. The inside of the building was dark. Wei made his way cautiously up the stairs, ears straining as he listened for any signs of people lurking in the dark. He had no doubt there were more people here than he'd seen; Leo Tong would have to be completely, stupidly arrogant to not have a larger force there. Then again, the fact that he was making a move on Wei at all in his own territory showed a high level of arrogance.

Not wanting to be caught off guard in the dark, Wei turned on the light of the stairwell. It gave away his approach, but so did the gunshots outside. Whoever else was there knew he was coming for them.

The knife flashed toward him as he reached the second landing. Wei barely had time to dodge it; he didn't get away without a thin cut on his bicep. The man stepped forward, striking out with the palm of the hand not holding the knife, hitting Wei's arm in just the right place to make him drop his gun. It clattered loudly as it struck the stairs.

Wei didn't have time to think; he acted on instinct, bringing his arms up, wrists together in a V-shape, and catching the wrist holding the knife before it could draw too close to him. His assailant was strong—very strong. Wei struggled to shove him away.

Stepping up onto the landing, Wei saw it was the man with the scar on his face. The same *puk gai* who sent someone after Noah with a knife.

"I've heard a lot of things about you, Wei Tseng," Scar Face said, voice as casual as if they'd run into each other at the supermarket. "You really are one intimidating fucker up close. But I gotta think that most of those rumors about you aren't true."

Wei's face remained impassive. "You're about to find out just how true they are." Wei cracked his knuckles and then his neck.

Scar Face chuckled. "Am I supposed to be scared?"

"I don't give a fuck if you're scared or not."

Scar Face lunged forward suddenly with the knife, hoping to catch Wei off guard. He did; only Wei's reflexes saved him from having the blade of the knife buried in his gut. He dodged to the side, bringing his fist forward in hopes of catching Scar Face in the jaw, but his opponent moved too quickly.

Scar Face came at him again, just as quickly, this time slicing outward in an arc. Wei wasn't as lucky this time; the blade cut through his shirt and drew blood across his stomach. Wei ignored the sting of the cut and pressed his advantage, following just behind the sweeping knife and lashing out with his fist. Scar Face was fast on his feet, and what should have been a full-on smack to the face was merely a glancing blow to the chin as he danced backward.

"Not so light on your feet, are you, Tseng?" Scar Face lashed out with the knife, reversing his hand midswipe and scoring a cut across Wei's cheek. He laughed maniacally when he saw the blood begin to drip down Wei's face. "Maybe now we'll have matching scars?"

Wei growled and brought his hands up in a boxer's guard, shifting his weight constantly from foot to foot, watching Scar Face's body for telltale indicators of movement. A lot of people carried knives to look dangerous and threatening, but didn't know how to properly use one in combat. Scar Face was different; he wielded the knife like it was an extension of himself, like he'd been born to it. He was exponentially more dangerous than those with guns had been.

Scar Face moved again, the knife coming upward, aimed just below his ribcage. Wei used his right arm to deflect the thrust, catching his wrist and twisting the arm with the hope of knocking the knife free. His left land lashed out in a violent backhand, sending Scar Face's head rocking back.

Scar Face jerked his arm free, elbowing Wei in the solar plexus and pushing him hard to the ground. He fell atop Wei, looking down on him with a sadistic grin on his face. "I'd hoped you would put up more of a fight than this, Tseng. And you're the fearsome leader of the Dragons? Hah!" He ran the sharp edge of the knife down Wei's jaw, stopping when the bloody point was hovering over Wei's pulse.

"Leo's going to be sad you're not alive to see the video we're going to make tonight, Tseng. Come to think of it, so am I." Scar Face leaned in close to Wei, keeping the knife pressed against his throat to speak directly into his ear. "I really wish you could see all of the things I'm going to do to that *gweilo* tonight." He gave an almost orgasmic shudder. "It's going to be magical."

The thought of the sick bastard putting his hands on Noah stoked the fierce anger that was building in Wei's gut, spreading it through his entire body. He brought his hands up too quickly for Scar Face to stop him, gripping his wrists and pulling the knife away from his neck as he twisted his lower body, gaining the leverage he needed to flip Scar Face over and end up on top of him.

Scar Face bucked beneath him, writhing to break free, but Wei just applied all of his weight in an effort to hold him down. Scar Face wrenched his wrist free of Wei's grasp and tried to stab at him, but his position gave him little power; Wei caught the wrist once more and turned it around until the knife was hovering over Scar Face's face.

Despite being in the disadvantageous position he was in, Scar Face laughed. "Are you going to kill me now, Tseng?"

"You don't think I would? You think you're the first arrogant gang banger to come at me like this? You think you and Tong are anywhere near as bad as the Nine Stars were? From what I remember, the Twisted Vipers played the bitch for the Nine Stars because you were afraid. Guess what? They're fucking gone—and you know who did it? Me. I personally put a bullet in the head of Uncle Bao. You're *nothing*, you understand? *Nothing*."

The rage within Wei was bellowing for him to do it, to force the knife down, to put an end to one of the people responsible for so much death and loss in his territory—not to mention the shit he'd probably done in Vipers territory, as well. How many lives would be avenged by this man's death? How many lives would be saved in the future? He'd killed before, for the greater good. He could do it again, and he doubted he'd lose any sleep over it.

Before he could act on that violent impulse, an agonized scream echoed in the hallway, catching his attention.

"Seems like Leo's started without me."

Wei couldn't waste any more time on someone like Scar Face, not when Noah needed him. Cursing under his breath, he took the knife from Scar Face's hand and grabbed him by the throat. He slammed his head hard into the wooden floor of the landing and then struck him in the temple with the hilt of the knife. Satisfied Scar Face was unconscious, he rose.

Please, he prayed, *please don't let me be too late.*

50

"You have any idea how much trouble you've caused me, *gweilo*?" Leo Tong was pacing back and forth in the room. The sounds of gunfire had died down outside, and Noah didn't think Tong was confident in the outcome.

Noah glared at Tong from where he lay on the floor. The fear that had faded when he'd heard the arrival of the Dragons had returned full force, especially when the gunfire started; he feared more for Wei's safety than for himself. His chest still ached from Tong's kick. He didn't dare attempt to get up; he didn't know what sort of hair trigger this guy had, didn't know what might set him off. It was never a good idea to agitate a cornered animal.

That's exactly what Leo Tong was, and they both knew it. As much as he tried to show he wasn't afraid of Wei, it was a lie. As he followed Tong's pacing, he caught sight of the needle that had fallen from Ming's hand. It wasn't so far from him...if he could get his hands on it, he might be able to turn the tide of the situation in his favor.

A loud thump from inside the building, very close from the sound of it, made Tong jump and turn to the door. Noah saw that as his chance and sat up, scooting across the floor, closer to the needle. It was almost within arm's reach when Leo turned from the door and saw him. Another violent kick, this time against his left shoulder, sent Noah sprawling onto his back once more.

"You trying to get away? You think because your fucking boyfriend is going to save you?" He kicked Noah hard in the side. "You're mine, *sei gei lou!*"

He brought his foot down hard on Noah's elbow. It hurt like hell, and Noah gritted his teeth against the cry of pain that wanted to tear forth. "Trying to play it tough, huh?" Tong ground his foot, pressing nearly all of his weight on Noah's arm.

It was agony, and Noah could not hold back the cry. He'd once seen someone break their elbow during one of his self-defense classes; it had been horrifying to watch. The guy was a self-defense pro, big and buff, and he still cried like a baby. Hopefully letting out the cry would satisfy Tong before he pushed it too far and broke the bone.

Blessedly, he seemed satisfied for the moment, letting up on the pressure. The pain echoed, slow to abate. Noah realized he was sweating and breathing heavily.

"Oh yeah," Tong said, voice a low rumble. "I'm going to enjoy making you scream in a hundred different ways."

"That's not going to happen, *ong lan gau!*"

A myriad of feelings surged through Noah as he turned to the doorway and saw Wei standing there, a knife in hand. First and foremost was relief; Wei's appearance meant he was safe. The second was worry; Wei was bleeding from more than one place that he could see. The third was fear—fear that Tong, who had a gun, would kill Wei, yes, but also fear of Wei. There was something cold and hard in his eyes at that moment, a look Noah hadn't seen before. It sent shivers down his spine. He hoped to never have that look aimed at him.

"I see you were able to join us," Tong said. There was a definite edge to his voice and eyes. "I'm so pleased. I would have hated for you to miss the festivities." He raised his gun, pointing it at Wei. "Drop the knife, Tseng." Wei glanced at Noah, eyes searching over him, seemingly making sure he was okay, before he finally dropped the knife. "All right, kick it behind you, out the door."

Wei did as instructed.

"You know, Tseng, you brought this on yourself."

Wei arched an eyebrow. "Is that so?"

"You fucking Dragons acting all superior, like you're better than everyone else. You think because you've held this territory for five years that you're unbreakable? Fucking arrogant prick. I tried to work with you, offered you a deal that would benefit us both, and you turned me down."

"*Yau mo gau lan chou?*" Wei took a step into the room, stopping when Tong brandished the gun again. "You and I both know this isn't about that deal. This is about you trying to prove yourself. You want to look like a big shot to the other red poles in the Vipers, when the truth is, you're just a fucking *jin jang*. You and every other Viper."

Noah saw Tong's hand that wasn't on the gun clench into a tight fist, muscles in his arm bulging. He really hoped Wei knew what he was doing; how far could he push before Tong reacted?

"I'm going to enjoy killing you, Wei Tseng. And you know what I'm going to do then?"

Tong took a menacing step toward Wei, who held his ground. Just behind Tong's foot, Noah caught sight of the needle dropped earlier. Glancing up to make sure Tong's attention was suitably distracted, Noah reached slowly for it.

"I'm going to hunt down and kill each and every Dragon, their lovers, their families, anyone who you ever cared about, anyone who was ever stupid enough to follow someone as weak and pathetic as you."

Noah lifted the needle, clutching it tightly in his hand. Wei caught his movements, eyes flicking toward him, and Noah glanced down at the needle and then up at Tong. Wei's head moved almost imperceptibly down and then back up; he understood.

"Big words from a nothing red pole," Wei taunted. "I'm so tired of listening to you run your mouth. You know what? *Diu lei lo mo chau hai.*"

Noah didn't know what Wei said, but the sound of it and the instant anger it incited in Tong told him it was bad. Tong made to raise the gun once again, damn near foaming at the mouth. Noah couldn't hesitate anymore; he jammed the needle into Tong's leg and depressed the plunger.

Tong cried out, more in surprise than anything else, and looked down at Noah, who flipped him off. That distraction was all Wei needed; he crossed the space between them in three big steps, wrestling the gun from Tong's grasp and smashing it into his face. Tong stumbled back, tripping over Noah. He crashed into the camera he'd set up, knocking it over and landing on top of it. Wei glared down at him.

"*Sik si la lei*, Tong."

Tong taken care of, Wei pulled Noah to his feet and right into his arms, holding him tightly against his chest. Noah wrapped his arms around Wei's waist, pressing himself against Wei as much as he could. Now that the situation seemed to have passed Noah found his entire body was trembling; he could barely stay on his feet. Wei's warmth, his scent, it comforted him like nothing else ever had.

"I was so fucking scared," Wei whispered, lips in Noah's hair above his ear. "I thought I was going to lose you, and it was all my fault."

"None of this was your fault," Noah said quickly, but Wei silenced him, covering his mouth with his hand.

"Being with me is always going to put you in danger, Noah. This won't be the last time someone targets me, and if you're with me, you're an easy weapon to use against me. When I realized you were—when I thought..." He trailed off, taking an unsteady breath before continuing. "I thought I'd never see you again, and I would never get the chance to tell you I love you."

Noah's eyes widened at the words, and his heart skipped a beat. His feelings for Wei were intense and deep, despite having developed over a short period of time. He'd always dismissed the idea of instant attraction, thinking it some ridiculous trope in movies; he'd certainly never experienced it, nor had he ever known anyone who had.

Meeting Wei made him realize that just because it hadn't happened to him yet didn't mean it wasn't real. His feelings for the other man were very real and very powerful. He didn't see the point in denying them.

"I love you, too," he said, butterflies in his stomach at the words.

Wei helped Noah out of the room, supporting him as he walked on weak and wobbly legs. Noah barely glanced at the unconscious form of Scar Face as they passed.

They were almost to the main door when Leo Tong, howling like a madman, came charging toward them down the stairs, the knife Wei dropped earlier in his hands. Without even hesitating, Wei raised his gun and fired. The bullet struck home in the center of Tong's forehead. Noah cried out, shielding his face against Wei's shoulder from the sight.

Above the ragged sounds of his own breathing, Noah heard the wail of approaching sirens.

"That'll be Hong," Wei murmured. "Let's get outside. I've had enough of this place."

51

Exhaustion set in once the adrenaline wore off, and Noah felt like he was a passive observer in everything. The first thing that happened when he went outside was Constance checked on him, looking him over for injuries. She applied alcohol to a cut on the back of his head while Wei continued to hold his hand tightly.

"Where is Winston?" Noah asked, voice slightly higher than usual. It might have been an odd question, but he desperately needed to focus on something mundane, or else he might fall apart.

"He and Raphael are keeping an eye on our bouncer friend," Wei said. "He's okay, don't worry. You think I would get him involved in this much danger when he's not even a Dragon yet? Constance would kill me."

"Damn right I would," Constance muttered. "I'm done. Just a small scratch where something hit you. You'll be fine."

"Thanks, Constance."

The first to arrive on the scene were police officers, led by Allen Hong. They got out of their cars, weapons drawn and trained on the Dragons. Hong approached Wei carefully, eyes examining what was around him. His face looked a little pale, his mouth set in a straight line.

"Flashback to five years ago?" Wei asked. His voice lacked any real challenge; he just sounded tired.

"This is nothing compared to your average night back then." Hong's eyes went straight to his sister and stayed there. Noah didn't know what was passing between them, but he felt like it was important. He turned to Noah then. "I told you the Dragons were dangerous."

"The Dragons saved my life, Inspector Hong. I owe them everything." Noah squeezed Wei's hand as he spoke.

Inspector Hong sighed. "We're going to need to start taking statements from everyone," he said.

"You should know there's a dead man inside the building."

Hong turned to face the building. "Is there, now?"

"He came at me and Noah with a knife, screaming like a madman. I had no choice."

"You never do." Hong motioned an officer over and sent him inside.

More sirens wailed as several ambulances pulled into the parking lot. They began seeing immediately to the wounded Twisted Vipers. Noah watched them work without any sympathy. Part of him felt resentment that they were helping these men, men who'd somehow played a part in the rape and murder of who knew how many girls—one of which included his sister.

It was a shameful thought, one that he would hold close to himself, never repeat to anyone else. It wasn't something that was true to his heart, and maybe in time it would pass, along with the rage, but at that moment, he wished each and every one of them were dead.

Hong led him to his car after that, sitting him down in the passenger seat and squatting down to not be intimidating as he questioned Noah about what'd went on. Wei watched on from a distance, himself answering questions being asked by a uniformed officer. All around the parking lot, the rest of the Dragons were doing the same.

You'd think they were the criminals and not the heroes, Noah thought.

Noah repeated his story several times, providing as much clarification as possible when Hong asked. He had a hard time talking about the video playing upstairs of his sister's rape and torture. Hong respected that, not prompting him on that particular topic.

The rising sun was slowly spreading pink fingers across the now slate-gray sky by the time the cops were satisfied. The stories all corroborated each other, and there was no reason for Hong or anyone else to suspect Leo Tong's death was anything but self-defense.

"We'll probably have more questions," Hong told Wei.

"You know where to find me," Wei replied. He wrapped his arm around Noah's shoulder, led him to Conroy's car, and helped him get inside. Wei got behind the wheel, his eyes still glued to Hong, who was at that moment talking to Constance. For Noah, both of their faces were too hard to read; he couldn't tell if it was a good conversation or a bad one.

"Let's get you to bed," Wei said at last, starting the car.

Noah leaned his head back against the seat, his eyes closing of their own volition. God, he couldn't remember ever being more tired. A low curse from Wei forced him to open his eyes. Just beyond the parking lot, there was an expensive black car coming to a stop, and a man in a business suit that fit much better than Leo Tong's had was standing there with his hands in his pockets. Seeing Wei behind the wheel, the man raised a hand almost tentatively.

"Who is that?" Noah asked, studying the man's lean, handsome face.

"That's Johnny Hwang." Wei's voice had gone ice-cold again, his eyes regaining that hard glint they'd had when facing Leo. "He's the dragonhead of the Twisted Vipers."

Noah tensed at that, fear flashing through him. He forced it down, though, reminding himself he was with Wei, and there were a dozen cops in the parking lot behind them. This Johnny Hwang guy would be stupid to start something here. Plus, he was alone.

Wei stopped the car, rolling his window down.

"Good morning, Wei." Johnny Hwang's voice was civil, casual, and polite.

"Not such a good morning, Johnny," Wei said, the challenge in his voice evident. "I just left a building full of *your* men making a move in *my* territory. And now the dragonhead of the Twisted Vipers himself stands before me. This has been a night full of surprises."

Johnny Hwang pursed his lips. "I'm here because I heard what went down, and I wanted to make absolutely sure you know this was *not* a move endorsed by the Twisted Vipers. Leo Tong got overambitious and made a unilateral decision without consulting me. If he had, I would have made it absolutely clear he wasn't to touch the Eastern District."

"How kind of you."

"I don't want conflict with the Dragons. I've been around a long time, Wei. I remember your fight with the Nine Stars. I have no desire to go to war with the Dragons."

Wei nodded his understanding. "Good. You keep your men on your side, and I'll stay on mine, and we won't have a problem."

"I'm very glad to hear it," Johnny Hwang straightened. "Have a good day, Wei."

"Johnny," Wei called, before Johnny Hwang could get into his car. "Let me be clear: if something like this happens again—shit, if I even *think* something like this is going on again, I'm coming for you. I will wipe you out. Hong Kong will forget the fucking Vipers ever existed. We clear?"

Johnny Hwang nodded his head slowly one time. "We're clear." Johnny got in his car and drove off, heading away from the Eastern District.

"He seemed surprisingly...civil," Noah observed.

"Johnny Hwang has a brain, unlike most of the idiots he leads. That's how he got to the top, and that's how he's stayed there. He was dragonhead when the Nine Stars were still in power. That's a long time to hold the reins in this place."

Noah yawned loudly and Wei patted his thigh, his hand remaining there. "Enough about this, though. Let's get you in bed."

52

It was six in the morning when they finally reached Wei's apartment, and Noah fell asleep as soon as his head struck the pillow. He was barely aware of the warmth of Wei's body sleeping next to him. His sleep was blissfully dreamless, his exhaustion so deep that even the horror of the previous night could not pierce it.

Barely four hours later, the sound of the apartment doorbell rudely yanked Noah back into the waking world. He felt like he'd only closed his eyes moments before. His sleep may have been dreamless, but it wasn't restful.

He shook Wei's shoulder to wake him. "Someone's at the door," he said, his voice groggy and heavy with sleep. Wei stirred with a grumble, his own exhaustion clear in the rapid blinking of his eyes.

He padded to the door, mumbling something about punching whoever it was in the face. Noah lay back down on the bed, eyes closed once more, certain it was probably one of the Dragons needing to see Wei after last night. He was surprised when he heard Inspector Hong's voice instead.

"Is Noah here?"

"He's sleeping." Though he didn't say it, his meaning was clear: *you're not talking to him.*

"It's okay, Wei," Noah said, walking around the stained-glass divide. He saw the discomfort on Hong's face, the way his hands clutched at a manila envelope, his eyes refusing to meet Noah's directly, and he knew. "It's about Lianne, isn't it?"

Hong nodded. Wei motioned toward the couch, but Hong shook his head. "We were able to interview a few of the men from last night. They gave us enough to go on, and we found a body matching the description of your sister. It was dumped in a construction site where the work had stopped after the company went bankrupt. We need you to identify the body. Normally we'd have you come down to the morgue and do this, but I took these photos instead. I wanted to spare you as much as I could."

Hands shaking, Noah reached out to take the manila envelope Hong offered him. He nearly dropped it before he could get it open. The top picture was of the corpse of a woman, sheet pulled down to expose from her face to the top of her breasts.

Noah couldn't bring himself to look at the face, didn't want to see it as anything but vibrant and full of life. He didn't want the dead, decaying image to replace his memories of her. He didn't need to see her face, anyway; the tattoo was there. Noah felt like he was unable to breathe. He closed the envelope and handed it back to Hong.

"Is it her?" Noah nodded. "Are you sure? You only looked at the top picture."

"I'm sure," Noah managed to say. "How did—how did she die?" He knew the answer, but he needed to hear it.

"Drug overdose," Hong replied. There was clear guilt in his voice. "There's plenty of bruise marks, and she had three broken ribs. Of course we've ruled it a homicide. We've reopened the other files, as well," he added to Wei. "Labeled them all homicides, as well."

"A bit late," Wei muttered, but Hong ignored the expected barb.

"How long has she been dead?" Noah asked, though he didn't want to hear the answer.

"About two weeks is our best guess."

Two weeks. So she'd been dead when he'd gotten to Hong Kong. He felt a sick sort of relief at that. It would have tortured him forever if he'd found out she'd been alive and in Hong Kong at the same time he was there and he hadn't saved her.

"Here's the number to contact to make arrangements for handling the body. I'm really, really sorry for your loss, Mr. Potter. Losing your sister like this... I can only imagine what you must be feeling."

Noah thought of Constance and realized Allen probably could. How afraid was he of losing Constance due to her involvement with the Dragons? But he couldn't think about that, not now. "Thank you, Inspector."

Hong turned to go.

"Dang is dirty, Inspector," Noah said to his back. "He was helping Leo Tong slip under the radar with those girls. He arranged for that building to be empty last night—a drug lab, or some other excuse to evacuate it. He's dirty. Be careful."

Allen glanced back at him over his shoulder. "Thanks."

Once Hong was gone, Noah stood. "I need to call my father. Do you think I can borrow your phone?"

Wei handed Noah his phone. "I'll take a shower, give you some privacy." He kissed Noah's cheek before making his way to the bathroom.

Noah waited until he heard the sound of the shower running before he dialed the number. He had to do it a second time, because he'd forgotten the international code. He didn't think about what time it was back home, didn't care, but if his father didn't answer... Noah didn't know how to handle this situation; he couldn't begin to guess how to go about getting a body flown back to America.

"This is Raymond Potter." The voice was unmistakably his father, strong and confident.

"Dad, it's me." His voice was shaking. It took him a moment to realize he was crying.

Noah hadn't called Raymond dad since he was a teenager, and that fact was not lost on his father. "What is it, Noah?"

"I've found... I just identified Lianne's body."

There was a moment of crushing silence, then. When Raymond spoke, his voice was heavy, like there was something lodged in his throat. A show of genuine emotion from Raymond Potter. "What happened?"

Noah explained as much as he could, speaking through the tears.

When he finished, Raymond took several deep, steadying breaths. "Send me the number you were given, and I'll take care of everything. Get a flight home as soon as you can."

"Okay. I'll be home in the next few days."

Noah heard the bathroom door open as the call came to an end. He wondered how long Wei had been finished with his shower and waiting for him to end the call. Wei, wearing nothing but gray boxer briefs, came up behind him, slipping his arms around him and pulling him against his chest.

"How are you doing? Sorry, dumb question."

"It's okay. I got what I wanted, I guess. I came here looking for Lianne, and I found her. Just not in the way I was expecting."

"What are you going to do next?"

That was a really good question, one Noah hadn't yet taken the time to consider fully. "I don't know, really. My father is going to arrange for

Lianne's body to be delivered back home for the funeral. I'll be going back in a few days to help with the arrangements for that. After that, I'm not sure."

Wei released Noah, turning him around so they were face to face. Noah was surprised by the uncertainty and nervousness he saw in the other man's face. "I know Hong Kong hasn't necessarily been good to you," Wei began, biting his lower lip. "But I have a bit of influence in the local immigration office; a few people there owe me some favors. If you wanted, I could get you a working visa. Constance has already offered to sponsor you; you'd work at the shop with her, and, uh, live here, with me. Only if you wanted to, I mean."

Return to Hong Kong after the funeral? His experiences in Hong Kong hadn't been great since his arrival, with his hunt for his sister and the events of the previous night. But it wasn't all bad. In Hong Kong he'd found something he hadn't expected: friendship and love. The Dragons were rough, there was no denying that, but he'd grown to really admire them in his short time with them. And then there was Wei. He'd said it the night before, and it still rang true today: he loved him.

What was there in America for him, really? A distant father whose only wish was for Noah to conform to his vision of how life should be? His sister had been the only good thing about his life there, and now she was gone. The only things back home were ghosts and memories, only the past.

In Hong Kong, he could see a future waiting for him.

The choice was surprisingly not difficult for him to make. "Asking me to move in with you, huh? Isn't that a little fast?"

"I mean, you could stay in the room over Constance's," Wei said quickly. "Or I could pay for a room for you—"

Noah silenced him with a kiss. "I'm kidding, idiot. I'd love to move in here with you, for as long as you're willing to have me."

Wei grinned. "Well, then, you're going to be here a long fucking time."

Epilogue

By noon every television station in Hong Kong was reporting the shootout in the Eastern District, but none of them revealed any information about who was involved. At least there was that.

Johnny Hwang sighed and muted the television on the wall opposite his desk. He set the remote down, drumming his fingers on the glass surface of the desk. He hadn't had any real hope of Tong and his idiots in North Point actually accomplishing the job, and he wasn't even upset that Wei Tseng killed that idiot Tong; it saved him the trouble, in the end. He couldn't have a failure like Tong sticking around.

Even though he was dead, Tong had fulfilled the purpose Hwang had in mind for him. Oh, he never told him anything directly, of course, but he'd seen the potential in him. Tong had this incredible hatred for the Dragons, and he was too ambitious by far. Putting him in power right next to Wei's territory, there was bound to be a clash. It came faster than Hwang expected, but that wasn't a bad thing. And thanks to that, he now knew the answer to a question he'd been asking himself for some time now.

It's been five years since the street war with the Nine Stars, and Hwang was wondering if the Dragons had lost any of the edge they'd had. Now he knew they hadn't.

Hwang rose from the desk, walking to the large floor-to-ceiling window facing the east. From his office, he could see the entirety of the city, depending which direction he faced. He'd planned it that way, using it as a daily reminder of what was rightfully his. The city was just waiting for someone with the balls to step up and take it. The old guard was arrogant, thinking themselves invincible. They'd grown complacent, which meant they'd grown stagnant.

Hwang was going to own that island; he would take the others down piece by piece. And he would start with the Dragons.

GLOSSARY

This is a list of the Cantonese phrases used throughout the book. It is by no means comprehensive, nor do I include tonal markings for ease of reading in the book itself. There are a lot of online resources for studying Cantonese if you are interested.

Da fei gei—Jerk off (literally translates as *shooting airplanes*)
Diu—Fuck (exclamation)
Diu lei—Fuck you!
Diu lei lo mo chau hai*—Fuck your mother's stinky vagina.
Dzu pa—Ugly girl (literally *porkchop*)
Fai di laa—Hurry up!
Ga tsan—Asshole
Gong dzau tin ha mou dik, dzou dzau mou lan wai lik—All talk, no action.
Gwei—White, foreign (literally *ghost*)
Gweilo—White guy, foreigner
Gwei mui—White girl
Ham sap lou—Horny bastard
Hou sei la lei—Drop dead, go to hell.
Jin jang—Low-life, pariah
Lan—Dick (body part)
Lei hou lin—You're beautiful.
Ong lan gau—Dumb fuck
Puk gai—Asshole, bastard
Sei—Damn (adjective)
Sei bat po—Damn bitch
Sei gei lou—Fag (derogatory)
Sei yan tau—Jerk
Sik si la lei—Go to hell.
Yau mo gau lan chou—You fucking kidding me?

*This is pretty much the worst insult you could possibly say to someone; it *will* get you attacked if you use it with a Cantonese-speaking person or on the streets of Hong Kong—this isn't even something you could say to your friends, jokingly.

ABOUT THE AUTHOR

J. C. Long is an American expat living in Japan, though he's also lived stints in Seoul, South Korea—no, he's not an army brat; he's an English teacher. He is also quite passionate about Welsh corgis and is convinced that anyone who does not like them is evil incarnate. His dramatic streak comes from his lifelong involvement in theatre. After living in several countries aside from the United States, J. C. is convinced that love is love, no matter where you are, and he is determined to write stories that demonstrate exactly that. J. C. Long's favorite things in the world are pictures of corgis, writing, and Korean food (not in that order...okay, in that order). J. C. spends his time when not writing by thinking about writing, coming up with new characters, attending Big Bang concerts, and wishing he was writing. The best way to get him to write faster is to motivate him with corgi pictures. Yes, that is a veiled hint.

Facebook: https://www.facebook.com/authorjclong
Twitter: @j_c_long_author
Website: http://www.jclong.org/
Email: jclongauthor@gmail.com

ALSO BY J.C. LONG

Unzipped Shorts

New Year's Eve Unzipped

Unzipping 7D

Coming Soon from J.C. Long

A Matter of Courage

Hong Kong Nights, Book 2

Blurb

Winston Chang has spent much of his young life admiring the Dragons who have kept his area safe and fought off the gangs that would bring violence to their area. Now that he's an adult, he wants nothing more than to join the Dragons and live up to those standards. The opportunity presents itself when his passion and knowledge of cars is just what the Dragons need.

One of their own has been killed and his death seems linked to his involvement with the illegal racing scene known as the Dark Streets. Winston is needed to infiltrate the scene and find out who is responsible and why. Steel has always been Winston's best friend, and Winston has always been there to get him out of trouble. Just as the stress in Winston's life reaches its peak, the relationship between Winston and Steel begins to change in ways neither of them expected.

Will Winston and Steel be able to find the courage to face not only the unknown killer stalking the Dark Streets racers, but also their growing feelings?

NINESTAR PRESS, LLC

www.ninestarpress.com

www.ingramcontent.com/pod-product-compliance
Lightning Source LLC
Chambersburg PA
CBHW021955170626
46808CB00001B/167